CW01180348

Death *Benefit*

Death *Benefit*

Are the dole cheats really making a killing?

Adrian P Fayter

Copyright © 2013 Adrian P Fayter

The moral right of the author has been asserted.

Apart from any fair dealing for the purposes of research or private study, or criticism or review, as permitted under the Copyright, Designs and Patents Act 1988, this publication may only be reproduced, stored or transmitted, in any form or by any means, with the prior permission in writing of the publishers, or in the case of reprographic reproduction in accordance with the terms of licences issued by the Copyright Licensing Agency. Enquiries concerning reproduction outside those terms should be sent to the publishers.

Matador
9 Priory Business Park
Kibworth Beauchamp
Leicestershire LE8 0RX, UK
Tel: (+44) 116 279 2299
Fax: (+44) 116 279 2277
Email: books@troubador.co.uk
Web: www.troubador.co.uk/matador

ISBN 978 1783061 297

British Library Cataloguing in Publication Data.
A catalogue record for this book is available from the British Library.

Typeset in Aldine401 BT Roman by Troubador Publishing Ltd
Printed and bound in the UK by TJ International, Padstow, Cornwall

Matador is an imprint of Troubador Publishing Ltd

To Debra
who also really appreciates a puzzle

AUTHOR'S NOTE

All characters, groups and businesses in this story are fictitious. They have no connection whatsoever with any real individuals, companies or political groups who may happen to have similar-sounding names or similar objectives.

PROLOGUE

The worst thing about doing a stakeout is the pressure it puts on your bladder. Except, of course, when something unusual happens; like stumbling across a warm corpse, for instance, or finding evidence of torture. Then things get much, *much* worse...

Normally, I bring a milk bottle with me, especially at this time of year, when the cold can eat through a tartan travel rug, jumbo corduroys and a pair of woolly long johns within ten minutes of killing the engine. But, by some miracle of staffing, that day I had a trainee out with me, so I was going to have to moderate my behaviour. Especially as I had already given her the rug.

'Can't we have the heating on?' she asked, through a small cloud of condensed breath. 'It's bloody freezing.'

I gave her a look that said, 'The age of chivalry is not dead, but it might as well be. You get the rug, half the cheese roll, most of the coffee and all of the benefit of my seven years investigating experience, and you haven't even smiled once. How about applying some of your Customer Care training to your colleague, then, eh?' Possibly this was too much for her to take in all at once, because she simply turned away and muttered 'freezing' again.

'We can only claim petrol expenses for the journey to and

from the job,' I said patiently, staring out into the dark. 'Oh, and for all those high speed car chases that happen, of course. I can't afford to run my engine for two hours just so I can be here.'

'If it was this cold in the office, we'd be allowed to go home.'

'Well, nobody's stopping you,' I wanted to say, which I admit is not my usual reaction to a strawberry blonde with good cheekbones and an endearing tendency to overdo the lip gloss. But when I'm suffering I prefer to suffer in silence. Maybe I'd have felt different if she'd offered to go Dutch on the travel rug, or even if she'd been better prepared for the night's work. (I know they've cut the induction course to a day and a half now, but, for God's sake, they hadn't even taught her to bring her own sandwiches!) Still, if she hadn't been there, of course, the whole affair would have turned out to be very different. Very different indeed...

'If you're lucky he'll be out in a minute,' I said.

'D'you think so? How d'you know?'

'The theory is he's on the night shift at Grannie Baker's.' I rolled my eyes. 'So he'd normally have to be there by eleven...'

'Wait a minute,' she said, checking her watch, 'it's only *ten* now.'

'Well, if he gets suspicious, he may leave early to lose the tail.'

'Come on! He won't suspect he's being tailed, will he?'

'Oh, you'd be surprised about these boys. How clued-up they are.' I didn't really mean this, but it sounded good. And, to be fair, you do get the odd one or two who are professional enough to lose an investigator in the blink of an eyelid. One nervous tic and they're gone…

I looked back out at the firmly closed front door across the street. It had bolts through it, as if someone had put on a steel plate or something to reinforce it at the back. Had they been there on my last visit? If so, I hadn't noticed. And this wasn't a particularly rough area: the houses were tiny terraces, but the majority were well kept. There were still some very elderly folk living along here; fortunately for us, since it was the only reason we had a parking space.

'And if we're *un*lucky, he won't be out 'til nearly eleven,' she said, sounding a bit despondent at the prospect.

'No. If we're *un*lucky he'll have swapped to the day shift and we'll be sitting here all night.'

'Bloody hell.'

'Either that or he's not working after all. And we'll be here all night.'

She shivered. 'How do you cope?'

'I'd try wearing trousers for a start.' I sighed. 'Lots of thin layers, like mountaineers do. Thermal underwear, or failing that, a pair of tights under your trousers…'

It was her turn to give *me* a look.

'Keep a fleece and a scarf in the car, even in summer…' I shook my head, patronisingly, I suppose. 'Welcome to the glamorous world of the Benefit Fraud Department,' I said.

It was then, or perhaps a moment or two later, when we heard the explosions.

There were screams, too – there must have been – although no-one else gave any sign of hearing them. Or was that just me, later, in my sleep?

CHAPTER ONE

It always starts with something small, something simple. Stupidly simple.

A tip off from a disgruntled neighbour, for example. (Now the Fraud Hotline is on telly all the time we get a lot more of these; and there's an email address, too, so you can conveniently shop your neighbours in between on-line stamp collecting and downloading pornography.) Often there's no real grounds for suspecting fraud in these cases: somebody's just pissed off about a noisy party or a dog crapping in their garden once too often. The fraud line offers a safe, anonymous way of getting back at your local troublemakers, plus the chance for a bitter little dig or two at anything or anyone else (scroungers, hoodies, poofs, Pakis, teenage mums or public sector employees) for whom you've developed an irrational hatred.

From my own point of view, most callers are worse than useless. Some panic and put the phone down as soon as they get through. Others come on all formal and self righteous, as if laying down a challenge: 'I wish to report Mr Joe Bloggs of 125 So-and-So Street, who is working while signing on as unemployed…' There! I've done it! Now, what are you going to do about it? Well, caller, nothing at all when it turns out, as it very often does, that the 'suspect' wasn't signing on in the first place, or was on some legitimate work experience scheme designed to help him back into a full time job. Caller, if you bothered to talk to your neighbours occasionally, instead of watching them through the net curtains, you might just have got to know that yourself...

Sometimes they get all defensive or apologetic: 'I don't normally do this sort of thing, but...' as if they think our staff will accuse them of being a busybody, or something. And this happens especially at the next stage, because, you see, a name and address isn't much good to us on its own. But when you start asking for more details – Who is he working for? What does he do? Or even just, What time does he normally leave in the mornings? – they never seem to know! Half the time they've no bloody evidence at all for their half-baked suspicions, and, naturally when they come to realise this, it makes them feel even more than ever like a nosy, interfering time-waster bearing an unfair grudge or two. It's no wonder they start blustering or suddenly put down the phone.

Unfortunately, while in previous years I could exercise some professional judgement over these duff referrals (and professionally file them under S H for shredder), recent targets from the Minister's office state that I have to follow up 96.5 per cent of fraud line registrations within fourteen days of receipt. And, of course, the percentage is set to rise year on year, too.

It's not only leads from members of the public that we are obliged to follow up, however. There are referrals from our own staff, small pieces of circumstantial evidence that a box clerk notices on signing day.

They train the clerks to do it, too. To look out for oil under the fingernails or paint on the claimants' hair and clothing – especially significant if the last declared job was as a mechanic or decorator. Or, if they look too smart, the clerks are supposed to ask, 'On your way to an interview, then, Mr Bloggs?' If not, why is he wearing a tie? Highly suspicious!

People consistently signing on late get referred to me, especially if they always come in at lunchtimes or at the end of the day. Anyone who seems to be in a hurry to get away comes under suspicion (that's most of them in my book, signing on can be an upsetting, stressful business at the best of times). Claimants rolling up in a taxi, likewise: we don't pay them enough for that luxury, do we?

You can tell the new boys and girls at the signing desks by the assiduous way they throw themselves into this task, by their disappointment when, a fortnight later, Mr Bloggs has finished doing up his kitchen and doesn't smell of white spirit any more, or when the guy with the oily hands turns out to be an ex-professor of environmental studies who travels everywhere on a dodgy second hand bicycle, and is a leading anti-road campaigner in his spare time. It gets even funnier when the clerks miss a real piece of evidence, like a forged signature on a coupon, although they are taught to look out for that too, of course...

It was exactly this sort of referral that started the whole Grannie Baker business. I was hanging round the front of house early on the Monday afternoon, trying to look busy while avoiding a number of phone calls that I was expecting, and weighing up how soon I could decently go for another tea break. I heard a polite cough and there was Ravi, a bright eighteen year old who has been with us on a temp agency contract for about a year and a half. His low pay and lack of pension and promotion prospects haven't dampened his enthusiasm yet – and I'd give him another six months before he even starts to be cynical. To be honest, if I'd known he was going to be on a box that day I'd have stayed upstairs and taken my chances on the phone.

'Hi, Larry,' he said, rather breathlessly, but then the poor lad does suffer from asthma. 'Could I have a word?'

'Well, I am a bit pushed for time at the moment.' I tapped my clipboard a few times in corroboration. 'Can it wait?'

'Oh. Sure. Sorry. Waiting for a client?'

'Er… Yeah. Yeah, I am.'

'Who's that, then, Larry? Anyone I know?'

Ravi, being a casual, helps out on nearly all the benefit desks, so he's got a good handle on the widest range of clients possible. Plus he seems to have some sort of photographic memory: give him a name and there's a 75 per cent chance that he'll get instant recall of the whole case.

'Cynthia McDonald-Cressie?'

'Thirty six Balmoral Terrace. Born 5 September 1962. Date of claim, 14 April this year. Qualifications, a degree in astrophysics. Last job, artist's model. Signed on late on two occasions, blamed hangover. Interviewed last week for a job at the dog biscuit factory. Overqualified.'

'Not anyone from my box, is it?' Ravi asked. 'I'm on Kiz to Murph this week,' he added helpfully.

I glanced down at the clipboard and studied a blank Fraud 1a form for a moment. 'Look,' I said, 'why don't you catch up with me later? Three o'clock-ish? OK?'

At twenty past three I sidled out of the gents' toilets and was heading up to the Adjudication Office, where the tea club are so efficient that they have bought a cappuccino machine *and* a toaster. Ravi appeared from nowhere, clutching a file. I tried to hide my pain.

'Are you stalking me?'

'You said three o'clock.'

'Come on then, let's see if we can scrounge an expresso from upstairs.'

'Good one. They had pain au chocolat last week, too.'

'Really? I didn't notice that.'

Ravi grinned. 'You have to get there early. With the post.'

I looked at him with new respect. 'You bring work for these people and they *feed* you?' And I was just wondering again whether Will would let me put in a request for an assistant, when Ravi spoiled things by handing me the file.

'It's this guy. Mr Mosley.'

I let the file dangle. 'Oh, yes?'

'I think he may be working.'

'Yes. Otherwise you wouldn't be hassling me, would you?'

'Nights.'

'Nights?'

'He signs on at eleven o'clock. Or he should do. But he usually comes in at three and he looks *completely knackered*. Why would he look tired when he doesn't have to get up early to come in?'

'Oh, Ravi.'

'No, there's more.'

'There'd better be.'

'I said, "Hello, Mr Mosley, you alright?" And he sort of grunted at me, and I said, "You're looking a bit tired today. Not feeling so good? Late night?" He looked quite worried at that.'

'I see.'

'He said, "Mind your own business, Paki boy, or it'll be the worse for you."'

'Very suspicious.'

'I know it doesn't sound much, but as a box clerk you get a sort of gut feeling about these things…'

Up in Adjudication, we helped ourselves to drinks and sat at a glass-topped coffee table that had been spread with glossy magazines, some of them less than a month old. It felt like a different world here. Downstairs nobody would think of bringing in any magazines, unless perhaps they were too lazy to take them to a recycling bin. And in the unlikely event that we all saved up for an expensive coffee machine, it's doubtful anyone would volunteer to keep it clean and perfectly polished.

'So, can you give me a description of this client?'

'Sure. Thirty years old. Five foot ten. Bald head. Blue eyes–'

'Tattoos, by any chance?'

'Yeah. A spider's web, just about here.' Ravi moved his index finger up and around behind his ear. 'Painful, eh? But easy to pick him out on a workplace visit.'

'Naturally bald, or shaven?'

'Um…'

'Or more of a number one all over?' I sighed again. 'Ravi, I'll tell you what I'll do. I'll pop down to the central file for you and grab a racial harassment report form. I personally don't feel you should have to put up with even one small derogatory comment on your ethnicity, but that doesn't mean I'm going to interview Mr Mosley under caution for totally the wrong reason. This is about the flimsiest evidence you could possibly come up with. Anyway,' I went on, 'I don't interview skinheads; they're too scary.'

Ravi looked genuinely disappointed, which knowing how

intelligent he is, surprised me. But then again, I have been seduced by gut instincts myself from time to time. Most investigators swear by them.

'Come on, Ravi,' I said, coaxingly. 'Even a Regional Director could see that you haven't got anything to go on.'

'I'd better get back to my filing,' Ravi said, ungraciously. Many more disappointments, I thought, and he'll start sounding like all the other bitter, put-upon box clerks. Which was a shame, but not really my problem.

'Don't you want your coffee?' I asked, innocently, handing him back the file.

★ ★ ★

Hindsight's a wonderful thing, isn't it? Of course, later I regretted not agreeing to follow up this lead for Ravi, because, on the face of it, a simple promise to add Mosley to my to-do list that afternoon would have let me off the whole affair. Some token agreement then could have buried him in my referral-slip mountain for weeks, well past the time when he could lead me into danger. But who knows? We all look back in judgement on all sorts of decisions, but we don't get to rewind the life video tape and check if our evaluation if right. Life's a complex series of actions and consequences, and we can't always sift out cause and effect in the simplistic way that our hindsight wants us to. I've always assumed that if I'd made a meaningless promise to Ravi, then Will wouldn't have spotted me slacking and therefore wouldn't have ordered me to make a full investigation. But of course there's no way of knowing how that alternative story might have played out. Maybe if I'd said yes early on, things would somehow have turned out even *worse*...

Anyway, that's one handy argument which can be applied to excuse any bad decision you've made. Alternatively, you just agree that there's no point in beating yourself up about it; especially when there are other people who are aiming to do just that.

CHAPTER TWO

Seven o'clock that evening found me on Mission Street with six tulips and a bottle of curaçao. Even half a mile from DoggieBest Ltd, the dusty, bonemeal aroma was still more than noticeable, and I held the flowers to my nose as I walked.

Laura had called shortly after I had slipped Ravi's noose by returning to the file-mountains on my desk. Out of the fire, back into the pan, that felt like. As I reached for the phone, the smallest of the three piles slid quietly to the floor, unluckily missing the bin by inches.

'Hi. 'S Laura.'

'Oh, hi. Hi. *Hi.*' I concentrated on sounding artlessly sympathetic. 'How are you?' Sympathetic but not pitying, that was it. Mustn't sound like I was expecting the worst. 'How are you?' It came out just right, I'd thought.

'I'm fine, Larry, considering, but what about you? You sound a bit strained. Bad day at work?'

'*Me?* Oh, well,' I improvised, 'you know what the pressure in this place is like.'

Laura had worked in benefits herself for a good few years (or, as she liked to put it, a 'terrible few years'); in fact she had been around for some time already when I was transferred over here. Despite her declared unhappiness for the job, she had only gathered the confidence to leave when her boyfriend Stephen (now *ex*-boyfriend Stephen) had suddenly revealed that he had been applying to art colleges across the UK with the intention of studying sculpture. He had gone earlier that autumn – to Grimsby College, the centre of a new abstract art movement, apparently - and Laura had followed him as far as the insurance call centre on the ring road industrial estate. She was on a night shift when he phoned her at work to end their relationship. The final indignity being that 'for training purposes,' every call is recorded…

'I was wondering… Are you busy tonight?'

My brain ran quickly through a few jokes about washing my hair or taking champagne with a pair of well-known teenage soap stars. I said, 'Er, no, I don't think so. Why?'

'D'you wanna come round for cocktails?'

'Cocktails,' I repeated, mock impressed. 'I'm impressed.'

'Stirred but not shaken,' she laughed. 'I'll cook as well if you want.' I made a mental note to call at Pizza Nirvana on the way.

'Great. Thanks.'

'Say seven? Bring some blue curakayoh.'

'What?'

'It's a liqueur. Also known as Blue Bols. Available at good wine stores and most large supermarkets.'

'Fine.' I grinned to myself. Foreign languages aren't Laura's strongest suit.

'Seven, then? I won't keep you – you've probably got some master criminal to catch.'

'Ha, ha.'

'See you later, then.'

'Take care,' I said, caringly.

By a five past seven I was turning into her driveway. Highfield Mansions had been repainted since my last visit: all exterior woodwork was now thickly overlaid with a dark green gloss which might just have originated at the Council's Parks and Gardens depot. A municipal colour scheme failed, however, to alter the image of the building. All other aspects of it combined to state unequivocally: Private Rented Accommodation, cheaper end.

Out of habit I gave the intercom an eight second blast, but there was no music playing today.

'I was meditating,' complained the voice box.

'Sorry.'

'Come up.'

The front door and I endured our usual battle of wills: since the paint job it seemed even harder to shoulder a passage into the building; no wonder both recent burglaries had been effected via ground floor windows to the rear. To prove a macho athleticism on my part, I took the stairs three at a time without tripping once.

'Hi.'

'Hi.' I attempted to breathe just a little more quietly. 'Good to see you.'

I leaned in hopefully, but Laura's lips gave me the shortest possible peck on the cheek; from her hair I breathed the truly intoxicating mix of kiwi fruit and cannabis smoke.

'*Larry,*' she protested, in that tone of voice that's supposed to convey gratitude, but always sounds to me like despair. 'You *shouldn't* have. Let me get them into water quick, before I forget.'

As always, Laura's flat felt cold and slightly damp, despite the gas fire blazing away on the far wall. Since she had secondary glazing and thick, if tasteless carpeting, I'd never been able to work this one out. Lack of effective roof insulation, probably. Stephen used to say it was the effect of living with a witch, but who is he to talk? After all, the acknowledged pride of his – admittedly impressive – vinyl and CD collection are the ancient picture discs by bands like Black Sabbath and The Grateful Dead. And if you believe Laura, his behaviour's been pretty satanic over the years.

I toasted myself against the fire while Laura hunted for a jam jar big enough for the flowers.

'Hungry?' she called.

'So, so.'

'You always say that. Are you dieting or something?'

'Dieting?' I ran my tongue over my upper teeth and swallowed a lingering taste of pepperoni and six cheese, Sicilian style. 'Real men never diet.'

'D'you think this'll be alright?' She held out a catering size pickled onion jar through the open kitchen door.

'Looks big enough, yeah.'

'Right.'

'If you turn the label to the wall, it shouldn't show too much.'

'Why don't you do the drinks while I arrange these?' She called from the sink. There was a clatter as she dropped the scissors onto the lino. I moved quickly into the kitchenette and breathed in deeply as she squeezed by.

'Where are your instructions?'

'What instructions?'

'For the cocktails.'

'I haven't got any.' I heard her moving around the living room, looking for a patch of daylight for the flowers. 'I just thought curaçao would be fun.'

'What am I supposed to be making then?'

'I dunno. Use your imagination. You can use anything that's there.'

'Great,' I mused. 'Probably a choice between Dubonnet and Vimto.'

Despite the promise of dinner, Laura was soon sidetracked into rolling a joint while telling me an unfunny story about her first attempt at a blue cocktail. Naturally she had done it in a tiny local pub offering a limited choice of booze to a very limited clientele. This was a place with original edition Babycham posters, where light and bitter was still a fashionable drink. 'We just stumbled on the place,' Laura had told me, explaining how she and a friend had accidentally become separated from a student group on a pub crawl. *Stumbled*, I thought to myself, is the operative word.

'So I go up to the bar and ask for Blue Bols, and he looks at me like I'm an idiot, and I'm going "Blue Bols!" for about the third time. "Have you got Blue Bols?" And he sticks his hands deep into his trouser pockets and says –'

'"Don't think so, darling, but as the wife's away you could check 'em for me."'

Laura was sniggering into her scratched champagne flute hard enough to spatter her shirt front. 'Marion went round the bar and started undoing the guy's belt,' she giggled, then stopped suddenly. 'We got thrown out soon after that.'

I lifted my glass to the light. 'You had a lucky escape then.' Laura stretched her hand across towards me.

Inhaling deeply, I waited for the familiar ebb and flow of dizziness and dislocation. I was relaxed in a way, but beneath the growing well-being induced by good quality North African resin, I recognised an undertow of unease. Laura wasn't easy to be with, really...

'Er... Look. Larry...'

Oh. Here we go, I thought, I must be psychic or something. Feel uneasy, then she's got something to say. I gave her a sharp look, or as sharp as you can on three dodgy cocktails and a puff of full strength joint. 'You're going to ask me a favour, aren't you?'

'Stephen's coming round later to pick up some things.'

'Ah.'

'Sorry, I should have said. I just felt I needed some moral support.'

'It's what friends are for,' I mumbled.

'I couldn't face him on my own.'

I wasn't too keen on facing him myself. Not that he was particularly threatening – unless he turned up with some butch heavy metal mates, of course, there was always the danger of that. But it was more the… the *disappointment* of the situation. You come for cocktails with a pretty girl and you end up playing gooseberry at the death of her last relationship. Dinner doesn't happen and the cocktails are undrinkable anyway. I mean, it's not exactly a result, is it?

'You will stay, won't you?'

'Of course I will. What time's he coming?' I asked, inhaling furiously.

'Half eight, nine.' Laura glanced at her watch. 'I should get cooking.'

'Don't worry. I'm not that hungry now.' Just this once I meant it.

'I'm sorry.' Laura bit her lip. 'I shouldn't have…' I didn't reply. 'Bastard!' Laura spat, suddenly. 'I wish I'd never met the bastard. Even when he's gone he's fucking things up for me.'

'Look, let's make this easier on all of us,' I said. 'Get his stuff into bin bags and leave it waiting downstairs in the hall. We don't even need to see him.'

'He'll knock anyway. He'll be convinced I'm holding on to something of his.'

'We don't have to answer.' I started to giggle. 'We can hide.' I had a brief image of us buried together under the duvet. 'What's he going to do? Kick the door down?'

'He's got a key.'

'Oh.'

'The landlord wanted to charge me fifty quid to change the locks,' said Laura defensively. 'I'm still disputing it.'

'Outrageous,' I agreed, though you could see the man's point of view. 'You should have told him your boyfriend's a psychopath. Does he want a corpse in his flat? Think of the redecorating bills. And it can be very hard to get another tenant after this sort of tragedy has occurred...

'Or,' I went on, remembering a previous thought, 'you could say Stephen was into Satanism. Your landlord wouldn't want the Devil summoned up in the flat; it would upset the neighbours.'

'Yes, the people downstairs complained about him playing Ozzy Osbourne once.'

'There you are then. Actually,' I continued, 'Satanists have a lot in common with obsessive record collectors. Rituals, arcane knowledge–'

'Don't!'

'The anoraks that they wear–'

Laura gave me a slap. 'It would get rid of him quicker if it was all packed up,' she said. 'But it's the records that he's coming for. Bin bags won't be any good.'

'Mmm. Got any spare cardboard boxes then?'

★ ★ ★

Six boxes laid out across the carpet, we stepped as one to the chipboard shelves. Close to, you began to see just how much music the man possessed: after all, even a four disc, 1970s concept album in a special edition padded box takes up only, say, three and a half centimetres of shelf width. You could fit hundreds of vinyl LPs into a single block of this storage unit, and CDs, of course, being so much shorter, could be double layered within the same space.

'How long would it take you to listen to all this?' I wondered. 'One at a time, straight through without skipping tracks? About a decade or so?'

'Hardly. Stephen will tell you if you ask him, though. He worked it out once.' I nodded. 'Now you know why there was always music on. All the time...'

'But it always seemed to me to be the same tracks.'

'Yeah. He had his favourites.'

'Bit of a waste if most of this never got listened to.'

'I dunno why you're so impressed,' Laura rankled. 'You've seen it plenty of times. You've had the guided tour, haven't you?'

'Yeah, but it must be more than, oh, two years ago. And I wasn't concentrating. I was waiting for him to offer me a beer. Which never came.'

Laura pulled a disc suddenly from the middle of a shelf. 'I'll be glad to be rid of this one.' She flapped it dangerously close to my face. 'If he'd stayed much longer I'd probably have smashed it.'

'Smash it now,' I said without thinking. 'It's the least of what he deserves.'

Outside, a wispy cloud had gradually spread itself across the sun; the pools of light cast by the small windows disappeared, leaving the flat interior uniformly dull. My tulips lost half their colour instantly.

Laura shook her head. 'I'm not going to bring myself down to that level. I want to keep the moral high ground.'

She looked up moodily and caught my eye. It was then we thought of it: Laura's act of revenge.

The idea itself was simple enough. We'd swap discs from cover to cover, CDs from box to box. Mix them all up. He'd get them home, get a beer, pull up an armchair and pull out his favourite album only to find inside, oh, I don't know, something he didn't like much, hopefully, something he regretted buying. Imagine the frustration! Unable to choose any music until every disc was checked and resorted!

Yet no real damage would have been done. The moral high ground would be well and truly kept.

'I'll let the next girl he's unfaithful to get the hammer out,' she said. 'It'll be nice to know she's got the option, whoever she is.'

'We could even be a bit witty about this,' I suggested, warming to the idea. 'Say we swap Elvis Presley for Elvis Costello. He sees Elvis on the label, puts it on, bang! Something's wrong but he can't quite get what it is. Like when you have a mouthful of tea, but you're expecting coffee...'

Laura was, for some odd reason, frowning at me. I went on, 'James Brown into James Blunt; The Rolling Stones into the Stone Ro...'

Laura shook her head. 'Random changes,' she said. 'Harder to put right.'

'Less interesting.'

'You really do appreciate a puzzle, don't you?' said Laura. 'In fact you can't do *anything* without making a puzzle out of it.'

'Is that supposed to be a compliment?'

'I'm not sure. It's one reason why you're still doing your job.'

'Funny, I thought I did the job because I need the money.'

'Bah,' she said, 'you love it really. You enjoy the challenge of a complicated case. And you're always so pleased when you get a result. Your little face just lights up with glee–'

'Get off. I'm not some saddo who only talks about his work, am I?'

'That's not what I am trying to say,' said Laura, not quite answering the question. I glanced down at her three quarters-full box and then at the two discs in my hands that I was puzzling over.

'Anyway, your motivation does you credit,' said Laura, surprising me with a sudden, more-or-less serious compliment.

'Thank you,' I said, trying hard to catch her eye. 'Would you like to be my boss?'

'Oh, go on then, if I must.'

'Great. Apparently I've been called in to see you first thing tomorrow morning. So it'd be so much easier if I could stay over tonight…' I paused, still watching her, but she was busily parcelling up more records. I suppose the real trouble with our relationship is that Laura thinks my flirting is just another ironic joke. Either that or she's just never fancied me in the slightest.

And then, fifty minutes later, Stephen surprised us by arriving early (and alone) in a taxi. Fortunately for us, with the meter running he was in an unobservant hurry to get away, and by ten o'clock I was eating burned burritos and salad, and wondering which of his thousands of songs he would try to listen to first.

CHAPTER THREE

'Mr Mosley? Mr Oswald Mosley?'

Before almost any other face I'd have had difficulty keeping a smirk off my lips. Oswald is such a ridiculously old-fashioned name as it is; Oswald *Mosley*, to those who know their history, is more ridiculous still.

But the figure in front of me wasn't built for mockery. Dark hair had been shaved right back to its lumpy skull; a blue spider's web crawled halfway up its throat. Suspicious eyes were buried in puffy flesh, bulging behind the pasty skin of a face that saw little daylight. The nose was broken, of course, but perhaps in three places; two front teeth were broken, too. Worst of all from my point of view, the face sat on a thick, thick neck, above limbs and a torso that, while rapidly running to fat, still held enough strength and anger to batter a pubful of policemen. Ravi was right: you wouldn't want to meet him up an alley on a dark night. I wasn't too crazy about this appointment in broad daylight, either.

'Who're you?'

I lifted my ID to his eye level and held it there. Close enough for him to read; not so close as to invade his personal space. I waited while he squinted at the small print. Just as I was beginning to think he might have a learning difficulty, his eyes made the telltale shift from the card into mine.

'I'm from the Jobcentre, Mr Mosley,' I said. I gave him

one of my most world-weary smiles. 'I'm afraid they've asked me to do some random checks. I'm sorry if I'm disturbing you?'

'What checks?' The piggy little eyes disappeared into his frowning face. 'What checks are these?'

'It's… Just a short questionnaire, really. To make sure some of their facts are correct.' I tried to look like a man who thought his instructions were rather embarrassing, and a bit of a waste of time. It's one technique to disarm a suspicious client. It wasn't hard: it wasn't at all far from the truth.

'Nothing to worry about, though. If I could pop in and take ten minutes of your time…'

Normally here I'd make a move for the door, or take a step forward at least, maybe stretch out an arm in an 'after you' gesture towards the interior. But with Mosley I stood where I was, maintaining firm but friendly eye contact (well, contact with the folds of skin where his eyes ought to have been); with open, relaxed body language, and a guileless half smile on my face. He's been signing on a while now, I told myself, he knows the score. He won't be unduly worried by a bit of rogue bureaucracy unexpectedly cropping up. It happens all the time! He'll take it in his stride. Come on, Oswald, I willed him, let's get in and get this over with…

'No.'

'I'm sorry?'

'It's not convenient.'

Damn! Now I was tempted to say 'OK, no problem' and walk away, but I knew if I left it now, I'd only have to waste another day later, because you could guarantee Will wouldn't forget about it. Having ordered the investigation to go ahead, he'd be on my back until I'd completed a thorough report, or at the very least something that appeared to be thorough. Our

Will can micro-manage with the best of them when he wants to, and the only escape is when some other unlucky bugger misses a monthly target and catches his eye.

'I'm sorry.' I sighed. 'I keep telling the supervisors we should phone first, but that's not the way they like to do it...' This sounded a bit too disingenuous, even for Oswald Mosley, so I hurriedly added, 'Look, if we can just get this out of the way now, we won't have to worry about making another appointment for you. You'd be doing me a favour, to be honest... *Help me to keep all the payments running smoothly...*' I added meaningfully.

I watched him weighing this up. He was within his rights to send me away, but surely he knew how to play the claim game by now? He could be called in to the office at an even less convenient time; he could find himself referred to a CV Clinic, Careers Guidance Interview or two-day Work Trial just because his file had sat open a few days longer than usual. The key to being a claimant is to know when to keep your head down and when to punch someone else's in. Only the mental cases enjoy picking a fight at every opportunity; most know just when they have to give a little bit.

'Right.' He fixed me with a hard look, then jerked his head. 'You'll have to wait while I put the dog out.'

When someone's guilty of benefit fraud they tend to argue and threaten; well, at the very start of the investigation they do. But there was no angry bluster from Mr Mosley, no whining or swearing about harassment, no vague threats to go to the papers or to his MP. And there were no wisecracks about living in a totalitarian state, either. Part of the reason was in evidence once I got inside: Oswald Mosley, like his namesake, was in favour of them.

'I'll make a cup of tea.'

This seemed unexpectedly civil, or maybe he did have something to hide, and wanted time to anticipate my questions, to prepare his story. That's probably what Ravi would have thought, but we're not working for MI5: my clients aren't often that clever.

I sat in a leather armchair and tried to ignore the fierce barking from the yard while I admired the décor and organisation of the room. Everything was neat, stylish and efficient, and it was only up close that you saw how cheap the materials were. The politicised image wasn't subtle, although in a way it was trying to be. It all looked like a budget-TV makeover designed by Martin Bormann's granddaughter. I was surprised. I'd expected to walk into a bit of a dump. This room didn't even smell of cigarettes, and there wasn't a lager tin or pizza box in sight.

One corner functioned as an office: a small unit with a miniature shredder was tucked in beside a heavy, old, steel filing cabinet that had been resprayed in silver. A row of reference books included both *Mein Kampf* and *Teach Yourself Non-Violent Direct Action*. A scuffed laptop sat open on the dining table along with some highlighter pens, and a sheaf of papers had been roughly stuffed into a cardboard folder. A road atlas had fallen off the shelf or table to form a tent shape on the floor.

The remainder of the room was taken up by two armchairs in black leather facing a widescreen TV, and, to one side, a glass fronted cabinet of the sort that an elderly maiden aunt would have for her collection of china dolls. There was nothing as fragile as china in this one, however.

'Milk or sugar?'

'Milk and two, thanks.' I was guessing that a man with his tattoos wouldn't be offering Lapsang, no matter how tidy his office, no matter how lovingly he spot-lit his Nazi bric-a-brac. 'Three in a mug.'

'*Shut up!*' he shouted, and I heard him kick the back door. The dog paused for a few seconds: possibly it needed to get its breath back.

I opened my leather-effect clipboard and flicked through a few flimsy sheets. The tea came in a cheap Royal Wedding mug that, though badly chipped, had outlasted by two decades the marriage it was designed to commemorate. I took a small mouthful and decided that the mug was the best thing about it.

'Thanks for agreeing to this, Mr Mosley,' I said. 'It does make it easier for everyone. Gets things out of the way promptly…' I smiled, but there was no response. I looked at my notes. 'So, it's Oswald Mosley, formerly known as Pete Biggs, and before that Lance Biggs. Current address, well, here, obviously… Thirty one Balmoral Terrace… Not on the phone here… Date of birth? Thanks. And you live alone, don't you? No dependants claimed for…'

'Correct.'

'Good…'

I sipped my tea. He didn't look like a skimmed milk man, I thought. Would there turn out to be a case here over undeclared income from a partner or lodger? It was a long time since we'd got someone on that account: not since Herman found twenty one pairs of lace knickers drying above Garth Thingummy's bath. And Garth would have got away with it if he had thought to claim he was a transvestite…

'Can you just tell me how long you've been claiming, Mr Mosley?'

'Since last May.'

'May the fifth, to be precise. Time flies, doesn't it? Be Christmas before we know it.'

Mosley was doing a good job of remaining impassive. I asked, 'And what were you doing immediately before the claim?'

'I moved here from Oldham.'

'And your job-?'

'I was at the university.'

I suppose some surprise showed on my face.

'*Cleaning,*' he sneered, irritation finally breaking through. 'Read your forms, pal, it's all down there, isn't it?'

I coughed. 'Well, I have to be sure I am interviewing the claimant in person.' For a moment, his blank look was back. 'I have to be sure it's really you.'

'Fucking hell, you only see me every other week! If you don't believe it's me, send that little Paki lad round. He knows me well enough by now.'

I sipped my tea non-committally until he settled back down into his chair. Very gently I said, 'And have you done any paid work in the last five months?'

'No.'

'Nothing part time, even?' I asked. 'Casual work counts as well, I'm afraid. You might not have realised that–'

'Nothing.'

I nodded sympathetically. 'Difficult to find the right job, isn't it?'

'You're the first person from the Jobcentre who's admitted that,' said Mosley, but in a tone that was careful rather than grateful.

'Even if the unemployment rate has dropped to less than two per cent.' I stared him out for a bit, and then, doing my best to sound genuinely interested, I asked, 'Why did you move here?'

'I've got... friends here. The cleaning company was

cutting costs. Oldham's fucked anyway. Too many... I thought it would be easier to get a job.'

'But you haven't found a job.'

'No.'

I paused for as long as I dared.

'What else d'you want me to say?' he said angrily. 'I haven't found a job. It's not for want of trying. I look at your boards: half the jobs there say "No visible tattoos." It's discrimination, that's what it is...'

I thought I'd mention this to Ravi; he was bright enough to understand the irony.

'What about *unpaid* work?'

'You don't need to know about that, do you? What I do in my spare time is up to me, isn't it?'

'Unfortunately it isn't as simple as that.'

'Why not? It wouldn't interfere with me looking for a job.'

I tried to look apologetic again, and considered telling him that I didn't make the rules. But he was quicker off the mark.

'Anyway, I haven't done any.'

'Right.' I busied myself looking through my papers, as if I were new to the job and didn't quite know what to do next. Then I looked up suddenly. 'Nice office space you've put together. Very professional.'

Oswald Mosley gave me a hard look. 'You know what they say,' he said, '"Looking for work is a job in itself." I like to be organised and methodical about it.'

'Nice tea,' I lied. 'Any chance of another one?' Mosley wiped his hands down his jeans and took my mug into the kitchen.

I wandered round the table and glanced at the laptop, but of course it was only displaying a screen saver (this one was a girl in a basque and fishnet stockings, with a military-style peaked cap on her head). I didn't quite dare touch the keyboard: you never know if these things are going to bleep at you, and the kitchen door was still ajar.

I opened the cardboard file. The top page was headed 'English Patriot's Party, Hampton Branch AGM'. There was a fluttering flag of St George logo. My eye caught Oswald Mosley's name under the heading 'Newsletters.' He had been asked by the committee to write fewer, to consider 'quality over quantity.' Under these minutes were some photos which hadn't come out properly: black with pairs of white circles, possibly taken at night. There was a graph of the exponential rise of immigration from Asia and Africa over the past ten years. The figures were not attributed to any source. There was also a business card with his name on it, of the sort you can print yourself from an arcade machine, or at home if you have the right software. I quickly wrote the mobile phone number onto my notepad.

I heard the kettle click off automatically and I was back in my seat before the fridge door thumped itself shut.

'It's my understanding, Mr Mosley,' I said, turning a page on the clipboard, 'that you always sign on late.'

'Yeah, I suppose I do.'

'Why is that?'

'The afternoon's much more convenient for me.'

'Mmm.' I nodded. 'What d'you do in the morning, then?'

'Stay in bed.'

I made a wry face. 'You don't strike me as being someone particularly lazy, though.'

Mosley wiped his hands again. 'I have trouble sleeping.'

'Oh, I'm sorry to hear that. My brother's an insomniac,' I improvised. 'It's a real curse. Of course, it's not so bad for him as he works nights.' I searched out Mosley's eyes in their folds of skin. 'He's been with quite a few different employers now, but nights, always nights…'

'Oh, yeah?'

'Have you ever worked nights yourself?'

There was a longish pause. 'Sorry?'

'Have you ever worked nights?'

'No… No I haven't.'

Again I gave him a long stare, raising my tea mug as an excuse to say nothing, although I really couldn't face drinking any more.

'Are there any more questions?' he asked. 'You said it wouldn't take long.'

'No,' I said. 'I can probably do the rest of the checklist from your original forms. That's red tape for you.' I stood up. 'Would you mind if I used your loo? All this tea…'

Upstairs, there was only one toothbrush by the basin, and one towel bathrobe on the door. But I was beginning to discount the live-in girlfriend idea anyway. Not because Mosley was such an ugly git – sexual dynamics can be so paradoxical that he could easily have had Miss UK on his arm – but, without being sexist or anything, how many women would keep a second-hand filing cabinet in the living room, even one with a reasonably attractive paint job? To my mind that was even more significant than the Death's Head riding crop, Tank Commander ceremonial spurs and all the other pieces in his collection. Depending on her politics, the poor girl might just put up with the boyfriend's eccentric collecting habits, but most women would rather chuck out the paperwork than make it the first thing that any party guests would see.

I sneaked a look in the bedrooms: given the attempt at cool downstairs, these were reassuringly threadbare and untidy. One of them was in use as a sort of gym, with weights, a floor to ceiling mirror and some sort of rowing machine, all straps and levers, leaning against the wall. There was an unmade bed piled up with black sheets. The other was where he slept, then: you could tell by the smell. I had a look round anyway. Dark brown duvet cover, saggy pillows, worn carpet. Nothing in these rooms, nor really in the rest of the house, had suggested any great influx of money. If Mosley was working, he was being ripped off.

He was scowling suspiciously as I came back into the living room, and I had the panicky thought that he had heard the bedroom floorboards creaking above his head. I nodded pleasantly at the display cabinet.

'Been collecting long?'

' 'Bout five years. On and off.'

'Where d'you keep the rest of it?'

He frowned. I said, 'If you've been collecting for five years, you must have more than this.'

'I sold some on a while back.'

'Oh.' I nodded nonchalantly. 'Are there a lot of buyers about for this sort of stuff, then?'

'There's never been more interest in the Third Reich,' said Mosley, with pride in his voice. 'It fascinates people.'

'I would have thought it was all a bit old hat.'

'What's different,' he said, 'is that historians are seeing it all in a new light. So much that was taken for granted is being re-evaluated.'

'I'll bet.'

'Look,' he went on, firmly, 'don't knock it. You're an intelligent bloke. You know that politicians lie. You know that you can't believe all you read in the papers.' He paused. 'Don't you?'

'Well… Yes.'

'Some lies just don't get found out for decades, that's all.'

'You must find it hard to let all this stuff go,' I said.

'What?'

'The memorabilia. Your collection. Don't you miss it when it's sold?'

'Nah, not really.'

'D'you make much of a profit?'

His piggy eyes gave me a careful look, and he paused before saying, 'Rarely,' and folding his arms.

'Shame,' I commiserated. 'Are you going to Great Escape 2000, by the way? Saturday, at the Exhibition Centre? There are loads of dealers there.' I tried a light emphasis on the word 'dealers', but Mosley remained poker faced.

'Couldn't afford to buy anything at the moment. I'm on the dole, aren't I?'

'I just wondered.'

'You're going, are you?'

'Er, yeah.' Suddenly I felt uneasy admitting this, as if it brought my interests dangerously close to his. 'I go for the lectures, though, not the second hand stuff.'

'They don't know what they're talking about, half these people. Get their facts wrong, miss things out…'

'There's some truth in that,' I acknowledged. 'Have you been before, then?

'Oh, I've been before,' said Mosley, as if it was obvious that he would. 'Last year I signed up for an Open College course with one of the lecturers.'

I tried to remember the exact rules on distance learning while claiming.

'It was a waste of money,' he continued. 'It wasn't what I expected.'

No, I thought, I don't suppose the syllabus covered holocaust revisionism.

'Look, Mr Mosley,' I said, maintaining the apologetic but honest approach, 'I'm afraid I've got some bad news. They've asked me to inform you that we are going to impose a weekly signing routine. That means–'

'I know what it means. I'll have to come in every Monday instead of every other.'

'Yes. I am sorry about this. If you carry on being late–'

There was a burst of fierce barking and scratching behind the door: the dog had managed to get into the kitchen and wanted to join us, quite possibly to defend its master from my sanctions. Mosley quelled it with a few loud words. 'You fucking people are the limit,' he said, finally losing his composure, though less aggressively than I had feared. 'It's harassment. You wouldn't do this if I was black.'

'You might think that,' I said nervously, 'but actually we harass everyone equally.' Mosley stared for a moment, and then, to my surprise, he laughed.

* * *

Like the clerks, Fraud officers tend to know when a client is lying. Or at least they think they do. 'You get a feel for it,' they say. 'It comes with experience.' Or even, 'You just *know*.' I love that. '*You just know.*' What are we, clairvoyant or something?

The trainers tell you to look out for certain signs of lying that psychologists have identified: undue sweating, wringing hands, fidgeting, tics and other nervous mannerisms. All the things that occur quite naturally, guilty conscience or no, when some hard nosed investigator turns up on your doorstep carrying the implicit threat of cutting off your income. Answering questions too quickly, too emphatically ('protesting too much') or not being able to answer at all are also suspicious. Well, that just about wraps it up, doesn't it? Job done! What a shame that body language and speech patterns on their own don't actually count as evidence. What a shame that a gut instinct isn't admissible.

My feeling was that Mosley was lying, but perhaps only to the extent that he was working very hard, *unpaid*, for his political ideals. Strictly speaking he should declare this, and be prepared to give it up if it clashed with a paid job, but it was hardly big deal, even to someone like Will. There was no obvious evidence that took me further towards a successful fraud investigation, anyway; even his business card had the union flag all over it.

So I nursed my professional pride with the assumption that even the stakeout of Mosley's house that Will had recommended was just another motion to go through before I could concentrate on another case. Now that I had completed the visit, he seemed a bit less threatening than I had first imagined, and even if he turned up at the convention at the weekend, I decided it wouldn't be a problem. People like Mosley were all show, weren't they? All image and not really a danger to anyone. You just get a feel for these things.

CHAPTER FOUR

I've never been happy parking in the central multi-storey.

For one thing, it's the worst piece of architecture this side of Birmingham, not discounting the flyover, the dog-biscuit works and the new shopping mall, which has plastic Corinthian columns *and* sheet metal flooring. One day, maybe, the 'ten storey, mouldy concrete' look will be back in vogue, but hopefully only for prisons of a repressive regime, not as the centrepiece of High Street redevelopment.

The interior, with its intricate twists and clever use of corner spaces, is an open invitation to vandalism. On the upper floors are bay after bay spread with cubes of shattered windscreen, or smothered in burnt out oil. Every wall and pillar is thick with graffiti, every staircase sticky with piss. Normally, I'll go out to the old gasworks site, or even drive around town for an hour looking for a meter, but today I had an appointment to keep. And the fact that I wasn't actually going to leave the car there didn't make me feel any better about it.

After all, hubcaps are easier to replace than, say, kneecaps…

I slowly nosed the Citroën into level nine, concentrating harder than the day I took my driving test, and feeling about as cool. Not that my old car couldn't take a few more scrapes – they'd only blend in with the damage I had already accrued – but if I ran into a gang of yobs… Well, the write off value of the vehicle was always going to be far less than my no-claims bonus. If anything serious happened to it, I'd be doing my stakeouts sitting on a bicycle.

There was no-one on the tenth floor. At least, no-one instantly visible, which wasn't saying much as there are plenty of nooks, crannies and pillars to use as hiding places, plenty of corners with the light fittings smashed to pieces. There were no cars parked there that evening, either. I killed the engine, wound the window quickly down and listened intently. Not a sound, bar some water seepage dripping. Good: nothing dangerous.

Then, feeling foolish as usual, I flashed my headlights three times: two long, one short. I wound up the window, checked the door locks and settled down to wait.

There's always a wait for Chandler to show himself. He's checking that I haven't been followed.

Why did I bother continuing with these assignations, I wondered. It had been months since Chandler had given me what I needed. Here I was in the ugliest spot in the county just to pander to his bizarre fantasies: meetings in the dark, code words and disguises, all the tradecraft of a spy movie, but thirty years out of date. It really was no good feeling sorry for him, or being weak and embarrassed about it myself. I was going to have to dump him, I told myself. No question; no more time to waste.

Ten minutes later I had my hand on the ignition key when I caught a sudden movement in the wing mirror, and felt a sharp pull at the door handle rocking the car. I flicked up the catch.

'Hello, Chandler.'

'Hello, Chief.' Chandler never refers to me by name. He thinks someone is bugging my car. 'Nice day.'

'Nice?' I said, surprised. 'It's freezing.'

'Good to see the sun, though.'

'It would be.' I looked out around the dark, dank walls. 'Is that what the hat's for, then? To keep the sun off?'

'Found it in the Oxfam shop. They threw it in for nothing with an old cigarette case I bought.'

You had to hand it to Chandler, he was really going for the image. I mean, the trenchcoat was normal enough, and people do occasionally wear a suit, collar and tie, though vintage gear is unusual on someone over twenty. But the genuine trilby, the steel case with the Camels in it, the Zippo lighter... The former addiction to bourbon, the – albeit inconsistent – American vocabulary...

Chandler, of course, didn't call himself an *informer*, but a gumshoe, a Private Eye, a Detective or even, God help us, a Dick.

'You weren't followed, were you?' he continued, more seriously. 'You took the long way round? Changed direction a few times?'

'I wasn't followed. Who's going to follow me? The last two leads you gave me were just blokes claiming for wives who had left them. We're not exactly dealing with the Mafia, are we?'

Chandler seemed to look a bit hurt at this, though it was difficult to tell under the hat. I went on irritably, 'the only people who might be remotely interested in your little tip offs are the clerks who haven't met their own targets for benefit disallowances this month.'

'There we are, then. Always best to be on the safe side.'

'What have you got for me this time?'

Chandler didn't answer straight away, but leaned forward and switched on the car radio. I was worried about my battery, but I couldn't be bothered to protest. Through an ugly crackle and hiss you could just make out the sound of an orchestra, with the strings, thin and strained amid the interference, coming to some sort of climax.

'Classical, classical. Doesn't anybody broadcast jazz any more?' He pressed the full range of buttons; only three were functioning at all.

'You won't get any sort of reception in here,' I complained, 'it's built like a World War Two concrete bunker.'

'That's OK. The static alone is enough to disrupt recording equipment.'

'Oh, yeah, and I s'pose the jazz will bore them into giving up, too.'

'I live on the streets, Chief,' said Chandler, hurt. 'And on the streets they have a saying: "A missing person is a person who let his guard drop."'

He settled back into my battered upholstery. 'Want to know about a claimant with a successful grocery delivery business?'

'Robin Smith,' I said. 'He shops for six elderly people on his estate, and for a bloke in a wheelchair. He doesn't charge for it, but since some of them insist, it's a straight donation to Age Concern. I turn a blind eye to him keeping the price of a pint.'

'There's a girl... Signs on Tuesdays. She's a nurse. Sally something... I could point her out to you.'

'And you'd be pointing out Sally MacIntyre. Not nursing. She's going to university to do physiotherapy. Her Careers Adviser set up a work placement for her. Unpaid. Declared to the clerks.'

I was beginning to feel I could give Ravi a run for his money here. Mr Memory the Second.

'Some of them gippos on the caravan park–'

I made a sort of loud harrumphing noise.

'I saw the lad from number fifty four at the Trade Counter in B and Q last week. Gary Price…'

I closed my eyes while he described the purchase of some innocent bricks and mortar.

I had first come across Chandler when he started signing on himself. At the time they were making investigators do new claims interviews: to 'nip any fraud in the bud,' as Will had put it, although the shortage of new claims advisers might also have had something to do with the policy.

Chandler's form stated that he had been a self-employed private investigator. This sounded interesting – it was even a line of work that I had vaguely wondered about for myself – so I got him talking about it.

He'd only really had a handful of cases, one of which was an unfaithful husband job. The guy was a cleaner at the art gallery and was actually discovered having sex in the Impressionist room, on the sofa in front of the Degas ballet girls. Not by Chandler, who was busy with surveillance at the man's local, but by the Curator and a visiting delegation from our twin town in Germany.

'If they'd been in the Installations Room, they might have got away with it,' I remember joking. 'They could have been taken for a piece of conceptual art. Or *contra*ceptual…'

Anyway, when Chandler let slip the name of the philanderer I realised he was one of our clients. He had been signing on the whole time. So the poor guy lost his job, was cautioned by the police for indecent behaviour, was told to sleep in the spare room until further notice, *and* was stung by yours truly for a large benefit repayment, though since he was now legitimately on the register, the money could only come off him at about two pounds a week from his giro; hardly worth the effort, really.

And Chandler had started life as a benefit supergrass.

To be fair, he had come up with the odd very hot tip over the years, even as he struggled to get sober and battle with eviction from his flat. But then the tower block was demolished and he became homeless, and as the economy picked up, claimant numbers began to fall, fake as well as genuine... And, well, let's face it, he hadn't really been much good in the first place... And so this was where we had ended up. Arguing over worthless information in a damp multi storey car park.

'Come on, Chandler,' I said, 'you'll have to do better than this. I'm not paying for any half-baked anecdotes about someone who could be working because he's got a purposeful look on his face these days.'

'I thought I was on a retainer anyway.'

'I'm not Inspector Morse, you know. More's the pity. I don't have a budget for this. I have to hide it in my expenses sheet, you know that.'

'Bloody skinflint organisation. Serve you right if I worked exclusively for the police, wouldn't it?'

Actually, I thought, I'd be delighted. It would save me the embarrassment of sacking you. But I wasn't getting my hopes up. I was dubious of Chandler's story about being on the police payroll, even though his knowledge was detailed and accurate on the subject of Witness Protection and the assignment of new identities. He'd obviously researched this, but if he was feeding them the same quality of information as mine, it was all academic anyway. Chandler with a new identity? For his sort of intelligence they wouldn't even pay for a new haircut. And Paul Wodehouse had talked about informers with me once or twice when drunk, but Chandler's description had never come up, much less his name.

'What I need,' I said patiently, 'is something big. Worth paying for. If it's an individual they've got to be earning a large salary and still claiming, or they've got to have been working for months, *years*. Better still, some sort of major scam. An employer with more than just one or two claimants on his payroll. Go and look into the local factories for me: I've been phoning them for months and they never return my calls. Grannie Baker's, maybe. Or DoggieBest... And I'm not interested in a student in a bassett hound costume handing out free samples on the High Street. I'm sorry mate, but if you can't get the right stuff you should go back to selling the Big Issue.'

Chandler looked away. He mumbled something like 'Below the belt.'

'Or if you want something easier, there's a claimant called Oswald Mosley. Tattooed and a skinhead haircut. I want him proved innocent as soon as possible.'

'Innocent?'

'I just want him out of my pending tray.'

'And you had the nerve to turn down my on stuff on Gary Price!'

'Look, Chandler,' I said, trying to sound regretful but not guilty, 'I've got work to do. Maybe it's time we called it a day.'

'I'll see you in a month, then,' he said coldly. 'Or I'll call you.'

'No, you see... I mean... Maybe you *are* better concentrating on one employer. You know, exclusively for the Old Bill... That is... Stop working for me.'

There was a long pause. What do I say now? I wondered. *See you around? Thanks for everything? Just get out and let me drive away quick before someone turns up and covers the car with graffiti?*

'Can I give you a lift anywhere?' I asked.

He shook his head. 'We shouldn't be seen together.'

'You're not taking this in, are you? It's not going to matter if anyone sees us driving out of here for once. As if it ever would've mattered anyway…'

Chandler looked up suddenly and under his hat his eyes were shining brightly.

'Grannie's,' he said. 'I might just have something. But it'll cost you. More than what you can hide with a sandwich lunch and a week's mileage. I'd need danger money.'

'Oh? And what sort of stuff have you got?'

'I'll phone you. Give me a few days. Usual code words when I call. It'll be double the usual fee.'

'To say that you must know something already. What is it?'

'I can't say anything yet. You can't be too careful.'

'Right, then. Fine.' It was best to humour him, I supposed. 'And,' I went on quickly, before he could reply, 'I'm not meeting in this dump again. There's no real reason why we can't meet somewhere comfortable. I know the pub is a bit of a risk, but what about a café somewhere?'

'A café!' Chandler scoffed. 'But you're right. We won't meet here. Out of town would be best. We probably can't manage out of the country.'

After Chandler had gone, I drove slowly and carefully out of the building, inserting my coins into the rusty auto barrier on the ground floor.

Danger money! Double the usual fee! What was he talking about? I couldn't believe he knew anything: Chandler needed cash constantly; he wasn't in a position to defer singing to me in order to raise the price. And he hadn't said anything, not even a hint before I had brought the subject up.

No, he was guessing, he was making it up. He was clutching at the straws I had tossed to him.

And if, as I expected, he came back with nothing worthwhile, would I have the heart to fire him and start fiddling my expenses back into my own pocket for a change?

The chance, as they say, would have been a fine thing.

CHAPTER FIVE

Question: 'Why is West Hampton, England more romantic than Agra, India?'
Answer: 'There's only one Taj Mahal in Agra.'

Not that you would call either of Hampton's Tajs romantic as such. One is in the classic style of flock wallpaper and mihrab-shaped alcoves built of heavily glossed MDF; the other is deep in a basement. The first shows you what you're missing, with its photos, paintings and cheap wall hangings of the real thing; the second shows you only bare walls, and they're lit by harsh, fluorescent tubes. The High Street Taj offers a reheated takeaway menu and overpriced beer and wine; the back street Taj serves good, authentic food, but alcohol is forbidden.

Neither could make a restaurant critic fall in love exactly; neither really lives up to the Seventeenth Century marble masterpiece of the same name. But nevertheless, couples come and go to both, and talk, and laugh, and hold hands across the linen-covered mahogany veneer, and so, if you think about it, they can both achieve romance, a little bit of romance at least, against all odds, by the sheer impetus of their customers' behaviour.

I was holding tightly onto that thought when Laura sent back her bhaji for the third time.

'What did you say his name was?' she asked me, as she

topped up both goblets with house Merlot. 'Oops.' She ducked her head to sip from her over-filled glass.

'Oswald Mosley.'

'Classy.'

'Much more imaginative than changing your name to Adolf.' I sat back and admired the glisten of her upper lip, without being too obvious about it. 'More patriotic, too.'

'You're not going to start defending him, are you?'

'Of course not. Patriotism is the last refuge of the scoundrel.'

She giggled. '"Last refuge." Does that make him a *refugee?* He wouldn't like that.'

'Asylum seeker. Worse.'

'People like that should be in an asylum. Locked up anyway.'

'I dunno,' I reflected. 'I could imagine him on the inside, but more as a jailer. Definitely as the jailer…'

Laura set down her empty glass. 'What's the matter?' she asked. 'Have I smudged my make up or something?'

'No, no. You're looking gorgeous as usual.'

'Thank you darling,' she said drily. 'Anyway, I hope you get him bang to rights.'

I shrugged. 'No evidence.' I turned in my seat and caught the eye of a waiter across the room. 'Could we have a carafe of water?' I mouthed, gesturing at our empty glasses. 'Honestly,' I said aloud. 'I've asked him twice.'

Laura only calls me 'darling' when she's getting drunk and enjoying herself (as opposed to *being* drunk and hating herself, which is the usual next stage of the process), so I was hoping that the food would come back quickly enough to soak up what she had already put away. I wanted to stop talking about work, but for some reason I was struggling: I knew she wouldn't be interested in my plans for the World War Two escape convention, but I didn't want to talk about *her*, either. The last thing I needed was another half cut rant about Stephen. And, of course, I had a hidden agenda to move our relationship on. I was fed up with offering a sympathetic ear and a shoulder to cry on; other parts of me wanted to have their turn.

But when you've been just good friends for so long, it's hard to know what exactly to say.

'Laura... Did you watch Coronation Street last night?' I asked.

'Yes. Good, wasn't it?'

'Mmm... That, er, that Ken, eh?' I chuckled. 'Poor guy, you know?'

'Ken wasn't in it last night.'

'Oh. Really? Come on, Ken's always in it, isn't he?'

'Last night was Marjorie's suicide attempt.' (She might not have said 'Marjorie,' but it was something similar, something a bit middle aged.) 'Ken's on holiday.'

'Ah. I must be thinking of another night.'

'You missed a treat, then.'

'What, *suicide*? *A treat?*'

'It was,' said Laura, and she was completely serious about this, 'too honest to be upsetting. It was a very honest performance. Moving. We all felt an affinity with her.'

I was beginning to think I should have started talking about the convention after all when her shoulders hunched suddenly and her head ducked, although not this time to drink.

'Sheet! Don't look round, whatever you do!' She lifted a hand to her face in that way people do when they think they could hide behind it: there it hovered uncertainly, more like a wave than a disguise. Probably as good a way as any of attracting attention to yourself.

And of course I turned around to look behind me: it's automatic when you get that sort of instruction.

'What?' I asked. Laura whispered at me. 'I'm not a lip-reader,' I complained. She leaned across the table to put her face close to mine and I smelled her kiwi shampoo again.

'At the front of house. It's *Stephen*,' she said.

Of course, that made me look again, while Laura cowered back in anguish. There he was, talking to the young lad at the counter and glancing at his watch. What was *he* doing here? A self-appointed expert on Indian food, he should have been round the corner at Taj number two. Then again, he should have been in Grimsby.

'What's he doing here?' I whispered, concerned by the two vacant tables either side of us, and wishing, not for the first time, that we had chosen an alcove. 'Why hasn't he gone back to college?'

'I think it's OK. It's OK. He's just come in for a takeaway. Just ignore him. He'll be off in a minute. A takeaway, that's all.'

I risked one more look. I wanted to be sure that was all.

Across a less than crowded room, Stephen caught my eye.

Well, naturally he had to come over; he couldn't risk looking like he was the embarrassed one. Or maybe he deliberately wanted to make Laura's paranoia worse... Or maybe he wanted to talk about his record collection.

'Larry,' he said carefully. 'Laura. Quite a coincidence.' His eyes moved to Laura and back, but I was wearing my best poker face, the one I use with difficult clients. This was a man who owned at least six different versions of the song 'Jealous Guy.' I didn't want to help him reach any conclusions, especially ones that I myself hadn't reached yet.

'So, Laura,' he continued. 'It'll be much easier for everyone if you apologise right away, won't it?'

'Apologise? What for?'

Stephen shook his head. 'I thought we were going to be grown-up about all this, but you've just proved how childish you are. I don't think it's anything to smile about,' he added, as Laura's hand rose again to her mouth. 'It could take weeks to sort it all out.'

'How come you're still here, Stephen?' I asked casually. 'Aren't you supposed to be hard at work again by now?'

'I'm seeing another artist who lives round here. We're collaborating on an installation.'

'Oh, an *installation*,' I said, nodding. 'And he'll be the one who likes worse-than-average quality takeaways, I suppose. Or have you got less snobby about this place recently?'

'*She*, actually,' he replied, with a little glance at Laura to see how she would take it. (I guessed he probably wasn't screwing her quite yet, then.)

A waiter had appeared at Stephen's side with a bottle of white wine. 'Are you joining this party, sir?' he asked, lowering the tray. 'Only you might want to order quite quickly–'

'Hold on, hold on,' I said, pointing to the wine, 'we didn't order this.'

'Yeah,' said Stephen. 'Good idea. I'll have a lager, please.'

'No way!' Laura squealed.

'But you asked me for it a few moments ago, sir.'

'Tiger beer, I think…'

'I said *water*, a carafe of *water*.'

'I'm sorry, sir.'

Laura's fingers closed around the neck of the bottle. 'He *won't* be joining us,' she said, firmly but drunkenly. 'He's *not* welcome. In fact, he's going any minute now.'

'Sorry, mate,' I said, 'it looks like that bottle will be joining us after all.' I nodded at the Chardonnay, which Laura was splashing furiously on top of the dribble of red in her glass. 'But *that* won't,' I added, jerking my thumb at Stephen. 'And you might want to see where the food's got to. You've been reheating it for twenty minutes now.'

'Yes, sir. I think this may be yours now.' A trolley was moving in closer, powered by a waiter who looked about twelve years old.

'So, Laura—'

'Stephen, I'm sorry I fucked around with your records,' she said, quickly and indistinctly. 'Now fuck off, please.'

'Oh, I think you can do better than that.'

'What are you going to do after your sculpture course, Stephen?' I said. 'Ever considered school teaching?'

'Professional artist, mate,' said Stephen, emphasising the 'mate.' 'Now, Laura…'

'Only you mentioned being grown up about things,' I went on. 'Maybe you think that means that *you* get to do all the telling off. Maybe you think *you're* so grown up that *you* always get to have the last word.'

Stephen paused and looked again from Laura to me. 'You were there the other night,' he said. 'You joined in the vandalism, did you?'

'No. Vandalism would have been smashing them to pieces.'

'Or was it your idea in the first place?'

'Well done, Steve. You might not want to be a teacher, but you can go to the top of the class.'

'No!' Laura protested, 'It wasn't Larry's idea, it was mine.'

'You're both as pathetic as each other!'

'Laura reached out and knocked over her glass for the

46

second time that evening. 'Why don't you just fuck off and leave us alone!'

Stephen saw the young waiter flinch, and caught the irritated glances of a couple at a table nearby. He took half a step backwards. 'Yeah, well,' he said, looking like he was thinking fast and hard, 'I wish you luck with her, mate.' I tensed as he patted my shoulder. 'Just don't take any of your stuff round to her place, that's all.' He turned away, and then back again. 'And don't ask for oral sex. She's a bit frigid about it.'

'You bastard!' Laura picked up a knife, although we all knew it was much too blunt to do anything with. 'You *know* that Larry's just a friend. When I've been… unhappy, he's been great. He's been a *rock…*'

'*Cock*, more like.'

'Right,' I said, pushing back my chair.

You could tell I had drunk exactly the right amount by the speed with which I moved. Too much and I would have been too slow to catch him; too little and I wouldn't even have tried.

My right hand shot out, grabbed his v-neck and pulled down, while my left cupped his balls and squeezed, not too hard, just the right side of painful. I looked straight into his eyes, and saw that he was at least as scared as I was. It gave me the confidence to go on, although frankly it was too late for any other option.

'I'm not taking you outside,' I hissed, 'because I haven't had dinner yet. On the other hand, I've been waiting so long that another ten minutes wouldn't make much difference. So if you don't want this very hot lamb phall shoved up your *arse*, you'll pick up your takeaway and fuck off right away. OK?'

'Is everything all right with your meal, sir?' asked a thin adolescent voice. I gave Stephen a little push.

'I haven't had a chance to taste it yet,' I said. 'Just hang on there a minute until I do.'

'You... I'll get you back for this,' said Stephen, slipping from grown up to child in six syllables. I ignored him as he moved off. From three tables away he had the last word.

'That's not a phall, it's a kurma! It's *mild*, you wimp!'

★ ★ ★

Why was I getting nowhere with Laura? I had plenty of time to ask myself the question. My last bus home was trapped by a lost articulated lorry, stuck in a street too narrow for it to turn. We waited, half blinded by its bright round pairs of halogen lights, until the driver finally got the message to dim them. The other passengers were shaking their heads, wondering how he'd imagined he could get to the factory this way. And why should ready-mixed garlic bread dough have to arrive in the middle of the night anyway?

I was shaking my head over my own thoughts.

Why was I getting nowhere with Laura? Partly bad luck; partly my own shyness. Interruptions or tantrums each time I even got near to making any sort of move. But more to the point was asking what Laura thought of me. *Just good friends...* That's what she said to Stephen. But if she was offered something else, would she be interested?

I couldn't guess. I didn't have enough clues.

CHAPTER SIX

A fraud investigator must learn to bury all his fears.

Or, to sound less of a drama queen about it, he must learn not to avoid the jobs he hates; otherwise he'd be hiding out in the toilets indefinitely.

Well, it might sound odd, but the job I hate the most isn't interviewing clients with a 'potentially violent' sticker on their file, nor even putting the screws on some weeping single mum who was just trying to make ends meet. What I hate is cold calling employers.

First, I'm at a disadvantage because I'm phoning to ask - no, *beg* - for their co-operation. Second, they always start by misunderstanding what I'm talking about, and third, they like to quote stupid clichés at me, like 'Time is money,' or 'I've got a business to run, here.' Fourth, they can't believe anyone could ever fool them, and so it stands to reason that no-one, not even a master of disguise, could be working for them incognito. Even if they seriously think that benefit fraud is *bringing the country to its knees* (another sad cliché: I've been known to try and get it into the conversation before they do in order to flatter them), they will be certain that this terrible problem is nothing to do with them. So in short, cold calling is nothing more than an embarrassment. And that's when you're lucky enough to actually speak to someone in authority; mostly you end up leaving messages that will never be acted upon, making calls that will never be returned.

'Reed Foods,' I thought the voice said, just as I had been about to put down the phone.

'Sorry, love. I thought I'd rung Grannie Baker's.'

'Yes.' There was a sigh like she had to explain it every time. 'This is the Grannie Baker factory. We're part of the Reed Food Group now.'

'Since when?' I asked.

'Last year, actually.'

'Paint's not dry on the signs yet, then?'

'Ain't got no signs.'

'Right.' I held the phone with my chin and wiped the palms of my hands down my trousers. 'Look, I'm not sure who exactly I need to speak to...' I heard her sigh again, less sympathetically than before. I hurriedly added, 'I'm calling from the Jobcentre, and–'

'I'll put you through.'

On hold, I doodled a Customer Charter on my blotter. (If you're wondering, it looks like a curly scroll, with gothic lettering and a seal at the bottom; maybe a few fancy calligraphic flourishes, if there's time to put them on. The words themselves are not important.)

Reed Food Group (or was it Reid, Read, Wreed?): I'd never heard of them. Not local, then. And I didn't recognise them from the national fraud database. I was surprised if it was a *group* to get such a remedial-class switchboard operator: in my experience, the larger the organisation, the more insistence on that *My-name-is-Mandy-How-can-I-help-you?* routine. In fact I was surprised to get an operator at all first go, instead of a recording and a series of hash key options. Now that sort of thing doesn't help *me:* there's never a 'If you are a benefit fraud officer wanting to check employee records press 99 now,' and if there were you'd have to spend half a day listening to all the other choices before it came up.

'Human Resources?'

'Oh, er, hello,' I said, trying to snap out of my daydream. 'Sorry, who have I been put through to?'

'Human Resources.'

'Ye-e-s... And your name is?'

'This is Sheena Hardy,' said the voice, somewhat reluctantly.

On my first day as a benefit clerk, I'd been taught to smile when speaking on the phone, as this is supposed to help you sound friendly and reassuring to the other person. I forced myself to make the effort now.

'Hello, Sheena, this is Larry Di Palma calling from the Jobcentre. I wonder if you can spare a few minutes to–'

'We haven't got any,' she interrupted.

'I'm sorry?'

'We haven't got any vacancies.'

'Well, I'm not actually–'

'It's a waste of time telling people to apply. I've had twenty letters this week and they all look like they were written by your advisers anyway. It's simply causing me unnecessary work.'

'Mmm,' I said, trying to keep my smile going. 'I'm sorry to hear that–'

'And the people we do interview are rubbish. Late. Unreliable. No commitment. They just don't want to work.'

'Could I just say–?'

'I really don't know why you people bother.'

'Perhaps I could just explain,' I said, loudly enough for several colleagues around me to turn their heads and smile. 'I work for the Fraud department. I'm not trying to *get* someone a job, I'm trying to *stop* people working. And claiming,' I added quickly, seeing more smiles across the room. 'Working and fraudulently claiming. Could I just take a moment to explain how you might be able to help?'

To be fair to Sheena, she did listen very patiently to about half of what I was saying before transferring the call; obviously she felt that workforce records were not within the remit of Human Resources. A nameless accountant, or possibly accounts clerk, or even perhaps a school pupil on work experience told me that it was nothing to do with him, but could one of the directors' secretaries help? Two further transfers later, the secretary said that Human Resources were responsible, but what with the restructuring of job roles I'd be better asking permission from 'Mr Wally,' and would I like to call again? I made some marginal notes that would look acceptable to Will, and gave the secretary an unconvincing promise that I would. There really was nothing more that I could possibly do.

★ ★ ★

'Doughnuts in the kitchen,' said Diana as I overtook her sending tremors down the partition wall ahead. I tried to be non-committal: 'Another birthday?'

'They're from the management team. To thank us all for our hard work last quarter. Marie got them.' Marie is Will's PA, or approximately one third of her is, as her time is shared across several projects and managers. Marie admires Will greatly.

'Did she buy them out of petty cash or out of Will's pocket?'

Diana gave me a look.

'It's a measure of how flattered we should feel,' I explained.

'I've really no idea.'

'Petty cash, then,' I decided. 'If Will had paid, Marie would have made sure it leaked out.'

'I hope you're going to have one. Save us girls from temptation.'

'Yes,' I said, 'we wouldn't want them to go to waste, would we?'

Di carried on to the lift and I stopped at the cooler to swallow a glass of ice cold water. What would we have got if we had actually *met* any targets last month? More expensive cakes? Or nothing at all? Well, I couldn't say that a free doughnut made me feel any better disposed towards Will's meddling with my casework, nor could I see seven major benchmarks being suddenly attained via a bout of comfort eating in the office. Not that it stopped me from heading for the kitchen immediately, though. As I said, it would be a shame to let any go to waste.

There are gaps in understanding between the sexes that may never be bridged, and the doughnut question is one of them. Why is it that all women make such a deal over cakes, chocolate or cream? With Diana, a certain obsessiveness is understandable, but most of the other women here have figures ranging from skinny to curvaceous, or, at the very worst, statuesque. One doughnut is not going to make a visible difference. And yet there's a whole litany to be gone through before taking a single bite:

'I shouldn't…'

'I mustn't…'

'I'll be told off at Weight Watchers.'

'You're alright, but I'm putting on the pounds…'
'It's not fair!'

Naturally when I got there, all that remained were four or five plates covered in sugar and blobs of jam. Carl and Sylvia were guiltily stuffing the last of the doughnuts into their mouths, *whole* in Carl's case, if his struggle to even begin chewing was any guide. I rooted around for some spare paper towels, not wanting it to look obvious why I'd come in, not wanting to look like the sort of loser who can't even get to the doughnuts on time.

'How are you two?' I asked.

'Mmm,' said Carl, nodding and rolling his eyes.

'Wish it was Friday,' said Sylvia.

'Bad day?'

'Bad? I've spent the whole morning with a Pakistani political refugee pretending he can't speak English, and his social worker who genuinely can't speak English. And no-one can advise me whether it's appropriate to offer him that vacancy we've got in an Indian restaurant.'

'Tricky,' I agreed, wetting my forefinger and sweeping up a line of crunchy sugar granules. My mind went back to our minor fracas the previous night, and also the long wait for food. But it wasn't the Taj that was recruiting. I'd seen the vacancy and I knew it was a restaurant out on the ring road, next to the multiplex cinema.

'I had to pass on my other clients to the rest of the team, and now we're all behind on paperwork.'

'Best to be careful,' said Carl indistinctly. 'Will won't want any bad press on the racial front.'

'How can we not be institutionally racist when we can't even get the simplest information? You ring the helpline and all they say is "Er… Good question."'

'Nightmare. Do you offend Asian cultural sensibilities by assuming they're all the same?' Carl swallowed with some difficulty. 'Or do you risk the backlash about Political Correctness gone mad?'

I nodded. 'They come over here, not taking our jobs...'

'It's not funny!'

'No, no, I'm serious,' I said. 'I can see a newspaper article now: "Jobcentre harasses white skinhead with Fraud visits and weekly signing, while letting off Asian man from even applying for a job." Well, put a bit more punchily, anyway.'

'Thanks, Larry, you've made me feel so much better.'

'Why didn't you just ask Ravi?'

'Ah,' said Carl triumphantly. 'There you go, assuming all Asians are the same.'

'He's a bright kid! He might be able to help!' I shrugged. 'Anyway, the buck stops with Will. Why are you stressing?'

'Are you kidding? If there *was* a complaint to the press, the buck stops with Will suspending the staff concerned pending a full enquiry.'

I nodded, accepting the watery Nescafe-substitute that Carl had made me unasked. It was no compensation for the lack of doughnut.

'In times of crisis,' Sylvia said, scowling over her bitter mugful, 'his first instinct is to be indecisive; his second is to cover his back.'

'Well, the guy's under a lot of pressure from senior management.'

'Carl, that's no excuse for being spineless ! If he can't stand the heat, he shouldn't be in... management.'

Carl gave me a raised eyebrow. 'You're bad tempered all of a sudden,' he said to Sylvia. 'Pre-menstrual, or something?'

'No,' I said, 'it's doughnut guilt.'

'Sexist pigs,' Sylvia admonished. 'Anyway, I put him in for a basic skills assessment. Waste of time, really.'

Carl looked at his watch. 'Shit, I've got to go,' he said. 'I'm supposed to be meeting those IT consultants at three. I couldn't get away last time, the number of questions they asked.'

'Your sacrifice will lead to better systems for us all,' I smiled.

'If it's that bloody Terry Shah again, I'll be here all night. He's obsessed with client's links to previous addresses and claims in other areas. And he doesn't even seem to know much about computers, either.'

'Well, at least *you* got a doughnut to keep you going!'

Back at my desk I found Will, who had a visitor with him: an attractive, young blonde woman in a new suit, cradling a leather clipboard in her arm. She looked like she had been writing down everything he said.

'Larry. Just the man I wanted to see,' said Will, sounding relaxed and genial for the sake of his guest.

'Larry, this is Helen Rossiter. She'll be joining us on an MBP 4 contract as of today. I'd like her to start her placement with Fraud.'

We shook hands and I wished I'd washed the sugar off more thoroughly. 'Fast turnaround,' I commented. 'You didn't mention this to me the other day.'

'Didn't I? I apologise. We had a lot of other things to cover, didn't we? And the confirmation from Regional Office came through very late… Helen will shadow you for some of the next three weeks. If you can copy me your diary, I'll integrate it into her ILP. OK?'

'Fine.' I smiled at her. 'It'll be a pleasure to take you out.' Helen thanked me politely, shifting her clipboard to a more comfortable position in front of her chest.

'Helen's done the MBP initial residential course, and Fraud Induction. So it makes sense to start with you.'

'Get the bad habits out of the way first, you mean.'

'I hear Herman has re-written the entire course. Maybe Helen can give *you* a few tips.'

'I wouldn't bank on it. He'll have renamed it Fraud 1:01 and they'll spend the time analysing American crime dramas on DVD.'

Will didn't laugh. 'I'm also delighted to have Helen here to help you. As I said the other day, we must get closer to our fraud targets. We can't afford to fail.'

'Yes, so you keep saying.'

'We'll catch up with you in due course, Larry.' He raised an arm behind Helen in one of those paternal, 'after you' gestures. 'Shall we continue? Oh, and Larry, can I have your report on the home visit you did as soon as possible? It might be interesting for Helen to see one completed. Thanks.'

I wandered back to my desk and sat looking at the mess of notes, post-its and papers that lay there. A new colleague at such short notice was a bit of a double-edged sword, I felt. It might be fun to have someone to work with for a change, but if Will was taking such a personal interest in her - escorting her round, doing the Individual Learning Plan himself - he would inevitably end up keeping even closer tabs on my work. If I'd been more paranoid I would have suspected him of engineering it this way, but of course that would have been an egotistical way of looking at it. He was just being welcoming to a new member of his staff. A new, young and very pretty member of his staff.

Still, I had a hunch she might be quite efficient, and I wondered how quickly I could get her on the phone doing my cold calls. I hadn't made much progress with Grannie

Baker's, and there was still the dog biscuit works to go… My immediate task, though, was to make my diary look like I was doing plenty of important work. It would be nice to impress my new junior, and I still had to cover my back for Will.

I rooted in my desk drawer. Better get it done before I went out for my next appointment. If I didn't get a move on, I'd end up taking work home with me or something, and that, as far as I was concerned, would be the worst failure of all.

★ ★ ★

Carl lifted his nose and sniffed the air. 'You know,' he said, 'I reckon the scent of frying onions is the strongest smell there is, the one that can travel the furthest. It's everywhere.'

We changed direction together without another word needing to be said. We caught the green man at the crossing and entered Market Square.

'Nah,' I said, 'It's the sheer number of vans. *They're* everywhere.'

Carl had joined me for a pint or two at the end of the day, and the alcohol had sharpened his appetite despite the doughnuts he had guzzled that afternoon. I suggested that since he had taken more than his share, he ought to pay for my takeaway, but all I got was a light punch on the arm by way of an answer.

We joined the end of a short queue. The Sultanahmet trailer is popular because it offers marinades and dips prepared by its parent-restaurant chefs, although it has all the usual plastic sauce bottles to choose from, too. But I like to think of it as the discerning man's kebab van. Carl, of course, will eat anywhere.

'Good job Sylvia's not with us,' Carl suggested. 'She'd be reminding us about having five fruit and veg a day.'

'You could always have a kebab *and* five gherkins to make it up.'

The regular tall, young, slightly melancholy guy was serving tonight. This lad was unfailingly polite and also scrupulous about washing his hands between customers. I like that, but it wasn't going down well with the man in the sheepskin coat who was ahead of us.

'Come on, Gunga Din,' he was calling, 'I'm double parked back there.'

The two German motorcyclists in front of him stepped aside and began to open their polystyrene trays.

'One moment, Sir,' said the boy, as he moved to the small handbasin at the back of the van. 'Reasons of hygiene. The rules are very strict.' He spoke with an accent and that strange, formal phrasing of someone well educated but not a native speaker of English. It made him sound like a fifty-five year old, though he was probably no more than nineteen or twenty.

'Christ! Don't bother with all that, Gunga, I'm not gonna get typhoid from a biker's tenner, am I?'

The young man returned to the counter. He looked upset, but still somehow dignified. Fortunately he had the advantage of height: not just the van, but his own six foot six or so. On the other hand, he was also sweating nervously.

'Now, Sir, how can I help? And, by the way, my name is Ali, as you can see if you read my badge.'

'Tch! No need to be touchy, son. I'll have a medium doner and a can of Coke.'

Carl was rifling through his wallet and licking his lips. The sheepskin guy turned around and caught my eye; he raised his brows in mock-innocent surprise. 'Can't take a joke, some of them,' he said.

'Actually,' I said, casually but loudly enough for all to hear, 'You might just want to read the poem some time.'

'Eh? What poem?'

'*Gunga Din.* The name's from a poem. I thought everybody knew that. Rudyard Kipling. It's a white soldier talking to an Indian servant.'

'Oh. I get you.' He turned away hurriedly and exchanged his cash for a poly-tray in a plastic bag. 'Keep the change,' he said: by my calculations it was all of five pence.

'Pay attention to the last line of the poem.'

'Right, right.' He was moving off like a man weighing up how weird it was to recommend poetry in a kebab queue.

I raised my voice again; this time the bikers looked up, too. 'The white guy says, "You're a *better man than I am,* Gunga Din." Got that? Next time you call someone Gunga Din, remember that!'

Carl slapped my shoulder, grinning. 'You tell him, mate. Now... Doner with extra hot chilli for me, I think.'

'No, no,' I said, 'this is the Sultanahmet. You want the authentic Turkish experience, with fresh tomato sauce and youghurt. Trust me. Two iskender kebabs, please, er... Ali.'

He gave a small, shy smile, the first I had seen in numerous visits to the van, and when ready, he assured us the kebabs were complimentary, although it took a bit of clarifying since he had never heard of the phrases 'freebie,' 'gratis' or 'on the house.' I hoped he wasn't going to pay for them himself, but since he was insisting I decided it would be insulting to refuse. Carl had a quick try of his kebab and told the boy it was excellent.

We strolled off into the dusk, with Carl deciding that serving in a burger van could well be the worst job ever, especially after pub closing time. We played 'Good job / Bad job' – the traditional Jobcentre guessing game – until our paths home diverged. As his bus approached, I told Carl that out of his list of ten bad jobs I had already done nine, and he was still doing the tenth.

'Depressing, isn't it?'

'Yeah,' said Carl. 'You know what we should do? Pretend to be claimants and refer ourselves to a retraining scheme as soon as possible!'

I gave him a salute as the bus pulled away. Retraining. If only we could really get away with a scam like that. If only the training schemes lasted long enough for people to actually learn something valuable…

But I could certainly have saved myself some heartache if I been able to follow up Carl's idea, couldn't I?

CHAPTER SEVEN

For about the hundredth time I reached out to wipe condensation from inside the windscreen.

'Doing a stakeout is a complete pain, to be honest,' I said. 'It's uncomfortable, boring, cold, usually; and you can't help thinking how much paperwork you could have caught up on in the meantime. And it is *so* labour intensive. It's just not a cost effective way to get someone off the register.'

I turned and looked into the shadows of her eyes. 'Sorry to be such a pessimist,' I said, failing to sound sorry at all.

'I wasn't expecting it to be a thrill-a-minute.' Helen pulled the travel rug higher up her legs. 'But when something *does* happen… Let's say he comes out, we're not exactly sure where he's going, he suspects he's got a tail and he's trying to shake us off… You did say he might be quite clued up…'

'Mmm. I was being sarcastic.'

'But following him to work! Watching as he confirms your suspicions, shooting the video evidence… Well, *I* think it's exciting, anyway.'

'Yeah, I can tell by the way you're trembling.'

'Shivering. Does the union Health and Safety Rep know you're working in these conditions?'

'I don't even know who the union Health and Safety Rep is.'

'It'll be in my induction pack,' she said helpfully. 'I can look it up when I get back.'

'Don't be surprised if it says 'Post Vacant', will you?'

I yawned, and watched the windscreen begin slowly to cloud over again. I was surprised that frost wasn't forming on the street outside, but maybe it was still too damp for that to happen. A good job, probably: an iced-up windscreen is the last thing you want on surveillance.

'Herman said you were a cynic,' said Helen. She paused while I looked up in surprise, as if she was weighing up exactly what to say next. 'He also said you're a very good investigator.'

'Herman!' I laughed. '*Herman* the ace trainer! Don't believe a word he said, the man's a lunatic. He thinks we're all James fucking Bond. Power mad, it's the half German in him. If he was complimenting *me* it was just a ploy to reflect kudos back on himself. Did he say "I taught Larry everything he knows" perhaps?'

'No, he just said I could learn a lot from shadowing someone like you.'

'And then he said we should all go out for a drink sometime because, between the two of us, we've so many stories to tell…'

'I don't think so–'

'But apparently I turned out to be busy, so he said he'd take you on his own?'

'Not at all.'

'But he did give you his mobile number? And tell you to call him for advice? *Any* time?'

Helen looked away. I laughed again. Despite myself I was pleased to be praised, and, though I hadn't realised it yet, I was pleased that Herman hadn't quite managed to charm his way into an instant date. Girls need protecting from the likes of Herman, if only to stop the rest of us feeling inadequate.

'Isn't *anything* going to happen?' Helen asked.

Though it was still not much after ten o'clock the street had been quiet for some time now, and we had been spared the usual stakeout embarrassment of gawping passers-by. Normally this can cause difficulties, though one advantage of having a woman in the car is that you are less likely to be suspected of casing the joint; I've had the police called many times, which really blows your cover. (The disadvantage is that any pre-teens about keep looking in at you in the hope you're about to start feeling each other up.)

The main reason for the quiet was the set of chipped concrete bollards at the street's bottom end: no through traffic came this way, and as Mosley lived only two doors from the boarded up end-of-terrace, few residents would either.

There had been no pedestrians: the pub and corner shop were at the other end of the road, and in any case, the cold was keeping people in. A row of four garages squatted beside the bollards, but there was no sign of life there. Indeed the only sign of life had been a tatty old two-stroke motorcycle which had just disappeared into the alleyway behind the houses. Even that went quietly: the rider had cut his engine at the turn, no doubt relying on momentum to take him home and save some fuel, although it had caused his pillion passenger to wobble and clutch at his shoulder bag.

I crossed and uncrossed my legs. 'Listen,' I said, 'I, er, I ought to scout round the back.'

'The back?'

'Standard procedure. The house backs onto that alleyway…'

'We know that,' said Helen. 'And we've got the exit to the

alley in view.' She pointed beyond the garages. 'I thought that's what you meant when we were deciding where to park earlier?'

'Ah,' I said. 'Yes. Right. But I should still have a quick look to verify it. And there's the question of an exit at the other end of the alley as well.'

'He lives at this end. Surely he wouldn't walk a hundred yards along a dark, mucky alley when he only has to come round the corner to be on the street? Or come out his front door?'

'True,' I said, thinking that with this sort of logic, Helen was not going to make a bad investigator herself. 'Unless he's trying to lose his tail.'

'You said you were being–'

'Look, I'm just going for a quick look, OK? Two minutes.'

I had just opened the door when we heard the bangs: two in quick succession, then a third after a brief pause. We looked at each other in surprise. I pulled the door to.

'What was that?' said Helen.

'I dunno.'

'It sounded like a gun to me.'

I made a face. 'Unlikely. Maybe it was that old motorbike backfiring. No, it's fireworks. Bangers already again. Bloody menace.'

'I hope they don't start chucking them near us.'

I grinned. 'Makes you jumpy, doesn't it, being on surveillance duties? You don't notice it at first, then bingo! Nerves kick in. Nothing to worry about really. If it's kids mucking about, they'll be off as soon as someone opens their door…'

But I waited five more minutes, partly just in case Helen really was getting nervous, but mainly because I didn't want fireworks flying about when I was having a wee. With no further bangs audible, I patted her arm, and said, 'See you in a couple of minutes.' Then I headed for the alleyway.

Fifty-nine seconds later I stepped out of the gap between two garages with a weight off my mind and out of my body. A cat half scared me to death and I guess the feeling was mutual: he raced off into the street, and I sought comfort from an ancient packet of soft mints from the bottom of my coat pocket (I've been using them since I gave up smoking). I struggled for an age over the glued-on wrappers and still ended up eating them with most of the paper on.

I carefully picked my way around the corner and along past the yard walls of Balmoral Terrace's houses, counting four to what should be Mosley's back gate. Most of the walls here were topped with glass or barbed wire; one gate had been barricaded with pieces of plank. The alley was filthy and neglected, and I guessed it wouldn't be much better at the nicer end of the street: there are limits to what even the most house proud pensioner is prepared to sweep. I could smell the gunpowder in the air, but there were no kids or teenagers to be seen.

Once again I worried about being taken for a burglar and then I started worrying about the dog. Nervous, I hung back. I didn't want the alarm being raised as I tiptoed up to his gate.

Because the gate itself was ajar.

I peeped in. The yard was quite visible by the kitchen strip lights, which shone dully through the rear window and brightly out of the wide open back door. Wide open in this freezing weather! I shook my head: people claiming benefits should be more careful about their heating bills. If I were Ravi, I thought wryly, that would count as another clue to Mosley having a second income.

The window was cloudy with condensation, but through the doorway I could see clearly back to the stacks of dirty plates and pans; even to the wallpaper, curling from the effect of damp. A rhombus of light lay over the junk-strewn yard, while in the shadows lurked a dilapidated lean-to: just the sort to have something nasty inside. I couldn't see my client, or any other person for that matter. Funny, I thought, his front room was so tidy and organised…

And then suddenly it came to me: door open, gate open… He's gone into the alleyway to throw out some rubbish or chase away the firework kids, and he'll be right back with the dog to find me in his yard!

'*What the fuck!*' I choked.

I had turned much too quickly and I bumped into a body close behind. In a terrified flurry of limbs I tried to jump backwards, then push past, then ward off an attack. But it was Helen. My hands dropped the instant I realised.

'Shit! What are you doing here?' I panted. 'I didn't hear you. You must have a tread like a cat! Bloody hell!'

I took a long look up and down the alley, but all was still quiet. I stepped into the shadow beyond the gate, and Helen followed, rubbing her upper arm.

'What's happened?' I asked. 'Any developments?'

'No, I just… You'd been longer than you said.' She looked a little upset, but I guess lashing out in a dark alley isn't the best way to make a new trainee feel welcome. 'You were past your *exit deadline*,' she continued. 'The Health and Safety guidelines clearly state–'

'Please tell me you haven't phoned the twenty four hour security helpline?' I pleaded. 'Those bozos will call the police out just to stop themselves getting bored! I haven't been *that* long…'

'You said no more than two minutes.'

'Fucking hell,' I said, 'I didn't mean *literally*.'

'I haven't phoned anywhere. I decided to come and have a look first. Maybe I'd better leave you to it: no-one's watching the front of the house.'

'No,' I said, 'don't worry.' I took her by the arm, gently, and led her through Mosley's gate. 'He won't go out the front with the back door wide open. But why's he left it like that?'

'Can't you smell it? Something's burning. He's letting out the smoke. What are we going to do now?'

'Burning? Like a chip pan? Do you think we should have a quick look? I don't want him burned to death just to get the unemployment figures down…'

★ ★ ★

We move swiftly and silently through the yard. Well, Helen does: I pause to move some rusty bike wheels and a bin bag from the path. I'm still worried about the dog: experience teaches you in these circumstances to be sure your escape route is clear. The bin bag is much heavier than I thought, and it scrapes wetly on the concrete.

Helen is at the door. We poke our noses into the kitchen and see that the cooker is off. There's no smoke. There are no flames.

'What now?' I put a finger to my lips and we listen carefully.

What am I hoping to hear? A dinner party? The tinkle of crystal glasses saying Mosley won't be out tonight and we can pack up and go home? Or the man and his mates waiting for the football, while he boasts in every detail about how he is cheating the benefits system, giving me all the leads I need?

We hear neither, of course. The house is quiet.

I've got a handkerchief over my mouth. 'You were right. He's burned the toast,' I say indistinctly.

'Not toast. Something more horrible.'

'Smells a bit like roast pork, or bacon…'

'Bacon!' Helen's getting excited. 'That means he's just had breakfast! And what do you do after breakfast? You go to work!'

'You should team up with Ravi sometime,' I whisper sourly.

'Let's take a look,' she suggests. I decide there's something else that I can blame Herman for.

We move forward as quietly as possible. Past the dirty plates and still steaming kettle, crossing the lino to strain our ears again before I push, ever so gently, one finger only, the door to the living room…

It's empty. I breathe out with relief. When I inhale it smells bad in here, too. Mosley has been working hard on his political campaigning. Papers are spread over the whole table and also on the sofa; box files are open and papers have been thrown about on the floor. His shelves are empty, even the top ones. The printer has exhausted its current paper supply, and the laptop has reverted to the screensaver, showing the blonde tart in faux leather military uniform. She's being suggestive with her baton.

Anyway, there's no evidence here: no overalls in a bag by the door, no packed lunch, no security badge on the table, no convenient note reminding him to give Joe Bloggs a lift to work today…

I'm feeling like someone who has gone skydiving for a dare. It's time to go home now, before I end up being talked into a second jump, this time without a parachute…

I think I hear boards creaking from upstairs.

Helen hasn't noticed. She's bending over, picking up an

old, discoloured steam iron that's been left on the floor. 'Still hot,' she murmurs, 'This *is* a fire hazard...' There's another creak from above.

I strain my ears for more: it's like some role reversal of those times you lie in bed wondering if it's burglars or the plumbing that woke you. Helen's now leaning over the table, scanning the paperwork. I touch her arm and mouth 'Time to go.' She looks pale. She nods.

From upstairs we hear a deep groan; then another, shorter, more intense; then one more, muffled. We back away towards the kitchen as quietly as we can. There's a heavy, jolting thump above us, as if someone kicked over a table up there, or fell out of bed. We run.

And it turns into a bit of cheap, silent comedy as we reach the back door together and get half stuck squeezing through. Helen takes my carefully cleared exit route and I fall over the bin bag. Its contents are soft and warm, but I haven't got time to be repulsed, I'm too busy running again and I'm feeling my arms for cuts: I don't want to go for a tetanus jab at this time of night.

Helen's waiting at the gate. She points back at an upstairs window. 'Look!' I do look and there's nothing there. 'Come on,' she insists. 'Before someone comes.'

★ ★ ★

Back in the Citroën I started the engine immediately and was relieved it fired first go: this was no night for calling the AA. In gear with the clutch down I paused to look again at the house, as if, illogically, seeking some final clue to the weird experience we've had. The curtains remained closed.

'What are you waiting for?'

I glanced at Helen, then engaged neutral and let the engine idle. 'Maybe we should continue our surveillance,' I suggested. I wasn't particularly serious, but Helen looked aghast. 'He still doesn't know we're here,' I explained.

'Are you kidding? Didn't you see the man in the balaclava?'

'No-o-o…'

'Looking out of the back bedroom window. He was only there for a second, but he must have seen us. Like some paramilitary! One of those full face jobs, with only the eyes showing– Ouch!' she cried as I changed gear and pulled away at speed. We reached the main road in moments. 'Well I'm glad I've convinced you to pay attention to our safety,' Helen concluded, adjusting her seatbelt. 'But shouldn't we call the police?'

'No. It's fine. The main thing is that we can knock off and go home. Mosley won't be going to work tonight.'

'What do you mean? Wasn't that a burglar in his house?'

'No, no, it's fine. Trust me. Let's just say I've been piecing together all the clues, and… Well, this is all a bit alien to me, but… Look, I don't know how to say this exactly…'

'*What* are you talking about?'

'Fancy a drink?' I asked, sweating. 'We can just get one in before last orders.'

'Fine. And then you can explain it all to me.'

I nodded, although I wasn't confident I could explain without some embarrassment my deductions regarding masks, screensavers, riding crops, magazines, groans and bedroom equipment. But that's team work for you. Helen was entitled to know how I could be sure that night that Mosley wouldn't be walking out of his door.

Just as later on she would be entitled to know which of my deductions were spot on, and which… were not.

CHAPTER EIGHT

For some people, the Second World War will never end.

And I don't mean the veterans, but men who were nowhere near even being born when the conflict was happening. They grew up with it, though, back in the 1960s and 1970s, watching the films, reading the comics, playing soldiers in the street. Their interest in it has stayed with them over the years, or has even grown over time; grown wider and deeper, all but taking them over in some sad cases, consuming time, energy and money. History, like sport and music, has its collectors, its fact-finders, its obsessives. That Saturday I was walking amongst them.

I was at *Great Escape 2000*, Britain's only national conference devoted to the theme of World War Two prisoners and their daring and ingenious escape attempts. Well, I've always been hooked on old war movies, and I always scan the TV pages hopefully for old favourites to add to my video collection. But this event isn't just for film buffs (though you could bet that most men here have seen all the films, many times). This event goes beyond fiction.

There are surprisingly erudite-sounding lectures, discussion groups and seminars, there are book-signings and self-published research papers available to buy. The Open University has a big stand halfway down the exhibition hall, as do our local Higher Education Institution and Further

Education College. There are specialist antique dealers, a pub quiz ('We welcome every Tom, Dick and Harry,' get it?) and the chance to pit your wits against the guards at Cyber-Colditz: you wear a virtual reality helmet complete with swastika and eagle badges; your handset is a model IV Lüger pistol.

There are screenings of classic movies, including some of the lesser known, plus even some foreign ones with subtitles. There's a paintball hall, an assault course and demonstrations by re-enactment societies. Fun for all the family!

Though not everyone brings the wife and kids. Great Escape started as a reunion for prisoner of war veterans, and you still see a few of them limping around the hall in their blazers and medals, swapping stories before dozing off in the tea tent. Then, obviously, a lot of tickets are sold to teachers and lecturers, writers and researchers: the history professionals. Not quite so many as you'd expect, though, and, compared to the amateurs, these people don't tend to show the same excitement at being there. Well, they are giving up their weekend for work, I guess.

There are school parties, scouts and army cadets, and skinheads buying Iron Crosses in the marketplace and trying hard to follow lectures called 'Death Camps: the German perspective.' (I was half wondering if Oswald Mosley would show up after all, but if he did, I wasn't planning to ask him where he had been the previous night.) But by far the largest number of visitors is made up of middle-aged men remembering the books and TV series of their childhood. Nostalgia is the biggest draw of all ...

In the bar I nodded to two semi-retired builders that I recognised from a discussion group the previous year. They had demonstrated a vast, if superficial, knowledge gleaned entirely from the internet and coffee table books, and they had kept two Oxford professors on the defensive for a full fifty minutes. They looked quite bullish now, in fact, but then this was a return to the scene of their triumph, and I guessed they were out to repeat it. After all, it must have felt so good to show off in front of people supposedly more knowledgeable than themselves. It must have made a change from showing off in front of their wives.

'Larry, isn't it?'

I'd have been more impressed at his memory if I hadn't been wearing a name badge from my 11 o'clock seminar.

'We met last year, didn't we? This is Colin, I'm Rhys.'

'Nice to see you again.' We shook hands.

'Enjoying it?'

'Yes, very much. Plenty to see, but not too crowded to get around.' I took a sip from my plastic beaker. 'The beer's as terrible as ever, though.'

'Worse than the secret home brew in Stalag Luft III,' said Rhys, and the three of us laughed in our different ways.

'Have you been to the memorabilia fair yet?' asked Colin. 'There's a chap wearing Gordon Jackson's trousers.'

I glanced at Rhys, but his face was blank. 'How the hell do they know?' I asked. 'Did he sew his name in them?'

'Authenticated by size and position of patching. Matched against stills from the film. And the actor's memoirs give a clue: he mentions how itchy they were.'

'I'm glad I'm not up against you in the pub quiz, Colin,' I said, taking another sip of the terrible beer. 'Especially if there's a round on famous trousers of World War Two.'

'I'm glad we met you, y'know,' Rhys was saying as he fumbled about in his portfolio. 'Can you remember the names of those professors from Oxford who chaired the debate we were in last year? I've been scanning the programme, but nothing seems to ring a bell.' He brandished the glossy booklet, perhaps hoping that the sight of it would jog my memory.

I shook my head. 'They probably heard you two were coming again. Decided to stay at home with a good book.'

'Encyclopaedia would be more to the point,' said Colin, smugly.

'There's someone from Cambridge here,' Rhys went on, 'but his session clashes with *The Wooden Horse.*'

'Classic,' I agreed, deciding to give the film a miss for once. 'You're keen on the seminars, aren't you?'

'We went to two last night,' said Colin. 'Run by some GCSE History teachers. Were you there?'

'No, I've only got a Saturday day pass.'

'You can judge the standard of the convention by the seminars,' Colin said pompously. 'And I like to make sure people get their facts right.'

'Doctor Wright was quite good,' said Rhys. 'For a woman.'

'For a woman who normally lectures on the Suffragettes.'

'Tetchy, though.'

'Heard the one about the female history professor?' Colin asked. 'Her boss asked her a lot of trick questions, and then jumped to conclusions when she got upset, not being able to answer. She had to spell it out for him: "Look, It's not my period."'

Colin and Rhys laughed heartily for a few moments.

'Didn't you have a photo on display last year?' I asked Rhys. 'From some sort of re-enactment, as I remember?'

'Ouch,' said Colin into his beer. I frowned questioningly.

'Ah, it's a bit of a sore point,' said Rhys. 'Yes, I came second in the photo competition. Two hundred quid and a year's supply of air freshener from the sponsor. Well, I spent the money upgrading some of my lenses. Lent the camera to… a colleague. He took it out at night and bloody dropped it!'

'Yes, Ouch,' I agreed. 'Is he going to pay for the damage?'

'I don't think he could afford it. Anyway, it was insured. It's the… the *inconvenience*. And the principle of it. You don't expect people to make promises and then let you down.'

I abandoned my beaker onto a clogged table and wondered how soon I could politely abandon the small talk; it looked as if others had failed to finish their drinks, too.

'What d'you think about next year's conference?' asked Colin.

'What about it?'

'Next year. Haven't you heard? They're opening it up. Not just the Second World War…'

'What, Vietnam ? They'd better not start showing *Rambo II* in place of *Secret Army*.' I was mildly concerned by this news; it's the old fashioned, British, black-and-white film atmosphere that I like about Great Escape. I really didn't want it to be watered down. Rhys was shaking his head. 'Not the Falklands, surely?' I pleaded. 'Not that guy who got out of Iraq in the first Gulf War? The one who gives speeches at big business dinners. I bet you'd never have got Guy Gibson doing that…'

'No, the idea is a convention on Escape as a general theme,' said Rhys, with a sort of sneer on the last two words.

'Not just wartime escapes at all,' said Colin.

'Fuck,' I said. 'What does that mean? They've got sponsored by a travel agency or something?'

I looked across the bar at two white haired men who were reminiscing about maps on silk handkerchiefs, compasses in shoe heels and Reichsmarks rolled up as fake cigarettes. Could 'escape as a general theme' really reflect what they had been through? Could it *respect* what they had been through? Call me old fashioned, but you know something's wrong when the words that spring to mind are 'History is not what it used to be…'

Rhys seemed to know a bit about what was going on. 'There are two groups pushing for this,' he said. 'The booksellers' forum, for a start. There's a lot of books on display which aren't really within the period.'

'Yeah, I bought *Napoleon's Hundred Days to Waterloo* here last year.'

'Not only military history,' Colin said. 'There's a book by a woman who married an Islamic fundamentalist and had to rescue her children from Iran. Or Algeria. Somewhere like that, anyway…'

'And a whole load of stuff on asylum seekers,' said Rhys, angrily. 'I mean, I know the booksellers have got to earn a living, but we don't want this event being swamped by other subjects.

'It's also the university that's behind the move. Last year there was a talk on "the Psychology of the Escaper". Well, now the other departments have discovered this event, they're asking why History should monopolise all the potential mature students there are to sign up. Sociology, Law, Psychology… They all want a piece of the action. Mind you, I don't think that many people here actually end up doing a course…'

'How do you know all this?' I asked. 'I don't suppose they're advertising it to the history buffs here today.'

Rhys laughed. 'Oh, I have my contacts,' he said. 'I walk the corridors of power…'

'Oh, like that is it?'

'I know one or two Town Councillors quite well,' Rhys explained. 'Well, in fact I know several, but some of them can't stand me. But one of the Councillors is on the Great Escape Conference Board. He has some sympathy with my views…' He shrugged. 'It's not that hard to find these things out. It's not like the Masons; they don't meet in secret. It's all public information if you know where to go.'

'Come on,' I said, 'it's all a bit third hand, isn't it? And I know what Boards are like: people make proposals that take forever to be agreed on.'

'I hope you're right,' said Rhys darkly. 'But I'm informed that if they bid for more Lottery money, they'll have to show Social Inclusiveness factors from the prescribed list. And there aren't many Black, disabled, lesbian ex-Prisoners of War around, are there?'

★ ★ ★

The army cadets were abseiling using knotted sheets and I put 50p in the corporal's bucket. Among the second hand bookstalls I spotted the book Colin had referred to; tucked in between the novels of an ex-SAS commando it didn't look particularly threatening. Nor did the little table staffed by people from Asylum Aid. After all, when you're a charity, you try to publicise your works at every big event you can, don't you?

I found a couple of out-of-print volumes from my 'wanted' list, and both at half the price I had been quoted on the net. I flicked contentedly through them while drinking tea and scones served by a pale woman in WRAC uniform. It was turning into a pleasant day…

'Hello, stranger. Mind if I join you?'

Detective Sergeant Paul Wodehouse shook my hand and sat down at my table. He was dressed in his civvies, which nowadays means jeans and polo shirt: his 'uniform' is the designer suits that these guys copy off the telly. He parked his Coke bottle and smiled.

'How's it going, Larry? Seen any claimants today?'

'Ha, ha. You know I'm interested in this stuff.' I pointed two fingers at him like a pistol. 'You on the other hand…' I fired and blew imaginary smoke from the barrel, 'Must be here on business. Because you hate history, and you couldn't even spot Heinrich Himmler in an identity parade.'

'‘Course I could! You can tell by the little moustache.' It wasn't quite clear if Paul was joking.

'How's the new flat?' I asked, in an attempt to be civil. Paul gave a smug smile and a thumbs up. 'New TV is very good. Twenty sports channels for a start. Massive fridge-freezer: holds a month's supply of lager. Leather sofas were delivered last week. You should get into a better place yourself.'

'Yeah, maybe.'

Paul decided to change the subject. 'What's the book? *The Man with no Friends*. Sounds like your autobiography…'

'It's about a gunner in a Lancaster bomber. All his crew were killed when the plane caught fire. He was on the run, all alone in Germany with lynch mobs and the Gestapo on his tail… Hence "no friends." It was twelve weeks before he was finally captured.'

'Aw, now you've given away the ending.'

'Yeah, like you wanted to borrow it when I've finished.'

Wodehouse grinned. 'Saw you earlier, actually. But I didn't want to interrupt. You were in the bar with a couple of fat guys.'

'You should have come over. You could have heard the story of Gordon Jackson's trousers.'

'What?'

'Famous actor. In the movie *The Great Escape*. The genuine trousers from the film were on sale here, apparently.'

'People really buy that crap?'

'I know. Collecting 'genuine' film props or 'genuine' historic artefacts… It's got to be a con, hasn't it? I wouldn't spend five quid on a 1940 battledress, so why would I spend five hundred on the one worn by Airey Neave on the day he got out of Colditz, even assuming you could be certain that it was the real one? Gordon Jackson's trousers! It's like medieval pilgrims queuing up to buy a piece of the True Cross…'

'They're what? Dealers?'

'No, just proud of the trivia they have memorised over the years. I've only met them twice, but if I don't bump into them until next year's conference it'll be a relief.'

'Oh. I thought they might be mates of yours.'

'No way!'

'You'd prefer to be the man with no friends.'

'Yeah.'

'Why?'

'I told you, because they are boring. Because they know enough about German army uniforms to put an Oxford professor under pressure, and that's what makes them happy. But who cares if it's three buttons on the cuff or four?'

Wodehouse sighed. 'All this Coke is bad for the teeth,' he said. 'Fancy a quick beer?'

'No, thanks, there's a few more things I'm going to see. What are you looking at next?'

'Oh, I've finished,' said Wodehouse, glancing at his watch. 'I've seen the people I needed to see. And I've got my wonderful free gift, a facsimile of an RAF evasion map printed on a handkerchief. What more could I want?'

'You should have come a few years back. The freebies were better then. I've got some bolt cutters that I still use... Or stay on today. Some of the seminars have their own giveaways.'

'Not tempting.' Paul put on a weak German accent. '*Nein, Englander,* for me now, ze conference is ofer, know what I mean?'

'You know what depresses me about all this?' I asked, mainly to myself. 'There's all sorts of people here with an interest that I share, but no-one's got a sense of humour about it.'

'Thanks very much,' said Wodehouse, although you'd have to say a lot worse to really offend him.

'Story of my life, really, isn't it?' I added, thinking aloud.

CHAPTER NINE

When you're single, your parents are always worrying about you. Worrying you'll be left on the shelf; worrying that you might be gay. When I ring to invite myself to my mother's house I can always sense the unspoken question, 'Aren't you bringing anyone?' And it's not just so she knows how many melon balls to prepare.

Mum lives with her second husband Kevin in a well-maintained semi within a pleasant cul-de-sac in Towbrough, and on the drive over I'm usually day dreaming that I've got Laura with me and they'll get on well together, and instead of feeling like I've got to justify myself all the time I'll be able to watch *Where Eagles Dare* on TV in peace. On this particular evening I didn't bother too much with the daydream because I was getting tired of being nowhere with Laura and it was obviously premature to daydream about Helen, but mainly because I broke the journey to knock on Oswald Mosley's door. I don't think I really knew why: was it Laura's comment about my love of puzzles, or did I just hope to get a look at Mosley's girlfriend (without, of course, her mask)?

Despite the detour to both front and rear of the little terraced house I made good time and arrived just as Kevin was opening the Shiraz. We had our usual conversation about how it would improve once it had breathed a bit longer, and how much more reliable most Aussie wines were compared to some of the French. Mum came out of the kitchen to give me a kiss and then disappeared again because she'd overdone it on the choice of vegetables and there was too much going on to pause, even for two seconds. Kevin thought he'd better help before she panicked. I flicked through the evening paper and drank my cool red wine. The evening was going well so far.

'How's the flat?' asked my mother once we were all sitting down to eat. She persists in calling my bed-sitter a flat, probably because the question 'How's your room?' wouldn't sound quite so worthwhile.

'Fine,' I said. 'No different. Nothing's changed.'

'Still getting on with your neighbours?' asked Kevin.

'Yes. They're fine.'

'That's a boon, isn't it? You don't want difficult neighbours when they're all around you, above and below as well. At least here we only have one party wall, whereas you've got a party ceiling and a party floor too…'

'Big problem when the parties start,' Mum said wittily.

'Lucky the rooms are too small for parties,' I said.

There was a pause and Kevin poured some more wine. I didn't want anyone to ask why I wasn't looking for better accommodation, so I told Mum her hair was looking nice. It was a mistake: her hairdresser also does Paul Wodehouse's auntie, and of course Paul had just moved into his new fucking penthouse suite with a million TV channels, so there was no escape from the subject.

'Maureen thinks he's working much too hard, you know. She hardly sees him, and when he took his parents over to her for Sunday lunch, it was Paul who fell asleep on the sofa, not any of the older generation!'

'That's hardly a crime on a Sunday,' said Kevin. 'Day of rest and all that.'

'Perhaps it's a good job you didn't end up in the police, Larry. Apparently they're making him travel constantly down to Harwich. Lovely new flat and he's stuck in a hotel half the week.'

'Not the weather for the seaside this week,' said Kevin.

'It's drugs, of course,' said Mum, with full confidence in her third hand information. 'No-one's supposed to know, though.'

'Don't worry,' I consoled her, 'his secret's safe with us.'

'But what a crazy idea! I mean, you can't get further from the sea than Hampton, can you? No wonder the poor boy's exhausted.'

'He didn't look too bad when I saw him yesterday,' I said. 'And Paul's not the only one working extra hours, you know. I called on a client on my way over here, for example.'

'Really?' said Kevin. 'You made good time, though.'

'He wasn't in,' I said lamely. 'The house was empty.'

'Maybe he was working extra hours as well,' joked Kevin. I decided it would be too complicated to explain why I doubted it.

As usual I had drunk too much to drive, so I was going to have to stay the night. This was a source of pleasure to Mum, who like any mother likes to have her grown up kids around. It was also a source of pleasure to Kevin, who had an excuse to open another bottle without being disapproved of.

We made some small talk about my brother Mike and his family, and Mum fished around to find out if I had seen my father and pretended to be outraged that he hadn't been in touch. The conversation drifted back to work and I found myself admitting that my new colleague was both female and young, and yes, she was also good-looking as a matter of fact. Mum stopped short of asking if she was unattached, but you could read her thoughts from the way she nodded and repeated 'How nice' throughout the conversation. Kevin, who had taken early retirement from college teaching the previous year, was no doubt remembering former strawberry blondes of his own, behind eyes that had glazed a bit from the wine.

'And is she good at the job?' my mother asked.

'I think she will be. She's certainly keen to learn, if a bit naive. But she's motivated.'

'That's nice.'

'Makes a change nowadays,' said Kevin. 'People aren't so keen to put the effort in. I used to see it in college. Over the last few years the overall level of motivation has been falling. It's laziness, combined with a lack of proper incentive. Why work hard for your A levels if your parents have already bought you all the computer games you need? You must see the same in your line of business, surely?'

'A lot of the unemployed just don't want to work, do they?' suggested Mum. She's said this so many times over the years that I sometimes think she's losing her memory, but really it's just a conversational habit. Unfortunately it's one that always winds me up.

'It's not that simple,' I said. 'The bureaucracy works against them. And many of them find it hard to get offered work because they come across so poorly. A lot are actually clinically depressed.'

'Depressed?' said Kevin. 'I don't want to minimise their difficulties,' he continued, doing just that, 'but British people are going soft. I came from a council estate, but my generation knew you had to work hard to make something of yourself.'

Kevin took another sip of his ten-pounds-a-bottle wine while I gently suggested that, as a teacher, he hadn't worked hard for thirty years only to be thrown on the scrap heap when production moved to Turkey or the Far East. Mum, as usual, was looking confused that someone working in benefit fraud should actually have any empathy with the unemployed. Or perhaps she was just worried I was going to spill red wine on her tablecloth.

'Look,' said Kevin, 'there's a family in this street who lost everything in the Bangladeshi floods years ago, and they came here with nothing. They now run a chain of newsagents. What's losing your job to losing your home and everything? You're talking about motivation. The immigrant families have it. They work hard because they've come from a terrible place.'

'Some of these unemployed men need a boot up the… bottom,' said Mum, who hasn't had a job for almost thirty years.

'A boot up the *bottom*? I suppose you think Kevin could have sorted out his lazy pupils quite easily if he'd been allowed to do that, do you? Maybe you think my boss should boot me around if I fail to meet his targets for the month?'

'Now I'm sure your mother didn't mean that–'

'Look, my job is hard enough without everyone coming up with comments that would disgrace some sort of fascist tabloid newspaper–'

'Have another glass of Shiraz,' said Kevin.

'I'll get the lemon meringue pie,' said my mother.

'How was that conference you went to?' asked Kevin. 'On World War Two, wasn't it? Prisoners of War?'

I took a deep draught of wine. 'Fascinating,' I said.

'By the way,' said Mum from the door, 'how's Laura these days? You could have invited her over, you know.'

★ ★ ★

Parents. How is it they can always make their children so... well, *childish*?

I'm sure that even if my mum and I shared identical opinions I would still end up losing my temper with her; it's quite possibly an inevitable part of the relationship. But the trouble with being a grown up child is that you feel guilty about it afterwards. Most especially at the point that your old bedroom stops spinning and sobriety returns.

I suppose by now she's used to me thoughtlessly chucking about words like 'ignorant,' 'judgemental' and 'fascist.' But that didn't make the last of those words any fairer. I mean, she wasn't collecting military uniforms and writing newsletters about deporting the unemployed, was she? And what fascist would be admiring of an Asian family's success against the odds? Whereas presumably Oswald Mosley would have resented it, either because workaholic Asians showed up his colleagues' failings, or because he believed newsagents had some sort of duty to be white.

Dusk had already been falling when I had parked up at the top end of Mosley's street. I walked carefully down to his house, which was in darkness, and firmly locked front and rear. I had knocked assertively, but with no real hope of a reply.

The front room curtains had been open, and I saw it was much tidier than on the night of our stakeout. Not only had the files and papers been moved off the table, chairs and floor, but they seemed to have left the room altogether. As far as I could make out in the dark, Mosley's shelves were empty. The laptop was gone, too.

Had he gone away, then? The letterbox flap was jammed open from the crush of envelopes in the little cage behind the door. But there was probably a free newspaper or a pile of pizza adverts further down; there was no reason to suppose it was full of several days' worth of letters. I tried pulling one out to look but only managed to tear off a corner and concertina what remained behind. Intercepting a client's post is strictly illegal and I usually only do it when I am convinced I'm getting a pay slip, so I made a run around the back before someone spotted me.

The kitchen was still a mess, although the yard seemed a bit different; not *tidy,* exactly, but with slightly more space than before. But there was nothing to see, nothing to indicate employment or otherwise. And no girlfriend, either. I had turned around to return to the car, with no particular sense of surprise, but still one of mild disappointment.

As I began to doze off, I remembered that somewhere I had a note of his mobile phone number, copied from a business card. Of course! But where was it? Not on the forms I had been filling in when I carried out the home visit: otherwise I would have noticed it and remembered it before now. Well, it would be on one of the sheets of paper cluttering up my desk. Probably best to see if I could find it: I couldn't see Will accepting that any client could be phone-less in this day and age. Still, I wasn't going to start thinking about that now; it was time to get some shut eye. I'd be back at work soon enough without trying to review cases in my sleep…

There couldn't be anything worse than dreaming about your boss, right?

Except for S & M nightmares about your clients.

CHAPTER TEN

'Don't you fucking threaten me, Bitch, or you'll be in fucking trouble.'

'I'm not threat–'

'Yes, you are. You said you'll stop my money.'

'If you'll just let me explain again–'

'Don't give me any of that "I don't make the rules" jobsworth crap. This is harassment. I'm gonna sue your ass off. Give me a complaints form. Go on, give me a complaints form.'

I squirmed in my seat. *Boy, he was good, this one.* We'd barely read him his rights before we had a three shot interview on our hands. I gripped my pen a little tighter.

'Please don't swear at me, Mr Smith,' said Helen. 'That is harassing *me.*'

Smith patted a hand around his huge Afro hair. 'What you gonna do about it? Send the police round to "have a word"? Look at the address, darling, read your local paper. Listen to the radio news about the estate. I don't think anyone's coming around to fucking get *me.*' He touched his hair again: it wasn't a sign of stress, more of complacency.

'If you swear at me again, I'll terminate the interview and withhold all payments pending... er, pending...'

Damn! And she had started the sentence so well...

'No. *Fucking.* Way.' Smith opened his jacket and pulled out a deep red wallet. A business card fluttered across the table and landed in front of Helen. Smith sat back and folded his arms.

'As you said, Girl, it's my right to be accompanied by a legal representative or "friend."'

Helen looked at the card and then turned and passed it back to me. I sighed and put the ILP assessment forms aside. There was a hint of sweat on her brow, I noticed, but then there had been a similar hint before she had even introduced herself to Smith. Formal interviews are always nerve wracking for the beginner.

Grant Leroy-Shaw, said the card. *Phd. Hampton Black Legal and Advice Services.* There was a phone number. No job title was shown. Nor, I noticed, any specific credentials in law.

'So phone him,' Smith said.

I stood up and moved forward very slowly. I placed the card carefully in front of Smith, making sure it was the correct way up for him, and even that it was square to the sides of the table. I said, as quietly as possible, 'The phone is right there.'

'You woken up at last? Gonna protect your girlfriend? Come on, darling,' he said to Helen, 'Get ringing.'

'I'm not your secretary.'

'You dragged me in here. You can make the call.'

'It's nine for an outside line.' I touched her lightly on the shoulder. 'Quick word? Excuse us for a moment, Mr Smith.'

We had reached the stairwell when the first tears came. I offered the box of tissues that I had taken from the interview room. We keep them there for overwrought clients. Or overwrought members of staff.

'What a bastard!' she choked. 'How do you handle this?'

'Tough nut, definitely. You were doing pretty well, though.'

'What do I do? Leave him until he phones his solicitor?'

'Unfortunately, I don't think we can make him wait too long,' I mused. 'He's the sort who will come out and start accosting the clerks and demanding to see the manager. Pushing in front of each queue. Showing off. No sense of shame. The opposite, really. One of the worst types to deal with.'

'Thanks. That really cheers me up.'

A couple of clerks came down the stairs, looked curiously at Helen and then moved on. I pretended to think.

'OK. If I break his nose, will you agree to lie to the police?'

'*What?*'

'Just kidding. Nose is too visible. Balls would be alright, though.'

Helen smiled, despite herself. I handed over the box. 'Come on. Ready to go back in?'

'Do I have to?'

'Yes. But I'll take over the interview.'

'Can I have a minute to redo my face?'

'You've got *one* minute. Just while I take a look at the video recorder. I've got a funny feeling it's going to be malfunctioning shortly.'

★ ★ ★

Back in the Cooler, Smith was talking on the phone, resting his size eleven trainers on the desk top. He glanced at us, then took his time putting his feet down while continuing his conversation. It wasn't about legal representation.

Helen sat on my chair by the door and I adjusted the broken blinds to make sure we were invisible to the outside world. I looked pointedly at Smith and he turned his head away. I waited about five seconds, then reached out to the phone cradle and cut off his call.

'Alright, Smith, you're free to go.'

For a moment he looked amazed, then pleased, then smug. He stood up and reached behind him for his leather jacket. Then something dawned.

'Are you releasing my payment?'

I inclined my head back towards Helen. 'I think "Darling" here explained about that, didn't she?'

'Fuck you, man! I'm gonna–'

'Shut up!'

Smith had made a mistake. He had stood up but hadn't moved away from the desk. His chair was behind him and one hand was still seeking out the arm of his coat. When I pushed him he was forced to sit down with a bump. I lifted my arm to show him the standard issue personal alarm in my hand and I spoke fast and loud over his protests.

'Sexual harassment of a female employee: on tape. Use of official telephone for private calls: on tape. Clear, compelling evidence of benefit fraud… You're in trouble, Smith. Try co-operating.'

'I'll see you sacked for assault.'

'The video tape's off, now, mate. And it's two professional words against one. One *fraudster*.'

'You're fucking dead meat, man.'

'Your National Insurance record shows payments from Hampton Borough Council. You're *employed* by the *Council*. Do you really think you can get away with it by threatening me?'

'I am not employed by the Council!'

'Really? Then let's clear this up without any more aggravation, shall we?'

★ ★ ★

Outside, the dim autumn sun was already beginning to slip down the sky. Under the harsh, yellow light in Interview room 3, known jokingly as The Cooler, I felt a pull of depression as my adrenaline level lowered itself. I heard someone saying goodbye loudly and contentedly: one of the box clerks taking flexi time to go shopping or just to get a break from the office. I cleared my throat.

'It's pretty simple. When we pay unemployment related benefits, we also credit National Insurance contributions. There's a duplication on your record.'

'Well, it's wrong. It must be another Jon Smith. It's not an unusual name, is it?'

'Another Jon *Maxwell* Smith?'

'Maybe there's more than one.'

'With the same date of birth?'

'It must be a case of identity fraud. Some other Jon Smith has borrowed my National Insurance number. Or maybe they're not even called Smith at all.'

'Why would they do that?'

'Because they're fucking signing on and they know what your computer records can do!'

I took a deep breath. 'Look, Mr Smith,' I said, 'we've checked the full details with the Council and we are aware of exactly which subcontractor employed you, which locations you worked at, and which site manager you reported to. We know you were paid in cash, and we assume that's how you came to think your little scam would work. We have successfully recorded at least part of this interview. Do I really have to arrange for your site supervisor to be shown the tapes and asked to confirm that you *are* the Jon Smith who did this work? And who was such a model employee that he was only late in once a fortnight, coincidentally on the same morning that *you* attend this office?'

'If it will clear my name, maybe you should show him the tape.'

'Don't even start on thinking that this… imaginary identity fraudster happens to *look* just like you, either.'

'Why not? White guys always say that we all look the fucking same.'

'Yes, and maybe you've suddenly remembered you have an identical twin as well.'

'Fuck you, man.'

'The choice is either that you write a statement and agree to repay benefit overpayments over a certain period of time. Or that we prosecute you. It has been known for jail sentences to be imposed…'

Smith grimaced and then took out his wallet for the second time. 'I'm going to phone my representative,' he said, looking at me as if he expected to be told he had forfeited the right due to his previous aggressive behaviour.

'Fine,' I said. 'We will set up a further appointment at his and your convenience.'

'Yeah, we'll deal with the assault next time,' said Smith, looking me in the eye.

I nodded. 'Nine for an outside line.' I couldn't think of anything else to reply.

★ ★ ★

'Was it OK, though?'
'Yeah, you were great.'
'Really?'
'Yeah really.'

'But I cried!'

'Actually,' I said, thoughtfully, 'I should have let you carry on. I've never tried tears as an interview technique before. Who knows how Smith might have reacted? He might have confessed to help cheer you up.'

'Now I know you're kidding.'

'No, you did well. That was what Herman used to call a three shot interview. You need three vodka shots afterwards... Seriously, you followed all the initial steps correctly, and you were dealing very well with his aggressive attitude. If you don't believe me, just watch the video of yourself.'

'This might seem a silly question...'

I smiled encouragingly. I love it when people say that: it makes me feel like a real expert.

'Identity fraud. It could be true, couldn't it?'

'Well, yes, in theory. What do you need to make a claim for benefits? Name, address, date of birth, National Insurance Number... Full details about the person. Things need to match up on all the databases. But we don't ask for ID, do we? No need for a passport or anything. So if you have all the facts, and if you get a posted giro, not a payment directly into the bank... It *could* be possible. But once his employer identifies his picture, he's stuffed.'

'We're not allowed to push people around, though.'

'No, definitely. Never touch a client. Obvious really.'

'But–'

'No,' I said firmly, 'never touch a client. Never in a million years. Never have that experience.'

Helen bit her lip and looked down at her lap. Well, the trouble is nowadays that every tiny bit of training and development includes issues like equality, fairness, ethics, human rights... It was likely she was thinking that I had put her in a difficult position, and in fact she was right. There was only one solution to this: to keep up the momentum of her learning experience, to keep on showing her the amoral reality of some of our work, to take her a little further into the twilight zone.

'While we're talking about experience,' I said, 'let me suggest something to you. I'll explain in a second, but how are you fixed for tomorrow night?'

CHAPTER ELEVEN

Every man needs a pub to call his own. His 'local,' where he is known as a regular drinker. There's a psychological benefit from being in familiar surroundings after a tough day at work; also, it helps you get served quicker at the bar. And, of course, you avoid that moment of anxiety that comes when entering a new or unknown pub, when you ask yourself 'How rough will it turn out to be here?' or possibly even, 'Why are they all staring at me?'

I have two locals (not counting the pubs around my bedsit, that is: they are local only by geography, not psychology, and there was a whole lot of staring last time I went in). Jobcentre employees tend to frequent the King's Head, since it is only eighty yards from the office door. We're all known there: the landlord will sometimes sit down to have a chat about the difficulty of retaining staff we send him; this usually happens five minutes into drinking-up time, after the lights have dimmed.

The pub of my choice, however, is known as the Dark Horse. It's tucked away beyond the town centre in a street of tired terraced housing, close to what looks like the only World War Two bomb site still in existence across the UK. There's a mix of college art students and pensioners who have been going there for decades. (Sometimes you also get a Real Ale fanatic or two, if they're still working from a guide book more than ten years old.) There's no TV, but a piano in the public bar and Wurlitzer juke box in the lounge. The landlady is in her late seventies and sounds very fierce, but you just know she has seen all types of customer and accepts every one, just so long as they are polite to her staff.

Above all, of course, the Dark Horse has that indefinable and elusive quality: true character. I like it best in mid-winter, with a real log fire illuminating the genuine sepia photographs on the walls, and in mid-week, when the proportion of sweet old senior citizens is highest. For me, it's the sort of place that makes you really *want* to be a regular, to eventually become one of its characters; to soak up, and then *become* a part of its history and ambience. So I always try to make a bit of small talk when Lilly isn't too busy, and I try to remember the names of the older customers, ready for the day when I might feel confident enough to use them.

The Horse is also about the only pub in the county where Chandler wouldn't look like a man in fancy dress. Lilly knows not to offer him alcohol, so for somewhere warmer than a car park, it's ideal. The only potential downside is being seen out drinking with him: I mean, I wouldn't want people to think he was my friend or anything.

Chandler's message had been waiting for us as we saw Jon Smith out of the building. It was in the usual cryptic crossword style, but luckily he'd left it in a sealed envelope, and so there was no need for me to feel embarrassed in front of the receptionist. On a torn-off piece of Poundland notebook he had written, 'Seven called to the bar for trial of new biscuit recipe, the fifteenth. C.' Well, this was our only 'bar' and seven o'clock was a reasonable time to meet. The note had been handed in on the fourteenth, so I had assumed the rendezvous was for the following day. I was guessing he had something on the dog biscuit works, although it could have been a number of other employers; hopefully it would make sense when he arrived. And hopefully I could talk him out of asking for danger money, too…

Helen had agreed to meet me just before seven, and while she strolled home to shower away the stress of a day in the Jobcentre, I had run to the bank to plead for an extension to my overdraft and the return of my withheld debit card. I had abandoned the idea of going back to the office to catch up – that would wait for a day or two – and after a fruitless search for a birthday present for my sister in law, I had crawled into the pub and sunk two pints in quick succession. I tried the crossword in the hope of impressing Helen with another talent, but by 6.40 I had hidden it under my coat. As the next few minutes ticked by, I found myself getting unaccountably nervous.

When Helen walked in she looked fantastic. Fantastic enough to make me wish I'd gone home and showered too before coming to the pub. Seeing her pause briefly at the doorway and look over the room, I could feel the sweat on my back, the grit on my collar, the black newsprint on my fingers and thumbs. She made me feel… *dirty*.

Girls have this secret way with make-up for the evening, don't they? No matter how pretty by daylight, the first time you see them made up for the night it's astonishing: suddenly they're riper, stronger, more knowing. Older, but in a good way. Sexier. On Helen, even at a room's distance, this showed, although to be strictly accurate, noticing her make-up came second to seeing how well her jeans fitted, and how perfect, under the short t-shirt and suede jacket, was the bare strip of belly and its piercing.

'Hi.'

'Hi.'

But this wasn't a date, so I wasn't sure if I was meant to compliment her. Instead, I said, 'Did you find it alright? Of course you did, you're here, and...' I glanced stupidly at my watch, 'You're on time... What can I get you to drink? You look great, by the way,' I added, making a late change of decision on the compliment front. After all, there's no bad time to praise a woman's appearance, is there? Apart from when it sounds like an afterthought, of course...

'Thanks,' said Helen. 'I just thought I'd freshen up a bit seeing as we're meeting somebody.'

I smiled. 'Somehow I don't think Chandler will have made the same effort.' I pulled out my wallet and gave a quick glance inside – a superstitious habit from way back. Helen said, 'Look, let me get you a drink, Larry. It's the least I can do after all your help.'

I scratched my head, which had begun to itch a little when she had come in. 'That's a rash offer,' I said, 'I don't do all that "No, no, let me, I insist" thing, you know. If you offer to buy a drink, then you do end up buying.'

'I *am* offering to buy.' She looked quizzical. 'What d'you want?'

'Oh...' I shrugged, 'A bottle of Bollinger, well chilled, a side order of caviare, a Monte Cristo... Pork scratchings...'

She gave the politest laugh I'd heard in ages. 'Come on, are you a lager man or a bitter man? Or a whisky man?'

'OK. A pint of Hornimand's.'

'Hornimand's. Right. A bitter man.'

'A bitter man,' I confirmed.

She was back quickly with the beer and a glass of wine, which, this being the Dark Horse, put me in mind of an old sit-com joke where the snobby, refined brother asks to see the wine list in a bar, looks thoughtfully at the card for a while, then says, 'I'll have the, er, *white.*' Helen laughed a little longer at this, and we made some polite talk about settling into the office, and I held back from bitching about people I don't like because I didn't want to prejudice her against me. We laughed cynically over some of the more obvious absurdities of the benefits system, and she got angry about the stress it was causing both clients and staff. I tried to reassure her that most people complained incessantly about their job, but very few made any effort at all to look elsewhere. She said that this didn't necessarily make it all right and I said that I agreed, although I didn't really.

I asked her about herself: hobbies, how she liked to relax. Helen got very shy and embarrassed to admit she had been learning karate, but not as embarrassed as me when I told her, for want of anything else at all impressive, that I had an interest in history.

'Really? What periods?'

I thought about Colin and Rhys, and the bargain Iron Crosses on sale at Escape 2000.

'Oh, any really. Well, not *any*, no, twentieth century. Oral history. Forgotten voices and all that. Anyway, let me get you a drink.'

'Just a soft drink for now. I don't want to be fuzzy when your, er, contact comes.'

I looked at my watch. 'He's late. I'm not entirely sure he's going to show,' I said, hopefully.

Being a regular doesn't help you get served quickly if there are casual bar staff on, and tonight there was a young Australian couple whose suntans showed how new to the area they were. It seemed to take me ages to catch the girl's eye, and then a voice said, 'Hello, Larry,' beside me.

'Pint of Hornimand's and an orange juice,' I said loudly and firmly, waiting until she had nodded before I turned my head.

Detective Sergeant Paul Woodhouse grinned wolfishly at me over his glass.

'Hello, Paul. How's it going?'

'Not bad, not bad. Enjoy the rest of the conference?'

I nodded. 'I went to the "POW Veterans in Conversation" seminar in the end. Very… interesting.' I cleared my throat.

'I'll bet. Those old farts must have some tales to tell, eh?'

I glanced down the bar where my Australian was swapping beauty tips with Hampton's only visible transvestite. She wouldn't get away with ignoring me if the boss was around, I thought miserably.

'On your own tonight?' asked Wodehouse, casually.

'Er… No. I'm with a colleague.'

'I didn't see you. Where are you sitting?'

'Over in the corner.' I reluctantly gave a backwards nod.

'No kidding? The girl in the red top? *Very* nice.'

'Mmm.' I raised my hand, a bit too hesitantly.

Paul leaned forward. 'Excuse me love,' he called loudly. 'We're still waiting for our drinks here.'

'Sorry, gents.'

'I'll get these, Larry,' said Wodehouse, setting down his own glass. 'I'm sure I owe you one from a few weeks back.'

Wodehouse actually owed me about eight, not that I'd been counting. 'No, no…' I tried to protest, but he had already pressed his cash into the barmaid's hand. Helpless, I watched him lift the orange juice and head for the corner while Sheila dealt with the till and topped up my pint, and he was settled on the banquette by the time I caught up, looking much like the winner of a police station sweepstake.

'Helen thought I was someone called Chandler,' he said, eyes twinkling. 'Anyone I know?'

'To do with work,' I said gruffly.

'In the pub? And they say the Civil Service isn't a cushy number.'

'Alternatively, you could call it working out of hours when most people are enjoying their leisure time,' Helen corrected.

'Touché.' Wodehouse grinned and sipped what remained in his glass. 'You claim time off in lieu for that, don't you?'

'And what do you do for a living?'

'Me? Oh, I'm in the investigation business myself as it happens.' He took a slim leather case from his inside pocket and passed her a business card. 'Slightly different focus, though. Up to a month ago I was on a murder case.'

'Did you solve it?'

'Oh, yes. The Peaseholme Estate is now a safer place than it was before.'

'But still not actually *safe*,' I said sourly. Slightly to my surprise they both laughed.

'What are you investigating now, then?' asked Helen.

'Not allowed to say. Let's call it traffic offences. I can't be specific.'

'Oh, well.' Helen lifted her glass. 'Cheers. Thanks for this, Larry.'

'Thank Paul,' I said. 'He insisted on buying.'

'Thanks for this, *Paul*.' She gave a little bow. 'How do you two know each other, anyway?'

'We go back a long way,' said Wodehouse, in what, from anyone else, could have sounded like a fond tone. 'Larry and I were both on the same recruitment and selection programme for Hamptonshire Police. Four days of interviews, group exercises, written tests, a medical... All at a residential centre in the middle of Wales with the heating broken down.' Wodehouse was laughing into his beer. 'You get a special sort of bond after that…'

I drank deeply from my own glass and tried to say something about water under the bridge.

'The first night, the first night, you know, Larry spent half an hour persuading us we should sneak out to the pub. Which was strictly against the rules, on pain of failing the programme I daresay. But after the day we'd all had, we were gagging for a drink. So out the window we go, like we're breaking out of the asylum, and we walk for forty minutes to the nearest village, and, guess what? No pub! Only God fearing chapel folk already tucked up in fucking bed! And we get back to the centre and someone's gone and shut the window, and we're locked out. Didn't help the team building exercises the next day, I can tell you. Boy, that was a struggle. No booze for four days! We more than made up for it on the train back, though, didn't we?'

'I didn't know you were in the police,' Helen said to me.

'I wasn't.'

'But..?'

'I failed the selection board.'

'Just for going out for a drink?' Helen was outraged.

'No, they never found out about that. We managed to break back in quite easily.'

'It was a tough course,' said Wodehouse. 'Plenty of good people didn't get in. I told him he should reapply for another intake, but he never did. Shame really. Yeah, it was tough.' He caught Helen's eye and held it a moment. 'I think only four people passed first time, you know.'

'And you've kept in touch ever since?'

'Yeah, we have…'

'We see each other for a drink now and then,' I admitted. 'Usually by accident.'

'I'd make it more regular, Larry, if you were always in such good company.' Paul winked and finished his lager. 'Who's for another one?'

It's not often that I really want to see Chandler, frankly, but that night I'd have been thrilled if he'd only walked in through the door. Anything to interrupt Paul Wodehouse and save me from being bored, embarrassed, *marginalized* by the turn of the conversation. But Chandler had failed to make the appointment. *Bastard*, I thought, I'll kill him when I see him…

Wodehouse had now charmed Helen into having a gin and tonic, but instead of taking our glasses to the bar he turned to me with an expectant look. I had been toying with my beer mat for some time now. '"The great white shark has fifty thousand teeth but no bones,"' I read. '"True or false?"'

'Actually, Larry, it's your round.'

'No, mate, the *last* round was mine.'

'*I* bought the last round!'

'Well, that's not my fault. You insisted. And you're the one who just offered, not me.'

'You tight bastard!'

I glanced at Helen, but I couldn't quite read her expression. I didn't really need to, though, to identify the lesser of two evils: getting stuck at the bar while Paul continued to monopolise the conversation was going to be preferable to getting 'tight bastard' digs and jokes 'til closing time. And to be honest, if the guy wanted a quiet moment to ask her for her phone number, he only had to wait until I went to the toilet. Though knowing Wodehouse, he'd be happy to do it in front of me anyway.

'Ha, ha,' I said humourlessly. 'Had you going there.'

The bar was quiet as I approached it, so I moved in quickly between two old guys on stools. The second barmaid managed the pints and a double Tanqueray without difficulty once I had pointed out the bottle and reminded her about topping up the bitter. I decided anyone could be as smooth as Wodehouse with a bit of effort, so I asked her if she'd like a drink herself.

'Thanks. I'll put a pound in the staff box for later if that's OK.'

'Where's Lilly today?' I said, referring to the landlady. (I'd never have dared to offer Lilly a drink.) 'Taking a well earned holiday at last?' Lilly was rarely absent, though she did tend to leave before drinking up time nowadays, and would curse the taxi company if her cab to her retirement flat was late.

'She's in hospital.'

I paused for thought. 'Nothing... serious, is it?' Lilly was a chain smoker, of course. My mind saw a hearse pulling away while the property developers hung around impatiently. Where would I find another local like this one?

'Varicose veins. Comes of standing behind a bar for sixty years.'

'There's a lesson to us all,' I said.

'Don't worry, love,' said one of the bar flies in a gravelly voice. 'You've a long way to go yet before that happens.'

'No worries,' said the girl. 'This is only a temporary job for me. I'll be starting my research project next September. I'm a microbiologist.'

The second bar fly stirred. 'When you're ready, love,' he said, 'I'll have another pint of bacteria from you.'

Back at the table, Detective Sergeant Wodehouse was praising sniffer dogs. Apparently they improved with age.

'They become more and more familiar with their favourite drug. More and more keen to find it.'

'It sounds like they get hooked.'

'Nah, they can't eat it or snort it. They're hooked on the chocolate drop reward if anything. Oh, thanks, Larry, that was quick.'

'Paul's been telling me about police interview techniques,' said Helen, taking her drink from my hand. 'It sounds fascinating.'

'Yeah, tough work beating a confession out of them,' I said. 'Hell for your knuckles.'

'You must have clients you wish you could give a good slap, though, don't you?' said Paul, denying nothing.

'Some of them deserve a slap for being stupid enough to get caught.'

Wodehouse glanced at his watch and frowned. 'I have to make a few phone calls,' he told Helen. 'Will you excuse me?' He patted her shoulder. 'See you in a few minutes.'

I drank deeply. 'Thanks for the drink,' said Helen. 'Lime's much better than lemon, isn't it? It makes a real difference.'

I smiled a little, and the conversation turned back to Jon Smith and interview techniques. I admitted that Paul was right: there were many similarities between our own approach and theirs. Some fraud officers deliberately use the jargon at every opportunity: 'helping us with our enquiries,' 'witness statements,' 'admissible evidence.' Reading the client his rights always sets the atmosphere, and the same questioning techniques are used, of course: basically to seek inconsistencies in the subject's story, point out any evidence gathered, and encourage an admission.

'They're not all as tough as our Mr Smith,' I said. 'Most of them crack when they see written proof in front of them.

Video evidence is even better. Sometimes they look totally crushed. It feels like you've made them accidentally walk into a cell door…'

I saw Wodehouse re-enter the bar and cross to the gents' toilets.

'Look,' I said. 'I don't know why you're so hung up on this. You're in your first two weeks of the job; of course everything seems like a challenge. And you're doing fine. If you were doing any better, I'd be seriously worried about getting replaced myself.'

'Thanks,' said Helen. 'But I want to do well, to learn fast. That's what being professional is all about, isn't it?'

'True,' I nodded, crossing my fingers under the table.

Helen smiled. 'Larry, I'm really grateful for today. And that you offered to look at my training course video with me. I'm sure it will be really helpful.'

'Glad to. Though I don't think I'll be able to add anything that Herman didn't say in feedback.'

'Is tonight still OK? We can dial a pizza or something if you haven't eaten.'

'It's fine,' I said. 'There's plenty of time. Chandler's missed his chance, anyhow.'

'I really appreciate it.'

'It'll be a pleasure.' Suddenly, my face fell. 'You weren't thinking of inviting Paul, were you?'

'No.' Helen smiled. 'I'm not ready to expose my weaknesses to him.'

'Why don't we make a move right away?' I suggested.

We crossed the room as Wodehouse came out of the gents' looking angry and concerned. For a mad moment I expected him to accuse me of stealing his girl, but he waved aside my unconvincing apologies about leaving him early and followed us into the car park. He drove off at speed, without offering us a lift.

'He didn't seem happy.'

'Beer disagreed with him, maybe,' I said.

'No,' said Helen, 'it's business for him. Work. Something unpleasant's come up.'

'Mmm.'

'I'm glad we don't have to deal with that stuff, really. Imagine questioning a murderer. Smith was bad enough… And seeing the results of violent crime… You know what, Larry, I know it must have been disappointing when you didn't get in the police, but I bet you're well out of it. It could be you driving off like that to God knows what crime scene. Maybe it was better you never reapplied for another selection course.'

I looked away down the dark street. 'I did reapply. Twice. Still failed.'

'Oh… Shit. I'm sorry.'

'Come on,' I said. 'Let's change the subject. I'll dive into the off licence and get a bottle of wine, and you can take me back to your place. You can expose your weaknesses to me…'

'I bet you say that to all the girls.'

I thought of Laura and nearly said, 'Some of them don't need any encouragement,' but luckily I stopped myself in time. She wouldn't have understood. It would have sounded like the sort of chat up line Herman might use. Instead, I went over to the off licence and rashly overspent on a bottle that Kevin had recommended to me. It looked like I'd be back at the bank tomorrow, but what the hell… With luck the evening might be worth it.

CHAPTER TWELVE

What woke me up? The cold, the hangover, the snoring? It doesn't matter: I was quickly aware of all three adding discomfort to the disorientation of waking in an unexpected place. A moment passed while I struggled to catch up.

Headache, thirst, full bladder. Not so unusual to wake this way, but harder to deal with when other things are so different. A strange bed, a cold room; half of me freezing, the other half warmed by a snoring body abutted to mine. My brain battling its own disbelief: this can't be right, this never happens. *Where am I?*

It was up to the most evocative of the human senses to help the brain out. Before even opening my eyes, I identified the dark, musky, sexy smell of skin and sweat, highlighted by notes of cannabis and kiwi fruit. And from knowing where I was, it was an immediate jump to remembering how I got there. I relaxed. Very slightly.

Then, quietly and gently, I clambered from the bed, waited to gain my balance, and felt my way cautiously to the door. Closing it quietly behind me, I went to the bathroom, then the kitchen tap, then the bathroom again. I squeezed some toothpaste onto a finger and tried to freshen my breath. Feeling grubby and cold, I decided to have a shower. Rubbing in the fruit shampoo, I imagined a knock on the door... 'Larry, I'm coming in, I'm desperate for a wee, shut your eyes...'

The shower was new and powerful (at odds with the cheap, tired furnishing of the rest of the flat) and invigorating enough to put breakfast back on the agenda. I hummed along to the kitchen radio as I assembled ingredients: free range bacon, nice, a day past sell-by only; tomatoes, wrinkly, can't tell when cooked; sliced bread, slice off the green spots, not done that in a while, takes me back; ground coffee, ancient, a purist would have kept it in the fridge or at least re-sealed the pack I s'pose, but no problem, it'll still taste of coffee, just...

I looked up and she was there, leaning against the door jamb, hair awry, eyes puffy, mascara still on her cheeks. Creased nightdress. Bang went my idea of waking her with a kiss, then. I gave her a smile.

'What are you doing?'

'Making breakfast, of course.'

'Oh, well. Help yourself.' Laura and hangovers don't go together very well. Surprising, since they've had so much practice.

'I'm making it for you.'

'God, *I* don't want any.'

'Come on, it'll do you good.'

'Maybe I'll have some coffee,' she said, spotting the cafétière. Milk slopped onto the work surface around the mugs. I deftly turned the bacon with her spatula.

'It's the most important meal of the day, you know.'

'You sound like my mum,' Laura complained. '"Eat your greens." "What time did you get in last night?" "You treat this place like a hotel."'

'Right,' I said, waving the spatula. 'You'll eat this up or I'll sma- I'll stop your pocket money. And afterwards you can tidy your room.'

Laura sat down. 'You didn't need to stay, you know. I'd have been alright.'

'Of course I had to stay,' I said. It didn't seem right to point out that I had stayed by accident, nodding off when I didn't mean to, in more clothes than I would have liked.

Laura lowered her head. 'I'm a mess, aren't I?' she said.

I shook my head. 'Brush you hair and you'll look fantastic.' I watched her try to smile. It hurt.

'*Inside* I'm a mess.'

'Hey,' I said, 'you're supposed to feel better after a good night's sleep.'

Laura wiped her eyes. 'Who put me in my nightie?'

'You did.' I concentrated on the frying pan. 'Unfortunately.'

'Ha, ha.'

'If it'd been me, I'd have chosen the red satin one. You know, not really long enough, looks like a mini skirt–'

'Stop it!'

'With the frilly knickers to go with–'

'Larry!'

'I turned and looked her in the eye. 'You still look pretty damned sexy in that thing, anyhow.'

'Larry.' For once I couldn't place the tone of her voice. I waited. 'Why are you here? Did you come over to ogle my tits or something? Is that it?'

I banged down the spatula in frustration.

'*You* asked *me* to come over. Remember? At half past one in the night. *You* were upset and needed company. *You* were scared. Then *you* got wasted and I had to help you get to bed. And now… Now you're sitting there with your nightdress half way up your knees… If you want to be comforted by someone who doesn't notice that sort of thing, then you should have asked a different friend.'

'I don't think I have any,' said Laura, and burst into tears.

★ ★ ★

When I had arrived the night before, Laura had already been letting her make-up run awhile; she looked like a sad-faced circus clown who'd been hit in the face with a floor mop. I knew better than to mention this, but I did take advantage of the circumstances by giving her a quick kiss and a hug.

'Thanks for coming, Larry,' she'd said in her pathos voice. I let her smear my shoulder with eye shadow and felt that odd mix of thrill and sadness run through me. We moved deeper into her sitting room.

'What's been scaring you?' I asked, referring to the answerphone message that had met me on arriving back home from Helen's. Laura pointed into a ceiling corner at the back of the room and for a second I imagined she'd called me across town in the middle of a blustery night to deal with a daddy long legs or a bigger than average moth. The corner, however, was empty.

'Listen.' I waited. 'In a minute…' I waited some more. 'It's intermittent,' she explained.

'I'll say it is.'

I was taking my coat off when Laura clutched excitedly at my arm. I frowned. The wind was getting up again, but what else? I strained my ears. Suddenly, there it was! A sort of rustling, tapping sound; very faint to be honest; I doubt I'd have even noticed it if she hadn't pointed it out to me. Just taking off my waterproofs obscured it. If you'd had the TV on it would have been inaudible. I gave her a sideways look.

She said anxiously, 'I thought it might be rats.'

'*Rats?*'

'In the eaves. Do I mean eaves? The loft space. You know…'

I listened again. 'It's very faint. They can't be very big rats.' Laura shivered as I spoke. 'Mice, maybe.'

'Ugh! Don't.'

'Baby rats–'

'Stop it!' She slapped my arm. Hard.

'You're the one who brought the subject up. Anyway, so what if there was something up there? They can't get in here, can they? What are they going to do: gnaw through the ceiling rose and abseil down the light flex? Take a dive from the light shade? "Look for a soft landing, boys! Aim for the pillow!"'

'You're horrible.' Laura was half laughing despite herself.

'You'll be fine,' I said. 'Just make sure you put all your food away and clean up any crumbs before bed, that's all.'

'Larry!'

'If it'll make you feel any better, I'll set a few traps for you…'

You know that bit in films where the bloke's being mean (jokily or seriously, whichever) and the girl sort of throws herself at him and starts pummelling away, and he has to grab her wrists to hold her off, and then it ends up in a passionate, writhing kiss? Well, that's what happened next, apart from the kissing bit, as she broke away too soon. I couldn't believe my bad luck: in one quick movement she was halfway to the kitchen and asking what I'd like to drink. And instead of following through, pressing home the advantage, forcing the issue one way or another, I panicked and said, 'Hang on, I think it's coming from the *outside*.'

Which is how, ten minutes later, I came to be hanging over a fire escape balustrade in a high wind at two in the morning, confidence boosted by a couple of stiff whiskies on top of the night's beer and wine, and hand to eye co-ordination impaired by the same. As I made the final stretch I was relying entirely on Laura to keep me from falling: there must be easier ways to get a girl's fingers into your trouser waist band, I was thinking, and warmer places to do it, too…

'Don't let go, whatever you do!'

'I won't!'

The wind blew grit into my eyes. My feet slipped an inch on the damp metal and my flailing hands scraped the brickwork for a hold. Laura pulled back: 'I've still got you.'

'Thanks so much,' I muttered, glancing dizzily down at the tops of the wheelie bins three storeys down. I launched myself again, grasped the length of twine I had been struggling for and reeled in what turned out to be a slowly deflating helium balloon and a sheet of A5 sized card. The fire escape wobbled under me; or perhaps it was just my legs.

Back inside, Laura poured me another whisky.

'What do I always say? You can't leave any puzzle unsolved, can you? Hercule bloody Poirot.'

I twiddled an imaginary waxed moustache. 'So, *mon amie*, the mystery, she is solved. The noise was of a card flapping inside the wall, in the space of a missing air brick, and brought there by a helium filled balloon!'

'Mister Poirot, how will I ever thank you?'

'Two mysteries, in fact,' I added. 'That great big hole in the wall is the reason it's so cold in here. Nothing but a thin plastic grill between you and the wind chill factor. And talk about a through draught. I'm surprised nobody's ever worked it out before.'

'No rats, anyway, thank God.'

'I didn't even know you had a fire escape running past your window,' I said, drinking.

'Oh, it's a statutory requirement. Didn't stop the landlord making a big fuss about it when he was showing us round, though. Should have been a warning to us really, shouldn't it? Hah! It's not going to be the height of luxury when the main selling point is the fire escape, is it?'

'Maybe he was just concerned about your safety.'

'"See the easily accessible fire escape." *Thanks*. He might as well have said, "Here we have windows, light switches and a floor to walk on. What more could anyone possibly want?" '

'It's not a bad little flat.'

'No, not bad. Apart from being dark, freezing, badly decorated, furnished with junk, it's not that bad at all.'

'It's in a good area. At least you don't have to worry about being mugged every time you go out of the door.'

'Oh, yeah. Wonderful. "The flat is equipped with a door, and you can actually go in and out of it." Paradise, eh?'

'It's better than my place.'

'It's not like having a house of your own, is it? A home with windows that let in some light. A garden, or even just a little yard with pots in. Hanging baskets. Why can't I just have some hanging baskets?'

My eye strayed to the jar where my tulips slumped, moulting. The water must have been too acid for them, after all. I didn't rate the chances of any plant life of Laura's, but I could see what she meant: you get out of your twenties, you're single again, you can't even begin to afford to buy a flat, you career is stalled, you feel a loser…

'I know,' I said gently, 'I know…'

The trick with being supportive of a depressed girl friend is to realise that you can't stop her from being depressed. You have to forget any notion of 'cheering her up.' You can nod empathically and pass the tissues, you can challenge errors and inconsistencies in what she says, and you can even crack a joke or two: it doesn't make any difference. Nor does trying to come up with practical solutions to her problems. No matter what you do, she'll just spill out all the things she's been wanting to say all along. It's a monologue (sometimes with actions: tears, foot stamping, smashed china). And a monologue needs an audience, not another participant. That's why this sort of support is called 'being there for someone.' You don't have to do anything practical at all. You just have to be there. That's all. And to believe that, much as it seems to the contrary, it helps.

But it is true that life hasn't treated Laura too well. She has a difficult relationship with her parents. At her first Jobcentre she was on the receiving end of some mild sexual harassment that ruined her confidence. (Can sexual harassment ever be *mild*? Well, it was comments, not action, but the manager concerned was also on the promotions panel, know what I mean?) And then there was her break up with Stephen... I sat on the arm of the sofa and rested my arm along its fraying top. I really did wish that I could help more. Vulnerability can make a girl attractive, but only up to a certain limit. If you want to be the knight in shining armour, your damsel has got to want to be rescued in the end. I stroked her hair.

'Help yourself to a top up,' Laura said, nodding towards the bottle and away from my hand. Then she stood up. 'Need a wee. 'Scuse me.' She weaved away towards the bathroom.

I sank into the warm patch of her seat and looked over the card we had found. It was one of those balloon race for charity efforts; the finder was asked to post it back with a note of where it had been found; the person whose balloon had gone furthest would win the prize. This one was in aid of the

Retired Donkey Sanctuary, Little Harborough. First prize was a four-foot cuddly Eeyore, with detachable tail.

Well, whoever had bought this balloon was unlikely to win. It had been set off from the charity car boot sale last weekend in the grounds of the District Hospital. It must have been all of three quarters of a mile from the outpatients' car park to the hole in Laura's wall. Of course, the balloon may have been blown about a bit before landing up there – it could have been to Benidorm and back for all anyone knew – but any round trip it may have made was not what was being measured. It was the result that was to be measured, not necessarily the distance travelled.

As in the donkey charity draw, so in life, I thought, and you didn't get much more profound than that at the end of a half bottle of Bells. And then I had stood up slowly: from the bathroom it had sounded as if Laura needed some practical help after all.

★ ★ ★

The morning's frustrations didn't end with Laura. I felt distinctly queasy for at least an hour (I put it down to the bacon, naturally). At the office I had mislaid Chandler's message, so I couldn't check the exact wording; it probably didn't matter, but I had been beginning to wonder if he had meant a different time or day. Will asked me to be around for the next day's signers, and I was pretty sure I knew why. Carl was moaning about the ICT specialists and how much information they needed.

In the afternoon, needing some daylight and fresh air, I went out to check up on Chandler. I found myself wishing that Helen had been free to go with me.

CHAPTER THIRTEEN

Everyone hates the homeless, me included.

Or rather, everyone hates *contact with* the homeless, me included. They make us feel guilty, don't they? And we think they look mental, and threatening. And they're often smashed out of their skulls at nine thirty a.m., which is twelve hours too early for any normal person to be in that sort of state. And they smell, and they beg instead of working... Yeah, admit it, we all hate them, don't we? Even though we wish, fervently, that we didn't.

Anyway, I was certainly hoping I wouldn't find any of them down at the Peterholme hostel. They're all signing on, of course, and I wouldn't want to be recognised.

Stung by the grit of passing lorries I waited patiently for the green man, then made my way past the plumbing centre's entrance, along the stretch of high security fencing, and up to Peterholme's gate. I hadn't dared park next door - the 'Customers Only, Clamping in Operation' signs had seen to that - and I had ended up on a meter half a mile away. The delay irritated me, but it would still be hours before the residents started queuing to be let back in. Time enough to get a message to Chandler without him thinking I was blowing his cover.

At the front door a wet cardboard sign directed me around the back. The back door was locked, but by inching round three wheelie bins which were blocking the pathway I discovered a possible way in: a new-looking glass door that displayed 'Fire Exit, Keep Clear' in large letters. A young man with blonde highlights in his hair was moving boxes about inside. I tapped on the glass and treated him to a three minute mime show for which he repaid me by opening the door six inches.

'Can I help you?' he asked, in the way that people direct this phrase at trespassers. I smiled and subtly rested my hand along the edge of the glass. 'Hello. I was looking for reception.'

'We don't have one.'

'That would explain why it was so difficult to find.'

Mr Highlights didn't share the joke. 'We're closed,' he said. 'What is it you actually want?'

I hate being obstructed by people who are younger that me, so I thought I'd bypass him and I asked to see the manager about a matter of some importance. This seemed to have the right effect as he told me to come in to the office.

He indicated a small door under a tall flight of stairs. If I had been asked to guess where it led I would have said 'broom cupboard.' I wasn't that far wrong.

I moved up to give him room to follow me inside. Helpfully, above the sticky brown tray with the kettle and Nescafe was a board with the names, photos and job titles of the hostel staff. I was talking to Darren Jones, Key Worker.

'Have a seat,' said Darren. 'How can we help?'

'Well, I was hoping to see the manager,' I reminded him. 'Mr… Ljudevitch?' I nodded at the board as I had a fair crack at the surname.

'I'm the only one here,' said Darren. 'Which makes me the duty manager. I'm pretty busy, so maybe you can tell me what you want.'

I was not feeling my mood improving. I took out my official identification card and held it up to him, making sure that my forefinger was underlining the words 'Senior Investigator.' I took my time replacing the card in my wallet. I said, 'I need to find out if someone is booked in here tonight. Chandler Wray.'

Darren was giving me a blank look. 'He has also used the name Malcolm Potts.'

I waited.

'We don't book. It's first come, first served. That's why there's a long queue by four o'clock.'

'OK, well maybe you can tell me if he stayed last night.'

'Look, Mr Di Palma,' said Darren firmly, 'I'll tell you straight off: I can't give you any information because it would break the confidentiality contract with our clients. Not to mention being a breach of the Data Protection Act if I happened to look it up. We have a relationship of trust with our residents and we can't discuss them with any third party without their consent.'

'I'm not asking you to *discuss* Chandler,' I said, 'I only want to know if he's still staying here.'

'That makes no difference, I'm afraid.'

'He... Didn't turn up for a meeting recently. I'm concerned about his wellbeing.'

'I didn't know you benefit blokes were so caring,' Darren commented disbelievingly. 'I'm sorry, I can't help.'

'I just need to know he hasn't been... run over by a bus!'

'Then maybe you should ring the hospital. Sorry.'

'Come on,' I cajoled. 'We have an information sharing protocol with Social Services and just about everyone else these days.'

'But not with us.'

'Well, what would you do if the police came round?'

'You're not the police. If you want to take it further, you'll have to speak to Mr Ljudevitch.'

'And when will he be available?'

'He's on holiday for two weeks.'

I sighed. It had been a mistake to try and impress him with my official credentials. The word 'investigator' is enough to scare off any key worker, because, for that 'relationship of trust' to survive, he's forced to always take the client's side. Maybe if he had believed it was a case of *paying* benefits he would have been prepared to bend the confidentiality code, although in Darren's case I doubted it; he seemed the type to get satisfaction from following very simple rules and therefore never being in the wrong.

'OK,' I said, 'if I write Chandler a note, could you pass it on to him if he's staying here?'

'I can't–'

'I'm not asking you to confirm if he's here or not here, I'm just asking that, in the hypothetical situation that he *is* here, you give him a note, and in the hypothetical situation that he *isn't*, you put the note in the office shredder. Surely that's a reasonable request?'

'All right. But I'm not confirming anything, either way.'

'Thank you.' I patted my pockets in relief. 'You don't have a pen I could borrow, do you?'

★ ★ ★

Now the thing about jobsworths is that they never really do it properly; they never, so to speak, see the job through.

I left Darren heading for the TV room, no doubt feeling pleased with himself for dealing with me in exactly the correct way, but if he'd really wanted to protect the confidentiality of his clients he should have made the effort to escort me all the way off the premises himself. Instead he asked me brusquely to see myself out. And left me alone before I had a chance to do so.

Upstairs I took a stroll around the dormitories. They were spartan, four-bed rooms with scuffed paintwork and bare light bulbs, but they were free of dust and mud, and of any sort of litter. The mattress covers had been freshly laundered, though most of the stains on them could never be removed. But naturally the rooms were empty. No belongings to be left during the day. So no clues about what Chandler had found out and then failed to bring me. I hadn't really expected anything like that. I headed for the sound of the vacuum cleaner, pulling a new pack of Benson and Hedges from my jacket on the way.

He'd been a small man to start with, but circumstances had reduced him further, it seemed. Quite possibly the manager (*not* Darren, of course) had let him stay behind cleaning for fear that he could no longer hack it on the streets. If so, my guess was that his fear was misplaced. Though thin and wrinkled, this guy was a survivor all right. Well, he'd not had much practice at anything else.

I put on the smile of a man who is pleased with the work going on around him.

'Harry, isn't it?' I said, extending my hand. 'Good to meet you.'

'I'm not Harry. My name's Lucas.' He gave me a suspicious, aggrieved look. I slapped my forehead.

'Lucas, I'm so sorry. Darren did tell me, but I'm hopeless at names. I must have been remembering a chap at the hostel in Stevenage by mistake. Funny how the mind works, isn't it?'

'I suppose.' Lucas made a face as if he didn't really know what to say.

'I thought I'd take a quick look around before I go back to Head Office. Everything's remarkably clean, I reckon. A lot of men might think that sort of work is beneath them, so it's a real credit to you that you're so thorough. Well done.'

'Yeah. Thanks.'

'I am serious, you know. I did a lot of cleaning work when I was younger and I know it can be easy to get fed up with it...'

'You're not allowed to smoke inside,' said Lucas, eyeing my cigarettes. I laughed.

'Of course not. I was going to ask if you wanted to join me for a quick one outside. Although between you and me, some rules are meant to be broken....' I tapped the side of my nose, and then regretted it as a piece of crass overacting, but Lucas didn't seem to have noticed. He had looked away and mumbled something about promises being made to be broken, too. But at any rate, the survivor in him had worked out that I was good for at least a free fag or two, so he led me down to the garden. Luckily Darren was nowhere to be seen.

'So, how d'you like it here?' I asked him once I had stopped coughing. 'Other residents friendly? Within the usual limits, I mean...'

'There's not much bullying or violence, if that's what you're after,' said Lucas. 'Compared to some places I've stayed.'

'Been here long?'

'Eighteen months on and off. If you're doing a report, you can say that the place is well run and the inmates are satisfied. And thanks for the new television.'

I grinned. 'You're very sharp. I'm just sorry I can't stay long enough to see some of the other residents. I have to get back for a meeting. Shame really, I was even hoping to catch up with a chap I knew from way back. Oh, but it must be two years or more... Chandler Wray. The only homeless man to always wear a suit. How is he?'

Lucas inhaled through his cigarette. 'I couldn't say.'

'Moved on, I suppose. Funny, though, I thought Darren said he was still using the hostel...'

'That's Darren's business.'

I turned and looked Lucas in the eye. 'Come on, I know there's a tradition for the homeless community to watch each others backs, but it's a lot of paranoid bollocks, isn't it? You'll be quoting the Data Protection Act next. I'm only asking after the guy, for goodness sake. What's the problem?'

'You're not from Head Office for a start,' said Lucas. 'They came last week.'

'Ah.'

'Yeah. So you're a journalist, or police, or benefits. You could also be a private investigator, but as Chandler doesn't have an ex-wife looking for him, that's the least likely choice.'

'I'm a friend of Chandler. Really, I am.'

Lucas made a dismissive gesture. 'Homeless people don't have friends. Not in the normal way. Everyone hates the homeless.'

'I know he wasn't in last night,' I lied. 'Possibly since a lot longer. I'm worried about his wellbeing.'

He looked at me. 'Have you ever offered Chandler a bed at your house? No? Then how can you say you're his friend?'

I looked down at my hands and I thought about how I had wanted to phase him out of my life.

'You're right,' I said. 'But I'd still like to know that he's

OK.' I threw the cigarette packet into his lap. 'Here, I'm trying to give up. Give Chandler my regards if he shows up tonight.' I started walking. I'd reached the wheelie bins before he called me back.

'Hey!'

'What?'

'How can I give him your regards? You haven't told me your name yet, you idiot!'

I smiled. 'Larry. Larry Di Palma.'

'You're right, Larry. I haven't seen Chandler for the last three nights. But that's nothing. It's not gonna be bad news. He was looking for a job.'

'A *job*? Is that likely?'

Lucas shrugged. 'Normally I'd say no. But he had a… work ethic, is it called? Anyway, he said he was going to go around the factories asking about jobs. Last time I saw him he was off to the dog food works. Didn't come back that night.'

'Asking *about* jobs…'

'What else would he be doing? He wouldn't be buying discounted dog biscuits in the factory outlet, would he?'

'But are you sure that DoggieBest was the last place he went to?'

'Certain. Grannie Baker's in the morning, DoggieBest in the afternoon. That's what he said.'

'Is that what you think has happened?' I asked. 'He's not come back to the hostel because he's got himself a job? And with the promise of wages, somewhere better to stay?'

'Oh, no. That's not what I meant. You can't get a job these days if you don't have a proper address. But people move on, find a new hostel… Try to go back to their relatives… Decide they need their own space (to you that means going back to sleeping in doorways). Just 'cos he hasn't been here for a day or two... It don't mean there's a problem.'

'Talking of problems...' I scratched my head in embarrassment. Lucas looked at me blankly. 'He wasn't... Falling off... You know...'

'Booze? He'd not touched a drop for months. But it never leaves you... I'd be lying if I said that the danger ever goes away completely.'

'Oh, well...' I shrugged. 'Thanks for the info, Lucas. I'd better leg it before Darren spots me still here. See you around, maybe.'

'Yeah, right, *maybe*. Ta for the fags, though.'

I walked back towards my car. So Chandler had told a fellow inmate where he was going, but being Chandler, he made it look like he wanted a job for himself. So... Assuming he *had* visited the two factories, there was something he had found out there that he thought he could get me to pay for. And yet for reasons unknown he hadn't turned up at the pub.

OK, then, I was no further forward for my brief visit to the land of the homeless. And I wouldn't get the information until he got in touch again. Nothing else to be done. There was no point in asking at the Dark Horse, not until Lilly was back behind the bar anyway.

I started the Citroën and headed back towards the office. I wondered if Helen would be calling in after her day at Regional Training, but I assumed not. After a hard day on client record databases she'd be heading straight home... Still, we'd had fun looking at her initial training video; it had been almost midnight when she had finally thrown me out...

A black BMW hooted impatiently: the filter was already green. Day dreaming again... Tired, too, after staying up to look after Laura. I really should be having a drink–free early night, shouldn't I?

So that was what I promised myself.

And to be fair, I did manage to get myself to bed by eleven thirty...

CHAPTER FOURTEEN

Hung over once again, and seriously in breach of the rules of flexitime, I found three telephone message stickers at my desk, each in the hand of a different switchboard operator. It seemed that 'Charles,' my father and someone who might possibly be called 'Karma' (there were question marks after the name, neatly combining uncertainty with abdication of responsibility) had all called while I had been struggling to lift the weight of my duvet. If Daphne had been in work there would no doubt have been a red flashing voicemail light too, and I would have had to spend twenty minutes looking for my last reminder memo on how to access it. But Daph was in Portugal, and the relief staff maintained a distinctly low-tech approach to telecommunications. I rang the switchboard.

'Did my dad really phone?' I asked. 'Only it would be the first time in a hundred years.'

'I don't know. I haven't been on here that long.'

Knowing Vicky, this wasn't a joke. I looked again at the handwriting on the message stickers. 'Karma, then. Who the hell is Karma?'

'That's what it sounded like.' Hearing my mood, Vicky fell back immediately on her main defence. 'It was a bad line.'

'Didn't you get a number?'

'No.'

'Why not?'

'It was a bad line.'

I rubbed my eyes and took a deep breath. Operators are not supposed to let a caller escape without taking a number, because a recent Quality Standard requires a hundred per cent response rate to enquiries, carried out within twenty four hours. This is ought to be a great rule for the incompetents among us who are always losing our address books, but the operators ignore any orders that interfere with the time needed for filing their nails or emailing dirty jokes to their boyfriends.

'You've done the Equal Opportunities course recently, haven't you?' I asked. 'Would you say that Karma is an Asian name? Or is it some new-age, postmodern hippy thing?'

'He didn't sound Asian,' said Vicky uncertainly. 'But I don't think we're supposed to say that. When I asked him to spell it, the phone went dead, though, so he could be an English as a Second Language person, couldn't he? Too embarrassed about spelling–'

'*He?*' I dropped the daydream about brown-skinned girls or hippie chicks and screwed up all three post-its. 'Don't worry, Vic, I've worked out who it is, and if he ever changes his name to Karma, he'll need to add the initials B-A-D first. I'll wait for him to call back.' I put the phone down and shook my head. Did I really have to start a full scale investigation each time I wanted to find out who my phone messages were from? 'Charles,' 'Father,' 'Karma...' How could three different people get *Chandler* so wrong?

(Pressure from above, indolence from below. If you believed in Karma, you'd assume my previous life must have been pretty bad: a minor criminal, a fraudster, perjurer, tax dodger, benefit cheat...)

Will had emailed for my report on the Mosley stakeout

and had clicked both the flag and the exclamation mark icons. To demonstrate independence I opened the Jon Smith file and spread the contents over the length of my desk. I had barely uncapped a fluorescent highlighter when the phone rang again. I sighed hello down the mouthpiece in my usual way.

'Larry?'

'Yes?'

'It's Helen.'

I may have sat a little straighter. 'Hi. How's it going down there?' Helen was familiarising herself with our quality systems on the front line signing desk, or, to put it another way, was covering for two box clerk colleagues who had phoned in sick.

'It's OK, thanks. Just need to pick your brains.'

'Fantastic.' I eyed the basketfuls of paperwork all around me. 'Don't tell me they gave you a fraud referral target just for a day shadowing the signing clerks?'

Sylvia walked past with raised eyebrows, miming a cup of coffee at me. I stuck a thumb in the air and mouthed 'thank you', just like we'd been taught on the Deaf Client Awareness Day, and then watched her check black or white by milking an invisible cow. I wondered when Will would bid for a proper sign language course for the Disability Team.

Helen said, 'There's a guy at my desk who's still got his make-up on.'

'Mmm?'

'He's not removed all his make-up. Easily done, as any girl will tell you... Now, if he's been working last night...'

'Has Herman come into the office, or something? Did he ring you?'

'What?'

'He's put you up to this, hasn't he?'

'I'm *serious*.'

'Then what are you talking about? A *guy* working nights in make-up?'

'Oh, didn't I say? He's an actor.'

I heard the clerks around her fall about laughing and I covered my eyes. There was a long pause.

'What's the matter?' Helen asked. 'I'm supposed to follow visual clues, aren't I?'

'Yes, yes. Never mind. Go ahead and question him if you want. You know, the usual casual type of thing: "I couldn't help noticing, Mr Depp, how good looking you are today…"'

From a distance someone said camply, 'Hello, darling, are you working?' I said suspiciously, 'You're not still at the desk with him, are you?'

'Of course not! I wouldn't phone my suspicions through with the client listening, would I?'

'No, fine. No. Just checking.'

'If he denies it I can always check the cast list at the Opera House, and any other local shows…'

'Very good,' I said. 'Very proactive. Don't be surprised if it's just some retro 1980s fashion thing.'

'I know. But I have to demonstrate my knowledge of different approaches when I get assessed.'

'And what approach is this?'

'Zero tolerance.'

'It wasn't on the syllabus when I trained.'

'Herman said it's the zeitgeist.'

'Herman just likes showing off his knowledge of foreign words.'

When Sylvia returned with my too-milky coffee I was back on the Jon Maxwell Smith case and I was holding the phone receiver about six inches away from my ear. She gave me a pout of sympathy as she dripped onto Smith's claim form and interview statement, and I thought, Good, at least somebody appreciates the work I do around here. I also thought that next time I'd mime back no more than two pulls of the udder.

At each tiny pause in the caller's diatribe I tried to squeeze in a brief response.

'That's inaccurate.'

'Untrue.'

'No evidence.'

'The recording equipment must be faulty.'

'*Now* who's being abusive?'

Grant Leroy-Shaw was lecturing me on the subject of compensation claims for alleged racial harassment, although he himself hadn't used the word 'alleged' quite yet. I had been mildly impressed at first by his confidence, and by his intimidatory use of legal jargon, but that had been nearly fifteen minutes ago. Still, it was a good job he had been put through to me; Will would have raided a decade's worth of petty cash to pay him off, and then blamed me for the whole situation. He wouldn't have lasted fifteen *seconds*.

'I'm afraid it really is a case of his word against ours, Mr Leroy-Shaw,' I said for the third time. 'One word against two.'

'It's *Doctor* Leroy-Shaw.'

'Really? I'm so sorry.'

'What you're saying is that it's one *black* word against two *white*.'

'That's irrelevant. Although factually correct.'

'And then there's the question of assault.'

'No evidence.'

'Listen, I *know* the policies you Civil Servants live by. You're guilty of gross misconduct, Di Palma. You could be sacked and lose your pension! How does that feel? You think your bosses will stand by you when I approach all my contacts in the local media? When the ombudsman takes my calls? When the Equality and Diversity Task Force come knocking on your office door? Think about it!'

'Yeah, well…' I hesitated. 'There's such a thing as slander, you know. I can sue you for defamation of character.'

'You've no chance.'

'I have to go now, Mr… *Dr* Leroy-Shaw. I'll confirm our meeting date with you and your client by email. Don't do anything rash until you've seen my evidence, will you?'

'Fuck you, Di Palma.'

'You too. Goodbye.'

★ ★ ★

I was trembling at the water cooler when Will appeared behind me in his usual silent way. 'Congratulations,' he said. 'We've got a result.'

On my present standing you'd assume he was being sarcastic (Hey, congratulations! We've got a result. *At last!*), but Will knows sarcasm is a form of bullying; he's been on the *Valuing your Workforce* seminars. Anyway, he's the sort of guy who is charming when he's getting his own way.

I tried to soak up the water from my sleeve with a paper towel.

'Who's *we?*' I asked, wondering if Will had forgotten the part of his training on avoiding *faint* praise.

'I'm sorry, did I startle you?'

'Yeah.' I dropped another towel on the damp patch on the carpet. 'I'm startled that I've done something right for a change.'

'Oh, don't be like that.' Will leaned forward and helped himself to a drink. 'I might have had to give you a push, but it was your work that achieved the outcome. Credit where it's due, after all…'

I glanced down the corridor and saw Ravi grinning sheepishly from the photocopier.

'This is about Mosley, isn't it?'

'Absolutely.'

'And?'

'Failed to sign. We've scared him off.' Will rocked back on his heels, smugly. 'Looks like young Ravi's hunch was correct.'

I caught 'young' Ravi's eye and with a backwards nod invited him over. He at least was looking embarrassed as he joined us, and well he might, I thought moodily. I knew for certain that Ravi hadn't informed the Fraud section of this latest development, partly because he hadn't spoken to me or dropped me a Failed to Sign memo, but also because it was too early for him to be sure of the facts. Yet he had gone blurting out his news to Will behind my back. If only he'd told me first, I would at least have had time to prepare myself.

It was now that Helen arrived with a couple of flimsies in her hand and a question mark on her face. I gave her a quick smile and said conversationally, 'I hear we've lost Mr Mosley, Ravi. Will was just complimenting you on your hunch about him.'

'Wow,' said Helen, 'that was quick.' Ravi blushed some more.

'You haven't passed me a Fats 99, though, have you?'

'Well, er…'

'No, no, you're right, of course,' I went on, looking at Will while I spoke. 'Because form FTS 99 is sent to Fraud *on closure of the claim* after the client fails to sign. And you haven't actually closed it yet, have you?'

Ravi coughed. 'No, we–'

'He's still got time to come in, hasn't he? He could be ill, he could have forgotten to come in, he could be down at the late-signers desk right now this minute, couldn't he, giving whatever excuse he has for not being here on the right day? We haven't got a result quite yet, in fact, have we?'

'You're forgetting that he's on weekly signing,' said Will. 'Which means–'

'Which means nothing. It doesn't make any difference, does it, Ravi? Except that perhaps we are having this conversation today and not in one week's time. Weekly or fortnightly, the claim won't be closed until five days after FTS.'

From the corner of my eye I saw that Helen had stepped back a little, with her actor's paperwork held unobtrusively at her side. She was, however, carefully following the logic of the argument. Will threw his plastic beaker into the bin.

'I must say I'm finding your attitude very negative,' he said exasperatedly. 'Alright, we shouldn't always count our chickens too soon. But what is the normal course of events when someone fails to sign after an investigator has called round? You don't need me to tell you: we don't see them again. This is just sour grapes on your part, Larry, because you've been against this one from the start.'

'Fine,' I said, 'you can believe he's gone off to his little night job and decided not to risk claiming any more. But there's no real evidence to support it.'

'Maybe I'll be the judge of that. When you turn in your report–'

'Oh, well, since we're closing the claim anyway…'

Will's body gave a little jerk, as if hit by a short electric shock. It might have been the static from the cheap carpet tiles, but I didn't really think so. 'No, no,' he said menacingly, 'you're not getting out of it that easily. You've done the observations and accrued the Time Off in Lieu. You'll do the paperwork as well. And I want it by tomorrow morning.'

'But it's–'

'No buts. Don't think we're dropping this one even if he does come back in. You'll get the claim closed permanently if it's the last thing you do.' Will stalked off down the corridor and we heard his door shut with a slam. The effect was dramatic: it doesn't take much to get the partition walls wobbling in this place, and across the open plan area we could see faces look up in surprise. Some of them stared in our direction.

'I thought when you do an MBA,' I said, as nonchalantly as I could, 'that you'd be taught to avoid clichés like the plague.'

'Ravi,' said Helen, after a moment's silence, 'has he failed to sign before?'

'Actually, yeah,' Ravi admitted. 'Of course he was always signing on late in the day, which was how I noticed... But actual fails to sign... Yeah, a few days late... At least twice during the claim, I'd say.'

'Mmm.'

That was all she said. 'Mmm.' But it was an Mmm full of meaning. Subtle; that sort of thing is effective in an interview under caution; it can really make a client sweat. And I couldn't help feeling pleased how it was implicitly supportive of me. 'Mmm.' Its only fault was that she hadn't got it in while Will was still in earshot. Oh, and the fact that she wasn't fooling anybody.

'Will's right,' I said. 'I'm just being pedantic: ninety-nine times out of a hundred, someone being investigated and fails to sign... That's it, they're gone.'

'He came and asked me specifically, you know,' Ravi said. 'He came to the signing desks the moment we'd shut for the day, wanting to know.'

Yeah, I thought irritably. But I bet you didn't mind being asked. You were probably flattered that he was so interested in your idea. I bet you didn't say, 'Hang on, Will, let's wait until we've closed the claim down before we celebrate.' I bet you didn't say, 'Look, this Employee of the Month stuff is too embarrassing, let's leave it, eh?' Oh, no.

I turned to Ravi and gave him a forgiving smile.

'He's really taking an interest in this one, isn't he?' Helen said. 'Does he often do that?'

'Not usually. But the Fraud figures are so low he's scared his productivity bonus is at stake.'

'They said on the induction course that it was a positive thing for a manager to be in close touch with the day to day work of his staff.'

'It's very positive,' I said, 'if he gets a better understanding of the work and its problems. I don't see much sign of that here.'

'I don't understand,' said Ravi. 'I mean, I know it's stressful having a senior officer breathing down your neck, but we got a result, didn't we? Well, OK, we're not completely certain he won't come back in before we close him down, but apart from that, well, we got the outcome. That's good, isn't it? We got a result.'

'Ah, but what result?' I raised my forefinger, and gave it a melancholy waggle under his nose. 'It's a lot of time an effort to reduce the register by one. Not very cost effective, is it?

Failed to sign: hardly worth having, is it? No repayment, is there? No money coming back.'

'It's better than nothing.'

'No, it's *worse*. In the time I've spent on this case, I could have made some progress on something bigger. I've got a cross-border multiple claim case on the go, but because it counts as someone else's principal target, Will doesn't give a fuck.' I took an angry drink of water. 'No, actually, I'm not being fair to Will,' I said, 'he wants the cross-border case sorted out *as well,* and he thinks I can somehow magic the time to do it out of thin air…'

Ravi was looking crestfallen and I felt marginally ashamed of myself. You don't always notice in these situations just how much you are raising your voice.

'Sorry, Rav,' I said. 'Anyway, at least he won't be around to call you a Paki bastard for a day or two. 'That might be worth the effort, I s'pose.'

Since the signing desks close so early, I was able to take Helen up to Adjudication for a properly made cappuccino.

'Did you nail the actor, then?' I asked.

Helen blushed. 'Amateur dramatics. Richard III. He even gave me a bit of a speech.'

'"We all have cause to wail the dimming of our shining star,"' I quoted casually. 'Poor bloke: trains for years at RADA and then ends up playing third spear carrier at the Queen's Heath Community Centre. Story of all our lives, really, though.'

'You were right. I was wasting my time.'

'No, on the contrary. Waste of time regarding fraud, perhaps. But why shouldn't the clerks ask a few casual questions about our clients' hobbies? Pass the time of day? Be civil? He was probably flattered. We don't always want to come across as a bunch of suspicious jobsworths who're just out to deny people their money.'

There was a pause. I put down my coffee. 'What?'

'I wasn't exactly *casual*…'

'Oh?'

'I took him along to the Cooler.'

'The *Cooler?*'

'After your feedback on the tapes, I thought I needed more practice.'

I laughed and shook my head at her, partly in admiration, partly in sympathy. 'Poor bloke!' I said again. 'But let's look on the bright side. You might even have managed to scare *him* off the unemployed register, too. Two results in one day! Will's going to be handing out the doughnuts again if this carries on. Speaking of which…'

A gentle smell of warm toast was wafting across to us, accompanied by the sound of a knife spreading home made strawberry jam. I stood up and put on my best needy-but-charming expression. Could I get a transfer to the Adjudication Office sometime soon? In the meantime, I would need a stack of carbohydrates to keep me going into the evening. Will wanted his reports, and with a fear of Dr Leroy-Shaw in the back of my mind, I couldn't afford to piss him off. If things went pear shaped, I might just need all the help I could get…

But asking Will for help? I sincerely hoped things wouldn't get that desperate.

★ ★ ★

In the back of my diary I had found one of those Jobcentre sticky post-it notes, one with the old 'Achieve it! Record it!'

strapline printed at the top. There was a mobile phone number in my handwriting, though no other information was present. But it looked nicely familiar.

'By such means,' I murmured, in a fair impression of Herman, 'Are hypotheses tested, and investigations solved...'

I rang the number. Not forgetting to conceal my own from the recipient: nobody ever answers if they know it's the Jobcentre calling.

'Hello?'

'Hello, is that Mr Mosley?'

There was a pause. 'Who is this?' The voice sounded familiar, but not quite right somehow...

'Mr Oswald Mosley?'

'Who are *you?*'

'Well, I–'

I was interrupted, hearing the crash of a door being thrown open, and an excitable voice in the background shouting, 'Galatasaray four, Beşiktaş zero! Paul, you owe me twenty- Oh, sorry, sorry, didn't realise you were–' But before he had gone any further I had rung off.

I looked again at the number. I could have sworn I had put Mosley's on a sticky, but it obviously wasn't this one. And I wasn't in the mood to confess my mistake to Paul Wodehouse, or to hear about his side bets on whichever match from his twenty sports channels he had been watching last night. (No, not even if, to quote Herman yet again, his loss was my little *schadenfreude*.)

'Ah, bollocks,' I said to myself, not for the first time that day.

So, without the right mobile number, only time would tell if Will or I was the better judge of Mosley. But then maybe it was better that way. As I had been saying to myself, I ought to pay a bit more attention to keeping Will happy, and that would not be the outcome of a successful call that found Mosley, say, in bed with a cold or stuck in a traffic jam. Not right after I had been challenging Will's assumptions in front of the most junior staff...

No, actually, losing Mosley's number might be a bit incompetent, but it was still a good move on my part!

Or so I imagined at the time...

CHAPTER FIFTEEN

It's always a mistake to take work home with you, but working late at the office is worse. Fortunately I've been quick to learn from my mistakes and in this area I'm almost infallible. Almost, that is, but not quite.

'Pub?' asked Vicky on her way past my desk.

I sighed. 'Backlog.'

'There's dedication for you.'

'Is... Who else is going?'

'Oh, the usual crowd. Maybe come a bit later when you've done enough?'

'*Had* enough, more likely...'

'Rather you than me,' said Vicky. 'Good luck.'

'Thanks. I may need it.'

With the phones silent and the last clerks gone, the atmosphere switched itself from hysteria to a relaxing calm and I settled into the series of checks, double-checks and cross references of which benefits procedures comprise. I made good progress at first, much better than ever. No distractions; I was free to focus exclusively on the work. Dedication in the true sense of the word! I'd have to try it more often. Feeling pleased with this insight I went to make myself a coffee.

An hour of data inputting and initialling little boxes is enough for anyone, so by half past seven I had taken my second break before moving on to opening the morning's post.

Now this did make me feel guilty. The Department's Quality Award insists that all incoming mail is sorted and on the recipient's desk by ten o'clock, and the admin assistants have to flog themselves to do it. There is no written rule about *dealing* with your post that promptly, but only because it was deemed too obvious even for the bozos who wrote the QA framework; it's kind of implied, isn't it, that if you get your post at ten, you don't wait nine and a half hours to start tearing open the envelopes. Thank goodness the award assessors would never know. Thank goodness the clerks wouldn't either.

Among the normal boring stuff was a padded envelope marked 'confidential' and containing only an unmarked cassette tape. It was addressed to me by name, which was unusual, at the 'Fruad Dept,' which was not: you'd be surprised how many public spirited citizens can't spell.

Or, of course, it could be a communication from Chandler. It was just the sort of nonsense he would dream up: a supposedly unattributable tape recording, no doubt with a series of complex instructions to pick up whatever evidence he imagined he had found. I could end up travelling in circles around Hampton like some demented orienteer, and at the end I'd find a pack of notes headed 'Memorise and destroy immediately.' I tutted. Still, the tape had caught my interest, and, as they say, there was only one way to find out…

On my way back from the training suite with a tape deck I met Irene, the cleaning supervisor, so I smiled and apologised for not having cleared my desk for dusting. You don't want to offend Irene: she's very strict, very proper and her husband knows the Regional Director well. Oh, and she takes personally every minor difficulty that she comes across.

'Did you solve your graffiti problem?' I asked considerately.

'There hasn't been any recurrence,' she replied in her usual sharp tone, 'but nobody's discovered who was responsible.' You could tell Irene thought this was a huge failing on the part of all concerned, her husband and his golfing friend included, but short of putting cameras in the toilet cubicles there was little anyone could have done. 'Fuck the Secretary of State' could be widely attributable after all.

'I don't expect to see that sort of language in a government building,' Irene said. 'I don't know what it says about the calibre of the employees.'

'Think yourself lucky you don't have to deal with our clients, Irene,' I told her gently.

Irene walked to the end of the open plan office and began emptying waste paper baskets into a bin bag. I felt a bit for her: she was supposed to be a supervisor but the calibre of her own staff meant that she was always covering their work. I climbed under my desk and plugged in the tape deck, then slipped in the tape itself, not noticing that the volume knob was turned to the maximum. I brushed dust from my knees, hoping Irene wouldn't notice and take it as some sort of criticism.

I pressed Play. Music filled the length of the room: we'd come in right in the middle of a song and an anguished, frustrated lyric, sung by a familiar male voice from years ago. The F-word at full volume had Irene frowning at me from claim cabinets Ng to Pow. I hit the 'stop' button.

'Sorry,' I called. 'Bit loud...' I turned to a quieter setting and pressed Play again. I listened some more. I knew this voice vaguely; the singer's name was on the tip of my tongue. But it didn't sound like Chandler's style. Any tape he reused was more likely to have 1940s jazz on it. I switched off in order to rewind right to the start.

I pressed Play for the third time and there was a long silence, then a few moments of crackle before the music began. That crackle took me right back, because you don't often hear the sound of a needle on vinyl these days, but why was it starting straight away? Where was the message? I gave a little groan of frustration. Should I have gone forward instead of back, and would I now have to trawl through the whole of the cassette to find it?

It wouldn't have mattered if I had tried: the communication, it turned out, was in the song itself.

It was a song entitled 'Laura.'

Oh, shit, I thought as I listened on, understanding dawning as the song continued. Very clever. The perfect message, in fact.

Because if you do happen to know it (and if you are old enough, or retro enough, or miserable-teen enough, you might just know this 1970s American ballad), then you'll remember that it is sung by a character who has been exploited by the neediness of 'Laura', and is feeling bruised and foolish as a result. Not a bad insult under the current circumstances.

I ejected the tape angrily. 'All right, Stephen,' I exclaimed aloud, 'you've made your point, you bastard.' There was the sound of a door slamming as Irene went back to the stairs. Well, I didn't have the patience to worry about whether I had offended her or not. I kicked the desk, though not too hard; I've done it before and it hurts. 'You think I'm shagging your ex-girlfriend and you're jealous, is that it? Why don't you stand up and fight like a man instead of hiding behind your music collection?'

Tape in pocket, I returned to my 'to do' pile, but my heart was no longer in it, even if everything else still was. I started packing up.

I hadn't come across the song before, at least as far as I could remember, but it was uncanny: the words could have been written for me in my present state. Now given what we had done to his record collection, it was easy to understand that Stephen might use it to try and get even (yeah, Steve, you tosser, I hope it took you *hours* to find the song you were looking for), but the question was… How much did he relate these lyrics to a relationship that he had barely witnessed? He knew me before as a friend of Laura, and he must have long suspected that I found her attractive, and he'd seen us having a curry together. He'd made some insulting cracks at the restaurant, true, but more directed at her than at me. He obviously assumed we were an item.

But why did he send me *this* song? Did he just pick the one with 'Laura' in the title, having no idea how apt it was? That would be too much of a coincidence. Or… Or did he know exactly what I was experiencing and had just the song to use to have a good dig at me? But how would he know what our relationship was really like? *Only if he had received similar treatment himself.*

All of which made me wonder if it was *Stephen* who was really the problem one in their relationship…

Where did that leave me? Well, right then it left me heading down the back staircase, having successfully moved three files, two pink forms and a memo into someone else's pigeonhole, *and* done enough data input to send me cross-eyed; not a bad evening's work, even if it did require no investigative skill whatsoever. Instead, it was the tape that was taxing my deductive reasoning and so I wasn't particularly paying attention to anything else. And that, when you exit into a narrow back street after dark, is another way that working late proves to be a mistake.

Some of the girls here never leave the office alone in case a client says boo to them on the outside, but we investigators are made of more blasé stuff. I barely glanced through the toughened glass of the staff exit; it hardly registered that the closest street lamp had been smashed out. I was out and the door shut fast behind me before I even saw them, rising from the window sill and throwing down their fags.

They came at me silently, competently, one from each side so there was nowhere to run. I backed against the door – if in doubt, cover your rear – and filled my lungs. If I could shout loud enough it would limit the time they had for me. Not that any witnesses would have much to describe: two men in black jeans and dark, hooded tops; plastic Halloween masks; thin gloves. Stocky, average height… It was scant consolation that neither appeared to be carrying a weapon.

When the first blow came I caught it with my raised briefcase and felt the structure of it collapse. Not quite so competent, then, if they needed more than one strike to put me out.

'Help! Help! I'm being mugged! Police! Help!'

I dodged a blow to the stomach which should have winded me, threw my shattered case aside and put my arms tight around the nearest mugger, who had made the error of lowering his hands. We struggled and stumbled together while his mate hesitated over where to swing. I carried on shouting and was aware of people hovering at the head of the alleyway: just three or four, perhaps, who would have liked to run off but would have been ashamed to do so. Not that they were brave enough to come rushing in. Someone was shouting urgently, 'Where's your mobile?'

The boys were getting in some punches now, although with the narrowness of the alley, the big bins in the way and me hugging tightly, there wasn't much momentum in the blows. If the one I held had dared to nut me I'd probably have been finished, but he concentrated on using his knees, and balls-protection was the one thing we all remembered from the investigator's self defence course. I wriggled and turned my legs, taking hit after hit on my bruised calves, while I tried, desperately, pathetically, *uselessly*, to get a hand up to eye-gouging height.

The second lad had picked up a brick and tried to rush me, but I was able to turn slightly and use his mate for a shield. The shield now had an arm free and was prising us apart while stamping on my feet at the same time. I took two more nasty blows and was able to judge the moment he would be off balance enough for me to knock him hard against the brickwork, but he was smart enough to keep his chin down and avoid bashing the back of his head. I had to pull hard to put him back between me and his partner, and my arms were very weak now. I couldn't do much more. He knew this and broke free, swinging a hurried punch which I dodged easily enough, although anything better timed would have had me. I raised my arms in front of my face…

There were two men in suits approaching hesitantly from the main road end, but what really swung it my way was Irene opening a window above us and screaming shrilly into the night. Evidently my attackers expected a woman's cry to bring more attention, or intervention, than mine, and with a final jostle they had passed me and were running for the dogleg leading to the tax office dropping-off point and their freedom.

'Hah!' I shouted excitedly. 'Easy! Two on one and still no problem! Wankers!' I added at their retreating backs while I sat down suddenly on the doorstep.

'You'll be OK now,' said one of the suits nervously. 'We've called the police.'

Irene appeared at the door behind me. 'Larry, are you all right?'

'I will be. Bit of a shock, that's all.'

'Who were they?'

'I... don't know.'

The two guys in suits were making some slow, gradual moves in a backwards direction. 'Er... We'll be off then,' one of them said apologetically. 'Hope you feel better soon.'

'Thanks. Thanks for coming down,' I said. I looked up towards the main road where the rest of the audience had dispersed. 'Not everyone would have bothered.'

'Oh, no problem.'

'Shouldn't they wait to give a statement to the police?' said Irene loudly. I watched them try to speed up without being obvious about it.

'The police won't do much,' I answered. 'I've half a mind to run along home myself. They haven't got anything to go on, have they?'

'Don't be silly. Those masks were very distinctive. Imagine if they've been wearing them for other attacks. The police would want to know. And then all it takes is for someone to have seen them taking the masks off... They'll check the CCTV footage...'

'Irene,' I said, 'you're wasted doing the cleaning. Why don't you apply for a job as an investigator?'

'You should come inside into the warm,' Irene said. 'It won't do you any good sitting down there. Why don't you have a nice cup of tea? Knowing the police, we've got a while to wait.'

I stood still while I found my balance. I was cold. I thought regretfully of a seat at the King's Head with Vicky and the rest of the clerical crowd. Still, there was one reason to feel cheerful about hanging around for the cops to show up, and that was to watch Irene giving out a series of suggestions on how they should deal with this case. Maybe her husband and the Regional Director would turn out to be pals with the Chief Constable or something, too. Despite aching so much, I was quite looking forward to seeing her in action.

CHAPTER SIXTEEN

The police had a new double act on that night and it wasn't an enjoyable one. Instead of good cop / bad cop, I'd got tall cop / short cop: five foot six paired with six foot four or thereabouts, which could have been funny except that both were at least fifteen stone, and both were playing *bad* cop: cold, slightly aggressive and very, *very* slow; as if they wanted to bore their suspects into submission. It was bad enough facing them as a victim of crime. God knows what it was like for any alleged perpetrators: they probably felt they were already serving a life sentence.

Irene had been spared the chance of keeping these guys in line. She wasn't even invited to the station, but gave notes to a beat WPC while I was driven off by a constable who might have never been trusted with the car keys before. Then, from the freshly painted reception area with its leatherette bench and customer charters, I was swiftly taken to a drab, bare interview room and abandoned. When a clerk with a tray came to ask what I wanted I said cocoa and my pyjamas please, but he didn't bother smiling and that seemed to set the tone for the rest of my stay.

It was twenty three minutes before the two officers came in. The tall, blond one mostly asked the questions and his bald number two took notes, although occasionally they swapped.

By now I was longing to get home, so I thought I'd keep my statement brief. It shouldn't have been hard – after all, the whole attack had been over in minutes – but the cops wanted to check my story thoroughly. They did this by stopping me frequently and repeating my own words back in question form. Every so often we paused so that the second officer could catch up with his shorthand.

'They were wearing Halloween masks?'

'Yes.'

'The masks were witches faces?'

'Yes.'

'You've seen the masks in Woolworth's, but you don't know if they came from there or somewhere else?'

'Correct.'

After we had covered the description of my attackers I thought of Irene and asked if there had been other reports of incidents involving the same men. This was received with stony looks and a refusal to comment, but at least nobody said, '*I'll* ask the questions, Sunshine.' My opinion was still that they could do nothing as they hadn't any real leads, and I wondered why they didn't let me go as soon as possible so they could knock off and go home or to the canteen. Maybe it was to do with overtime payments, or maybe they got a weird thrill from prolonging the interview, who could tell? It wasn't as if they seemed particularly keen.

There were one or two aspects to my story that raised a flicker of interest, however. For example the fact that neither attacker had said a single word.

'They didn't ask for money or anything?'

'No,' I explained again. 'No threats, no demands, no swearing. Nothing.'

'And no way of telling if they had a regional or foreign

accent. And they wore masks and gloves. No bare skin was visible?'

'Correct.'

'They could have been foreign, then?' suggested the second officer, looking up from his pad.

'Well, there's no way of telling, is there?' I said irritably. 'Look, I've already told you that the most likely explanation is that it was a pair of claimants with a grudge. They saw the lights on, thought they'd hang around and take their frustration out on someone. It happens…'

The tall blond cop looked down at his own notes and nodded. 'Someone whose money got stopped.'

'Or didn't get any in the first place. Or who gets a letter saying he has an entitlement to benefit, which gets his hopes up, followed by a second letter saying his benefit is disallowed…' The two policemen exchanged glances. 'Yes,' I continued, 'it is *technically* possible to be "entitled" but not to receive anything. In my experience it's these bureaucratic… nonsenses that annoy our clients the most. Most of them limit themselves to shouting and banging on the counter, but,' I shrugged, 'sometimes they think they'll take it further…'

There was a knock on the door and a young WPC entered with a tray of drinks. Both of my interviewers spooned in three sugars, and when I tasted mine I could see why. Fortunately the chocolate biscuits helped to disguise the taste and there were enough of them to take the edge off my hunger. I hadn't eaten since lunchtime and I'd been feeling it for almost as long.

'Is there anyone you can think of who might bear a grudge against *you* personally?' asked the first cop.

Oddly enough, my first thought was of Stephen, although physical violence didn't seem to sit well with the pitying attitude behind the 'Laura' tape. It would have been an interesting form of revenge to have these guys send Grimsby Police to caution him, but I'm not really the feuding type; I prefer a quiet life. Anyway, I wasn't so sure it was a question of revenge: you *could* see the tape as a sort of sympathetic warning… And I'm not so dumb as to put my personal life into a police file, obviously. I tried to look blank at them.

'Come on,' he pressed. 'You're in the fraud department, aren't you? There must be some unhappy bunnies out there because of you. What are your current cases?'

'Well…' I sipped at my horrible tea. 'I suppose there's Jon Smith.'

'Has he threatened you?'

'No more than normal.'

'What does that mean?'

'Oh, you know… "Fuck you, you're dead, Motherfucker… I know where you live…" That sort of thing. A lot of people get a bit mouthy. Of course, they don't know where we live at all…'

'But they know where you work.'

'Obviously.'

'Any other suspicious ones?'

'There's one bloke I was checking on. Personally I didn't think there was a case for it, but my boss disagreed and ordered me to carry out an investigation.'

The taller cop raised an eyebrow and I felt for the first time that I had attracted some sympathy. I continued.

'I followed some of the usual procedures. A visit to him at home, attempts to contact his alleged employer. We even watched his house. I didn't find any evidence of benefit fraud, but he failed to sign soon afterwards.'

'He failed to sign on as unemployed. So he just didn't turn up for his money?'

'Well, the payment goes directly into a bank account, of course. But, yes, he didn't turn up on the day he was due in.'

'So he could have been innocent of fraud, but you managed to scare him off. That's enough to make anyone give you a punch in the face, isn't it?'

'Maybe. But anyone hard enough to come and beat me up isn't going to be scared off the unemployment register that easily. And I only decided to work late at the last minute. How could he be sure when I would come out? I would still assume the attack was opportunistic.'

My interviewer let his fingers drum lightly on the table top. 'What's his name, this bloke you were investigating?' he asked.

'Mosley. Oswald Mosley.'

'And did he strike you as a violent type? Did he ever threaten you?'

'No, he didn't threaten me. Violent? Well, he's a skinhead with a tattoo on his neck, and he's a member of a far right political group. He keeps a display of whips and things in a cabinet…' I forced myself to stop. Hunger and tiredness were making me babble, and if I wasn't careful I'd end up confessing about trespassing in Mosley's house and listening to him having sado-masochistic sex upstairs. If the cops repeated all that back to me I'd be here until dawn broke.

'I've no idea how violent he really is,' I admitted. 'Run him through your computer and see.'

'Thank you for the suggestion,' said the tall cop. He looked at his watch uninterestedly. 'I think that will be all for now. We'll be in touch. If we need anything else.'

The shorter policeman looked up from his notebook. 'Perhaps you would care to wait in the reception area, Mr Di Palma, while we get your statement typed up ready to be signed.'

I wondered if a bit of name dropping might help speed

up the process. 'Is Detective Sergeant Wodehouse around tonight?' I asked.

'Wodehouse? Why?'

'He's a friend of mine. I've known him years in fact. I thought I'd drop in on him for a chat seeing as I've got to hang around the station a while longer.'

There was a short pause, then the second cop shut his notebook. 'I could ask the desk officer to phone upstairs I suppose,' he said grudgingly.

'Thanks,' I said, deciding that this must be the 'good cop' after all, or as near to it as I was going to get.

★ ★ ★

I was flicking listlessly through some glossy brochures in the reception area when a slap on my shoulder announced the arrival of Paul Wodehouse. He seemed genuinely pleased to see me, and for once the feeling was mutual.

'Larry,' he chided, 'what d'you mean by getting yourself mugged and bringing us a load of work to do?' He smirked and fingered the silk of his tie. 'I wouldn't have expected it of you, you know.'

'Oh, you know. Didn't see them coming. Mind on other things…'

'Still fascinated by our recruitment literature, I see,' he commented, nodding at the brochure in my hands.

'Is that what it is? I should have guessed, but Urdu's never been my strong point.'

'We've got them in Turkish, Arabic and Polish, too, you know. Here.' He placed some forms on the counter for me to sign. 'We can go and have a drink when you've done that.'

I read with care, but it still didn't take me long. My

lengthy stay in the interview room had resulted in two short paragraphs summarising an attack by persons unknown.

'Hardly worth coming in for, was it?'

'I nearly did a runner along with all the witnesses. But our cleaning supervisor insisted I stay. And then she told me she was locking up and I'd have to go off to the station! Hence forty minutes with your boys. I don't suppose they'll get any joy with investigating this one, will they?'

'Investigating? Don't make me laugh. Don't tell me they agreed they were actually going to do anything about this?'

Wodehouse had passed the papers back to the desk sergeant and we now left the painfully bright strip lighting of the police station for the sulphurous glow of the streets. It had turned bitter; there would be frost by the early morning. I was getting a headache. Delayed shock and dehydration, I guessed.

'Well,' I said slowly, 'I suggested they could run a name or two through the criminal records database. Your tall colleague was determined to pump me for anyone who could have a grudge against me personally, so I told him about a couple of clients: one live, one failed to sign.'

Paul Wodehouse successfully combined a tut and a sneer. 'I guess they thought they had better offer to do *something*. Respectable civil servant attacked after a hard day saving the taxpayer's money. It wouldn't go down too well if you got the usual brush off we give to any old member of the public, would it? They probably thought your boss would complain.'

'Will they call me in again if they find someone's got a record? For further questions? Or to let me know?'

'I doubt it. They might never even get around to doing it. Look, they didn't even mention him on the statement you just signed, did they? Just something about persons unknown with a grudge against the benefit office staff.'

We crossed the road and Wodehouse held open the door of the pub for me. It was one of those mock-Irish chains where you find yourself ordering Guinness for a change and then regretting it when you see how they've bumped up the price. I supposed this was the coppers' local, but no-one greeted us except the barman. His accent was more Durban than Dublin, and in my view he was still as authentic as anything in the room.

'Actually, I'd quite like to know if Mosley has a record,' I mused aloud. 'Out of pure nosiness… And the fact that he's bound to make a new benefit claim again sometime soon.'

'Mosley? Is that what your client's called?' Paul was looking at me with narrowed eyes. I nodded.

'Neo-Nazi type. Scared the life out of me when I had to do a home visit.'

'You've been investigating a neo-Nazi called *Mosley?*'

'Do all policemen do this nowadays?' I asked. 'Keep on repeating what's just been said, but in the form of a question? Your mates spent the entire interview doing it.'

'I don't know what you mean.' He took a long pull at his pint. His hand was shaking and I wondered whether he was working too hard these days; I'd noticed the bags under his eyes back at the station, and he'd rushed off on police business when he was halfway through chatting up Helen the other night. But it's not really the thing for male acquaintances to express concern for each other's mental health, so I told him about Mosley instead.

'Look, this is off the record, right?' I continued. 'We're doing this stakeout at Mosley's house, ten in the evening, me and Helen, because the theory is that he's working nights.' I paused to drink. 'He's left the back door open, so we poke our heads inside. There's noises upstairs. I can hear a sort of groaning. He's only left the door wide open while he's upstairs having sex!'

'Oh, no.'

'Honest, he's on the job! Only not in the way we expected. Not only that, but it's kinky S and M stuff. He's got the magazines, women in uniform, that sort of thing. And when he looks out of the window as we're leaving, he's wearing a mask, those ones like a full face balaclava! Or *she* is…

'That's one for the memoirs anyway,' I concluded, rather lamely as Wodehouse had gone quiet and was staring into space. It wasn't the reaction I'd expected. He usually lapped up crude stories that he could pass on to the lads, and he was the originator of several urban myths that had done the rounds locally. All to do with sex.

I wondered again if he was depressed: the stress management course we had all been bullied into doing had identified loss of humour as a prime symptom. Or maybe he was weighing up if he should caution me for trespassing, or entering without owner's consent, or whatever they call it these days.

'Are you OK?' I asked.

'Hmm? Oh, sorry, I've just remembered something important that I forgot to do this afternoon. Sorry. Good story, Larry,' he said unconvincingly, 'I bet you get as much excitement in your job as we do after all.'

'At half the pay…'

'I'm going to have to go in a minute,' said Wodehouse, taking a few last gulps, but failing to finish his pint. 'What was the other client you were talking to the officers about?'

'He's called Jon Smith.'

'Oh, well, *he* should be easy to find. And they're in this together, are they?'

'No, no. They're just both on my books for different reasons. There's no connection. Smith's Black, he wouldn't team up with a neo-Nazi, even to get his revenge on me.'

'Listen,' said Paul, standing up and wiping his brow. 'Why don't *I* check for you whether anyone is going to follow up these leads? Don't start hassling the officers yourself, it'll just piss them off.'

'Well, thanks. It's not *that* important, though. If you're under pressure…'

'I'll do my best. Can't have a mate being attacked in the street. But that is the only reason, Larry. Don't ever start asking for inside info just to make your job easier, will you?'

'Come on, even I know better than that.'

'And this Mosley guy. Failed to sign. So you've closed your file on him? He's off your books, is he?'

'There's not much else I could do, to be honest. And it was all a waste of time, except for getting a funny story out of it. But that is off the record as I said, OK? I can't risk my boss finding out that I went inside his house without the correct permission.'

'No problem. Keep quiet about it, that's definitely your best bet. Nice to see you again, Larry.' He patted my shoulder. 'Don't work too hard.'

'Watch that yourself,' I said.

I sipped at my pint. Wodehouse definitely had a problem, I had decided: he hadn't asked me about Helen, had he? He hadn't even mentioned her. Knowing Paul, I would have thought that forgetting about an attractive girl was a sure indicator of other things taking over his life.

I can't pretend though, that this idea didn't provide me with a small warm glow inside.

CHAPTER SEVENTEEN

'All great investigators have the sort of mind that constantly goes off at a tangent. I myself am no exception.'

Herman would use these words whenever he felt got at for not completing his paperwork; most days, in fact, unless he was using a similar pompous phrase like 'filing is for the little people,' or 'I demand a secretary to do all that.' And they say the Germans don't do irony... Still, the point is that getting sidetracked isn't all bad, that it can be healthy to leave off the dull, everyday tasks to jump-start a new project, that going off at a tangent can be creative and dynamic, the sign of an entrepreneur who constantly seeks new ways to find information, to experiment and to achieve...

I revisited these thoughts as I sat through the EPP meeting that I had entered on a whim. And I told myself that next time I wouldn't be so bloody silly.

Why was I here? Laura's words echoed: 'You just can't let go, can you?' But it wasn't quite that simple. I wanted to find Oswald Mosley because I had been forced into the investigation against my will. This wasn't about puzzles. This was about autonomy and professional status. Self determination, *freedom*... (The same abstracts, funnily enough, that kept leaping from the mouths of the Party members present.)

It was about personal pride. Or personal pig-headedness.

I'd imagined a crowded hall - well, say twenty or so

people – where I could simply slip in unnoticed, sit at the back for a while, and then slip out again. Mosley, surely a member of the committee given all the work he did, would be on the top table, at a distance, and wouldn't be likely to recognise me. Or if he did, I could claim I was genuinely interested in the meeting.

Of course it was a stupid idea which just demonstrates how a tangent should not be followed without at least a short pause for thought. What could I possibly find out? He would either be there or not. And unless the committee proposed him a vote of thanks for his efforts before wishing him well in his new job / new term at college / new life in Australia, then I wouldn't be any the wiser about his circumstances. I certainly wasn't going to accost him while he was surrounded by all his skinhead mates to demand why he had failed to sign on. But all this didn't cross my mind until the meeting was in full flow, and by then it was too late.

I'd found the English Patriot's Party meeting by accident while scanning the small ads in the back of the Chronicle: they list all the public meetings of political groups, probably as a way of filling up advertising space they haven't sold. As usual I was checking the memorabilia columns for World War Two bargains that I could chuckle over or imagine selling on at a profit, although it's all hideously overpriced these days and there's much more on the internet anyway.

The meeting was billed for 7.30 pm in the function room of the Kent Street Working Men's Club, which isn't all that far from my bedsit and is probably why it registered with me in the first place. Not that I took much notice at the time. I didn't think of going to it until I was practically passing the doorway on my way home from the chip shop, which happened to be at seven twenty-five.

'No chips in the function room,' said the tired-looking little man at a table in the corridor. I swallowed a couple more quickly, burning my tongue in the process.

'Hang on,' I said, 'it's a *function* room. Surely they have food in there all the time.'

'Not chips. Too greasy and smelly. Anyway, you can't have a serious meeting while people are eating, can you? Are you a member?'

'No, just... interested.'

He frowned suspiciously. 'You're not from the Chronicle, are you?'

'You mean a journalist? No. Why?'

'They're running a hate campaign against us.'

'Really?' The Chron was very even-handed in all its reporting and editorials. They'd been sued by a councillor recently and had no choice. 'But they advertised the meeting for you nevertheless,' I said.

'There's a collection for Party funds,' said the doorman. 'Three pounds.'

'Cheaper than a night at the movies,' I said.

In the event it was more like a Samuel Beckett play, full of strange repetitions and nothing really happening. We had minutes of the last meeting, corrections to the minutes, matters arising from the minutes, moves to take the agenda in a different order, points of order, and a reference to the constitution, of which nobody had a copy.

And all this before the meeting had really started.

No wonder they were all obsessed with losing their 'freedom.'

Everyone was friendly enough though, especially Rhys from Escape 2000, who came and shook my hand as soon as I went in. So much for sneaking in anonymously then, although I couldn't have managed it anyway: there were only seven people round the table and one behind the serving hatch making instant coffee, and it was a sixteen yard walk from the door to the nearest chairs. Oswald Mosley was not there.

'Nice to see you again, Larry,' said Rhys, handing me a printed agenda. 'Good to have new fighters for the cause coming in.'

'Well, I'm interested in your policies,' I said carefully, 'but I'm not sure I'm ready to sign up just yet…'

'A sceptic, eh?' said a man with a beard close by. 'We'll soon cleanse you of that. I'm an anti-sceptic, you see…' I smiled at him politely.

Rhys tapped his pile of unwanted agenda sheets. 'This *is* a business meeting,' he apologised. 'Don't expect too much. If you come when we next have a regional speaker you might find it more… inspirational…'

He wasn't kidding. This turned out just like any committee meeting of under-supported fringe groups across the country. Whether they are political parties, church committees, residents' associations or charities, the same depressing aspects apply: the vacant posts (Press Officer, Membership Secretary), the brief, sad Treasurer's Report ('Balance of account, thirty-one pounds, nineteen'), the apparent lack of achievement ('The Zimbabwean Embassy demo is cancelled due to lack of support'). No wonder they got hung up on the minutiae of procedure: it was the only way to keep a pretence of importance about the whole business.

But somehow I was too embarrassed to leave. I kept saying to myself, 'five more minutes,' and then feeling too self conscious to stand up while someone was talking. Then there was a coffee break, so I thought I might as well get a free drink out of it, especially as they had blown half the night's collection on posh Austrian chocolate biscuits. Then the subject of newsletters came up, so I hung on longer and found to my surprise that there was no mention of Oswald Mosley. None at all. And yet according to the previous minutes I had seen in his house, Communications Officer was the very role he had been carrying out. It was weird.

At the end of the meeting there was an embarrassing rush for the door. Rhys made a blow for personal freedom by lighting an extra length cigarette. 'Sorry about that,' he whispered. 'They do go on a bit.'

'Not at all. It's an important philosophical point, isn't it? Can you really elect an MEP if you are committed to pulling out of the EU altogether? What would he actually *do*?'

'I wouldn't mind all the discussion,' Rhys continued, 'if we actually had a volunteer to be a candidate.'

'Ah.'

'I don't suppose you'd be interested yourself?'

The doorman, who had been introduced as Tim, came over and sat down. 'He says the Chronicle advertised this meeting,' he told Rhys, nodding his head to indicate me. 'Didn't bring anyone else in, did it?'

'It was only two lines,' I explained. 'In the notices.'

'You see what we have to put up with? That's why no-one comes.'

Rhys rolled his eyes at me. 'Public information, Tim,' he explained. 'It's not like we paid for an advert. It's not like we sent them a nice press release to copy out. Although we could if we had a Press Officer.' He began to gather up his papers. I decided to take a risk with the thread of the conversation.

'It was an impulse that brought me here,' I said casually.

'But I'd heard about the EPP from someone I know slightly. Someone who drinks in the same pub. I thought he might be here, actually.'

'Who's that, then?' asked Rhys.

'I know him as... er, Oz,' I said. 'Short for Oswald–'

'Oswald *Mosley*?'

'That's it. He is a member, isn't he?'

Rhys exchanged glances with Tim the doorman, then sucked thoughtfully on his fag. 'Yes,' he agreed at last, 'He is a member.'

'Doesn't he come to meetings? Or is he on holiday or something?'

Tim coughed and looked down into his cash box, as if seeking solace in the twenty-five or so pounds it contained. Rhys looked at the ceiling. 'Let's just say we *assume* he's on holiday at the moment.'

'Oh, well...' I turned and pulled my coat off the back of the chair. 'As I say, I don't know him very well. Anyway, thanks for the meeting...'

Rhys was still looking at the ceiling as I left the hall but we crossed paths again on my way out of the gents' toilets a few minutes later, and he persuaded me to join him across the road for a drink. He told me that Colin was getting up a petition regarding the changes proposed to next year's escape convention; their original complaint having elicited a brusque letter citing 'financial necessity' for the expansion into other subject areas.

Rhys was angry at the disrespect he thought this showed the veterans, especially those who had successfully got out of their Prisoner of War camps, and for whom the convention was originally created. I thought it was touching how he idolised these old men on the strength of a single act of great courage far back in their youth, and I thought how this symbolised perfectly the nostalgia and fear of change that sent men like him into the English Patriot's Party.

I bought him a beer in return and the extra alcohol seemed to loosen him up. He apologised for appearing rude earlier on.

'There's been a bit of trouble with Oswald Mosley just lately,' he explained. 'In fact, I wouldn't mind betting he only encouraged you to come to a meeting because he wanted to increase his own base of support.'

'What, a sort of split in the local Party?'

'Yeah. I shouldn't gossip about it though, seeing as you're not a member. But there has been some ill feeling.'

'Has he been thrown out, then?'

'Oh, no, no. I told you he's still a member. There have been some expulsions recently, though. But there have to be all sorts of procedures. We have a very comprehensive rule book, you know. Some people are pretty angry with Oswald. I am myself. He never really apologised about my camera.

'You see,' Rhys continued firmly, while shifting into a more comfortable position in his chair, 'You see, political power comes through the accepted political processes. England isn't some banana republic. You can't engineer a coup d'état. You can't *buy* seats on the Parish Council. At least not as a simple cash transaction.'

'Especially if you have no cash.'

Rhys looked at me for a moment. 'So you have to get votes. You have to get members. You have to campaign. It takes patience. The younger guys didn't last the course.'

'They left?'

'They were expelled. Five of them got into a fight with

some North African boys. Got arrested, kept telling the police they were political prisoners.'

'Brought the Party into disrepute?'

'Worse. They started showing off. Making things up. Fucking bravado! They made all sorts of crazy claims. Colin and Tim were arrested for incitement to racial hatred. It took forty eight hours to get them out. Stupid little bastards,' Rhys said dismissively. 'They could have been fighting for a cause, but they just wanted to fight for fun.'

I let lie the ambiguity of the word 'fighting.'

'You know, those five lads had started turning up at meetings all wearing matching black shirts.' He laughed bitterly. 'Blackshirts! They wouldn't have lasted a week! No self discipline, no respect for authority, no work ethic. Blackshirts! They'd be better suited to football shirts.'

Mosley, Rhys told me, was somewhat different to the hooligans, but while having sympathy for both sides, he had blamed the older, more politically-minded faction for the collapse in membership. Other people had walked out in frustration, and the number of regular members had never been large. The Party was having to start from scratch again, and Mosley was impatient.

'He wants power, I'll give him that,' Rhys said over a third pint. 'He sees the value in winning elections. But at heart he's a direct-action man, you can tell. And all that Nazi memorabilia he keeps. It's a skeleton in the cupboard for anyone with serious ambitions.'

'He'd do better to have Gordon Jackson's trousers,' I said, but Rhys didn't respond; maybe he didn't hear me.

'I tell you, if the Chronicle did get wind of that, then all Tim's oversensitivity would be justified. It would be such an obviously good story.'

'He told me he did a lot of work for the EPP, though,' I said, trying to sound casual. 'Newsletters, membership lists… I was surprised he had time to earn a living on top of it…'

'Yeah, I can see it would be sad for him if he did end up giving up. He took it hard when some of the younger ones were saying *he*'d betrayed *them* by staying with us. He never betrayed them, he supported them. He got some death threats, same as I did–'

'*Death threats?*'

Rhys looked up, embarrassed. 'Oh, it was all bullshit. Nothing to worry about. Idle threats. Besides,' he added unselfconsciously, 'the guy who made the threats is in prison now, for beating up a Paki student in Leicester. Same again?'

'No,' I said, 'I've got to get home.' But I decided Rhys was talkative enough for me to probe further. 'You don't know why Oswald didn't come tonight, then? He *was* expected?'

'No, not really. He was perfectly entitled to come, but last time he left in a bit of a huff. We'd spent weeks all trying to be pleasant after the expulsions. Oswald had said he was working on a project that would get the active wing back to being interested and would swing the voters locally onto our side. He wanted some money to help him. He'd already borrowed my camera. He wanted to keep it all secret, so we refused. Well, you heard, we've only thirty quid in the bank anyway.'

Rhys finished his pint and wiped his mouth. 'No doubt it was all rubbish, and that's another reason why we haven't heard from him. Embarrassed. Anyway, it's been nice to see you again, Larry.'

Rhys fished in his wallet for a business card ('Rhys Godfrey, Drainage Solutions') and scribbled on the back the dates of the next two meetings. 'Come again,' he urged. 'I know it sounds a bit doom and gloom, but, well, we're in the right… We've got to protect our own culture, we've got to value our history. *You* know that. You're interested in these things…'

'What was the project, though?' I asked.

Rhys shook his head. 'No idea. "Top secret." The prat.'

'You're the Chair! He must have told you something?'

'No. All hush-hush. You see he didn't trust us after we forced out his mates… Anyway, why are we talking so much about him? Come to another meeting. Or give me a bell about the convention. Colin will be delighted if you sign the petition.'

'Rhys,' I called as he started walking away. 'Does he have a job? Oswald Mosley. What does he do for a living?'

Rhys turned and came back to the table. He looked at me suspiciously, as if he couldn't work out why I was asking. 'He works in a factory.'

'Which one?'

'I don't know. I'm not sure he ever said.'

'Days or nights?'

'No idea. No, days I should think. Because he came round to my house once directly from work. My wife said he smelled a bit. Of tinned meat. Or maybe meat pies.' Rhys laughed. 'Thinks he's the new *Sir* Oswald Mosley and he smells of meat pies!'

CHAPTER EIGHTEEN

'Now don't say I never bring you little presents any more.'

Di looked down at her desk and up again into my eyes. 'What's this for?'

'It's a present.'

'What for?'

'Because... Well alright, actually because it's more use to you than to me, but... What's the matter? Is it the wrong flavour or something?'

Sharon turned to look from the adjacent desk. 'Larry...' she hissed in an urgent tone. I ignored her.

'*DoggieBest Lamb chunks*?' There was a slight catch in Di's voice.

'Alright, alright. I didn't realise your Hamish was so fussy.'

'Hamish,' said Diane, levering herself up from her chair, 'is a Cornish Rex.'

'Yes?'

'It's a type of *cat*.'

'Ah, bollocks.' I slumped into Di's seat as she stomped off towards the ladies' toilets. Sharon was smiling, but it was a sad sort of smile, and she was shaking her head.

'You idiot, Larry.'

'But it's an easy mistake to make! I thought she had a dog! She told Carl that Hamish gets on with the Labrador next door. It's fucking well called *Rex*. How am I supposed guess

172

it's a bloody feline? Anyway, I'm not saying it has to eat the stuff—'

'It's not that. You don't give *dog food* to a woman who hasn't got a boyfriend and is self conscious about her weight problem. Especially at lunchtime.'

'What? No! You *are* kidding. I'm not—'

'Women are very sensitive about this sort of thing.'

'For God's sake, surely she doesn't think—'

'No, I'm sure she knows you well enough by now Larry. It's just the surprise and confusion upsetting her. She'll be fine. Eventually…'

I picked up Diane's pen and wrote 'Sorry about the pet food mistake' on the nearest sheet. Then I put it in a speech bubble and drew a cat's head underneath. I gave the cat a human body and a big piece of paper in its hand with FTS 99 on it. I looked around for a highlighter pen to colour it in.

'Why have you been buying dog food anyway?' asked Sharon.

'I didn't buy it. It was a free gift. From a visit to an employer.'

'Cheapskate.'

'Fuck this,' I said, 'I'll leave it on the PI desk for one of the dog-on-a-rope homeless guys on Friday. They'll appreciate it if no-one else does. And if it's the wrong brand they can swap it for a can of cider.'

Sharon cleared her throat. 'I like your picture, Larry,' she said, 'but you've done it on the back of Di's Annual Review form. And I don't think Will has signed it yet.'

★ ★ ★

Ray Model had a metronome on his desk. From the way he had talked I'd half expected him to set it ticking. He'd already had his secretary explain that we had no more than fifteen minutes before the Board meeting at nine thirty a.m. Which might have also explained the expensive suit he was wearing, though I had a hunch he always dressed like that.

'So to summarise,' he had said, as he looked me up and down for the fiftieth time, 'you are asking me to check our employee records in order to identify any matches with benefit claimants.'

'Yes.' I'd agreed, while wishing I was a bit more of a morning type of person, or at least looked like one. Maybe I should have put on a clean shirt...

'And what's in it for me?'

'I beg your pardon?'

'What is the advantage for me? For my company? What does DoggieBest Limited get out of this?'

'Well... It's more a case of general economic advantage. Benefit claims fall: less cost to the taxpayer. Companies, and individuals like you and me.'

'But there's no... pardon the pun, straightforward cost-benefit analysis we can do?'

'Well, no.'

'Despite the cost of the man-hours, *person-hours* that my staff would use up.'

'There is such a thing as... civic duty, too.'

'Yes, I suppose there is.'

But Model wasn't looking like a man motivated by civic duty, or indeed any other phrase that doesn't figure in a business plan or, more especially, an executive Curriculum Vitae. Ten years younger and he would have made a fair stab at one of those business-oriented reality TV shows, but as it was he was doing it the longer way round. He had already used phrases like 'When I was at Microsoft,' just to make clear that he hadn't always worked for an independent pet food factory. After a couple of years here I guessed he would elbow his way back into a major national or multinational company, but some rungs further up the corporate ladder.

'I could use up valuable admin time and end up losing some experienced workers, too.'

I was way ahead of him, but I gave him the usual questioning frown anyway.

'If they were committing fraud I'd have to sack them. It would be gross misconduct. Unless you suggest I gave them a second chance, as it were. Kept them on out of—'

'Civic duty,' I sighed.

'Knowing I'd shopped them. Mmm. Not sure their production levels would rise, actually…'

Model made one of those steeples with his fingers and smiled politely at me. This was the crux, of course. His motivation was all about raising production levels, or lowering costs, or both. Or at least making it appear that way. He needed a nice little project for his CV. Something to impress the headhunters when he next put out a feeler or two. Our agreed fifteen minutes was just an outside bet that I might have had something useful to offer *him,* but it had turned out that I wanted a favour myself. If he was disappointed, though, he was hiding it well.

He had paused, as if thinking deeply, then pulled a notepad across his desk in a single, decisive movement. 'OK,' he said, 'I'll take some advice from colleagues. I'd like to help. I'll have my secretary email you.' He made a slight movement to stand, and I recognised my cue.

At the door, he asked, as if a complete afterthought, whether there were still any subsidised work placement schemes run by our Department. He had come across them 'When I was with M & S.'

I gave him Will's name and referred him to the relevant pages of the national website. And I wondered whether Will would agree that a Fraud check of *all* employees should be a prerequisite for him to boost his workforce with half a dozen claimants who wouldn't need paying for six months. It seemed a good enough quid pro quo to me. And I didn't think Model would play ball otherwise. Without an incentive I could see that employee relations, or the trade union, or the Data Protection Act would *regrettably* get in the way of anything he could do for us. Well, never mind, even Herman has no real answer to the 'What's in it for me?' question, except that he's much better at the moral blackmail side of things than I am.

'Sandra, would you be a love and gift wrap the metronome for me?' Model said to his secretary. 'I'm taking it tonight. Oh, and perhaps Mr Di Palma would like a present, too? Do we have any marketing packs with the new sales brochures? Pleasure to meet you, Larry. Sorry to have to rush off. If you need anything, leave a message on Sandra's voicemail: it's picked up daily.'

I took my carrier bag of glossy leaflets and nearly dropped the can of dog food that came with it. In some ways I quite liked Ray Model. He certainly had a very polite way of saying 'Don't call us, we'll email you.' And the clock showed that he had found me seventeen minutes of his time.

★ ★ ★

But that afternoon, conversely, Will Snelle had lost all of his customary politeness, or 'Person Centred Human Resources Management Style', as he might have referred to it. There were no niceties like an offer of a coffee or even water. He was holding a sheet of paper. He was waving it under my nose; I could practically feel the draft.

'I need you to explain something,' he was saying in a slightly strangled tone of voice.

'If it's about the cat, I'm sorry,' I said.

'Cat?'

'Yes. Well, it's supposed to be a cat. Maybe you can't tell. It has a human body, after all.' Will was looking as if his breakdown had finally started. 'On the Annual Review document,' I explained, though as I did so I had realised this was not to do with my drawing. It was just under an hour since Diane had run to the Ladies'. She quite possibly wasn't even back at her desk yet.

'This isn't an Annual Review,' said Will, 'It's a *writ.*'

'Ah.'

'It refers to our new trainee.'

'Really?'

'And to you.'

It was time to relieve Will of some of his burden, if only to get to know the worst without delay. I slowly stretched out and took the thick cream-coloured sheet from his fingers. It was high quality, embossed paper, laser-printed with one of those fake handwriting fonts. It had been signed in a flourish by *Dr* Leroy-Shaw. I went hot and cold, and then as I read, I smiled to myself.

'It's not a writ,' I said. 'It's just a letter.'

'They are going to do us for racial harassment!'

'Unfortunately for them, they don't have a shred of evidence.'

'Are you sure?'

'Maybe I'll sue them for defamation of character. Or assault, even. That might have been Smith the other night, trying to put the frighteners on me. I said so at the time. I'll ring up DS Wodehouse–'

'It's a disaster! He says they are going to the press!'

'Which just goes to show how shaky this is. You can't give your story to the papers before you give it to your solicitor.'

'Of course, of course.' Will sat back in his chair, looking ashen but noticeably less tense. I don't often feel sorry for the man, but I did at that moment. Something made me think of Helen and her complaints about the cold weather and Health and Safety regulations. Maybe she had some sort of 'Stress at Work' leaflet I could copy and post under Will's door. We didn't actually want to lose him. There were worse people waiting for promotion, after all. I could name three managers of local satellite offices straight away, and that was without even considering our own collection of team leaders. Unless, of course, Will was a very good actor and this was a new management technique for getting your staff on your side. *Sob Your Way to Success,* it would make a good business self help book.

'I don't need this, you know,' Will said plaintively. I went over to his coffee machine and poured two cups. It was lukewarm, but better than nothing.

'Targets are down,' Will said. 'Out of the nine Major Benchmarks, this month we are on target to achieve three.'

'Oh,' I said, in a suitably sympathetic way. I handed him his drink.

'Our average over the past six months has been three point six.'

'I see.'

'The Minister's overarching target was, quite naturally, to achieve an overall improvement in all nine.'

'Mmm…'

'Of the three Major Benchmarks relating to Investigation…' Here Will paused and looked up at me, 'We achieved none.'

'Oh.' Or maybe *oh, shit* would have been more apt. I had hoped he was just thinking aloud, but even under stress Will can't stop instructing his staff. He seems to think it motivates people.

'And in two out of the three, you are well below the percentage improvement needed. Well below.'

'Right…' I particularly admired Will's shift from 'we' to 'you' at this stage of the conversation, and I immediately felt less sorry for him. Ironically this cheered me up.

'I understand,' I said. 'Three out of nine Major Benchmarks isn't good, obviously.'

'No.'

'How did we do on the Minor Benchmark?'

'Well above target,' said Will, his head in his hands.

'Look, you want my advice?' I said, since I was keen to change the subject from missed fraud targets. 'Ring up Human Resources. And guess what? They'll tell you to send Leroy a letter saying you are conducting an investigation. Then just ignore him. We've got Smith bang to rights. No-one's going to take his claims seriously when they know he's being prosecuted for fraud. It'll be obvious to the thickest magistrate that it's a ploy.'

'And you say there's no evidence?'

'Of course not!'

'No, of course. You're right, Larry. I'm being stupid. What am I panicking for?'

'Exactly–'

'I mean, we video tape interviews anyway, don't we?'

Will met my gaze, and in lieu of a reply I fished out my handkerchief and pretended to sneeze. This didn't seem a good moment to admit that the second half of the interview had not been taped. Lost evidence never quite convinces the legal profession, either, does it?

'Good. Thank you, Larry, that's very helpful. And there's still no sign of your Mr Mosley, either, is there? So well done on that, too. But we do need to improve on attaining targets. I'm relying on it next month. Helen will be more up to speed then, so no excuses.'

Will gave me a smile that was almost back to his normal person-centred-manager self. At the door, I said, 'There's a drawing… a doodle on Di's Annual Review paperwork. I'm afraid it's my fault.'

I slipped out while Will was still looking perplexed. It's the best way to make a confession. And now I had more work to do on the Smith case: I couldn't afford to see this one as just the usual mundane cutting through red tape.

There was also the question of cutting through video tape.

CHAPTER NINETEEN

If I'd been more awake, I'd have seen who it was right away. If I were fitter, I'd have caught him up sooner. If I'd made the questions simpler, quicker to answer I might have found out something before he went off again. (Though I don't know how much simpler you can get than 'Where the fuck have you been?') But as usual I was just that tiny bit too diffident. Too slow.

★ ★ ★

I'd had an afternoon with the video recorder and a mini screwdriver, and a teatime watching a documentary and listening to a football being kicked against the outside wall of the flats. I'd spent a pleasant half hour reading *The Man with No Friends* although the thrills of the author's dive from a stricken Lancaster bomber were offset by his descriptions of the airmen's fear of fire. Who would have guessed that the smell of burning in wartime can put a man off his roast pork dinner for life? As always, the sacrifice of that generation made my own problems seem just a little pathetic.

I wanted a shot of the hard stuff and the bedsit bottle was down to its last finger, so I took a walk to Max's. The early evening had given us warm autumnal sunshine for a change, and I slung my jacket over my shoulder. I even put on my sunglasses, though it was more for fun than necessity.

People joke that I don't move to a better flat because there aren't any with an off-licence so close (ha, ha, I tell them, I'm moving in above the adult movie store next, or opposite the sixth formers' netball pitch). But of course the only reason my friends even notice Max's is because it's a rarity. Offies have gone the way of all the old-fashioned shops; everyone's going to Tesco. Max stays in profit due to mugs like me who are habitually too lazy – or too drunk – to go further afield. That and his under-the-counter cannabis dealing, of course.

The last time I'd been in, Max gave me grief for saying I couldn't afford 15 year old malts any more. You have to hand it to him, he knows what tempts every customer and just what sales pitch to use: jokey sarcasm with a hint of bullying gets me every time, and I'd dithered weakly over an expensive compromise. So this time I was concentrating on the special offers in the window and simply felt, rather than saw the tallish, track-suited figure who pushed past out of the doorway. Or rather *smelled not saw* would be more accurate. I don't drink much Tennessee whisky but I would have sworn he was sweating pure Jack Daniel's.

'Not another one,' Max complained as I entered.

'Mmm?' I avoided his eye as I'm not convinced he doesn't practise hypnotism to maximise sales.

'Another one who doesn't know what he wants. That last bloke asked the price of every size and brand of bourbon I've got. Then he wanted a little taste of all the ryes. *Then* it turns out he doesn't even have his wallet on him.'

I moved across to the bargain bins and picked up a bottle marked 'Highland Fling'.

'Oh, you'd enjoy that.' Max stood back and pulled in his belly in mock outrage. 'Tastes like it was distilled in Ghana.'

'It ought to be in my price range, then.'

'Silly bugger had had enough anyway. Pissed as a newt. No money, kept checking his pockets and frowning, and then stopping to look out of the window! All the twelve year olds are a fiver off, you know.'

'I need something that's a fiver *in total…*'

'Only one thing worse than an aggressive drunk if you ask me. A paranoid one. Said he was being followed!'

I felt a rush of blood to my head. Smells like American whisky, afraid of being followed… The tracksuit was all wrong, and the lapse into drinking was itself very questionable, but I was out the shop like a sprinter, and still moving like an end-of-marathon runner a hundred yards down the street. He was still in sight, just, at the far end of Cutler Street, moving in the direction of the Gasworks car park.

Having closed part of the gap, I slowed to match his pace, and only partly to get my breath back. No, I wasn't a hundred per cent sure I had the right man, and though staring at the back of his head from a distance wasn't really going to help me, at least it gave a moment's thinking time. Of course I could simply try to follow unobserved until his final destination, but if I was right, this would mean a long, random meander, calling at all points where he could try to beg a free drink. This was not at all how I wanted to spend my night…

He began to turn and I melted into the doorway of a boarded-up shop. He crossed the road, then stopped suddenly and knelt as if tying his shoelaces, or, in this case, adjusting a Velcro strap. Paranoid drunk, I thought. Using forty year old techniques to watch his tail. Would he stop to light a cigarette? (My own training had hardly been more sophisticated; though for health and safety reasons, lighting a fag was not permitted. Herman used to tell us to open a bag of crisps, although nowadays surely one would be told to pause to open an individual portion of fruit…)

And then he turned to enter the old Gasworks site. The traffic was quieter here as the main road is shielded by a derelict water tower, and the workers on the trading estate had driven off home. I remembered another tip of Herman's: if ambient noise drops, be quieter yourself. Beware of sneezing, farting and footsteps. Don't open that packet of crisps!

But it was immaterial now. I didn't need to stay incognito. It was the location that did it for me. Synchronicity: we were always fated to meet in car parks. It must be him. I made a new attempt at running; I waved and called his name.

'Chandler? It's me. Larry.'

He turned and looked at me with glazed eyes. Was he just drunk, or was there something else? And that tracksuit. You couldn't imagine an athlete in it. To me it looked a bit, well, *institutional.*

'You look rough. Are you OK? Why didn't you turn up at the Dark Horse the other night?'

Some boy racer was gunning his motor down Peppermint Road, but otherwise the car park was still. Chandler blinked. 'Larry,' he said. 'I *knew* someone was following me! I could sense it all the way from–' He flinched suddenly. 'You're not one of them, are you?'

'One of who?'

'You don't have a drink on you, do you? A beer? Anything?'

'You're supposed to be reformed.'

'Just one little beer wouldn't hurt.'

'One of who, Chandler? Who's been following you?' I raised my voice, partly to try and focus him, partly because the boy racer had reached the entrance and was pulling a handbrake turn through the gate. I moved in behind a Range Rover without thinking about it.

'They took me in.' Chandler shielded his eyes. The late sun was in his face; it accentuated all the bags and wrinkles. 'For my own safety…'

The car pulled up with a scream, dangerously close. I turned angrily, but instead of young men in a beat-up stolen vehicle, I took in a smart, black BMW and, clambering quickly out, a small Asian man in a dark suit. I glanced back at Chandler: he was running towards the pedestrian exit on the far side. The Asian man followed. I followed.

It wasn't much of a head start for Chandler and although he was fast for a middle aged alcoholic, we caught him easily. Or at least the stranger did. He was holding Chandler's arm, firmly but not at all roughly, as I slid to a halt.

'What are you doing?' I gasped. 'Let go of him!'

'I'm very sorry, Sir. It's not safe for him to be out.' He turned his back on me and spoke calmly. 'Chandler, I don't really approve of this, but I have been given permission for you to have something to drink. I am going to give you a lift back. I'm sure you should eat a little, too.'

'Lift? Where are you taking him?'

'Unfortunately…' He gave me a long and confident stare, 'Our service follows very strict policies on confidentiality.'

'You can't just kidnap him on the street!'

'Of course not. This is England, not Afghanistan. Chandler, please reassure this gentleman that you are coming quite voluntarily.'

Chandler licked his lips nervously. 'You say I'm allowed to have a drink?'

'Correct.'

'Alright.' He looked downwards, as if suddenly ashamed of his weakness. 'Sorry to cause trouble.' The comment could have been addressed to either of us, or even both.

'Look, who *are* you?' I asked.

'Well, I could ask you the same question.'

'I'm…' I stopped, finding it hard to explain our exact relationship to a stranger. 'I'm a colleague. A former colleague… A friend…'

'Unless you can prove you are his next of kin, then there's nothing I can say.'

We had reached the car. The investigator in me was looking for clues: belongings on the back seat, parking permit on the windscreen… I'd already memorised the registration number. 'Chandler,' I said, 'you ran away a moment ago. Who *is* this man?'

'This is Mr Shah.'

'Where is he taking you?'

'It's OK, Larry.' Chandler slid into the back seat. 'He said I could have something to drink.'

I opened my mouth again, but the engine was running and the electric windows shot up. Then, as the car started to move, Chandler turned his head to face me, lifted a cupped hand to his ear and mouthed something. I shook my head. He did it again.

Voicemail.

He lowered his hand and his eyes glazed over again. I saw Shah look in his mirror, although whether he was checking on Chandler or me would have been hard to say.

★ ★ ★

Helen's mobile gives you twenty rings before the voicemail kicks in. I knew this because I had tried her number four or five times and I'd been counting since the second attempt.

So maybe time had got on a bit when she finally picked up; certainly I'd made some inroads into my Ghanaian whisky, which tasted just as Max had promised.

'Hi, Helen. At last!'

'Who is this?'

'It's me, Larry.'

'*Larry*. What are you doing? Stalking me? I've had seven missed calls. I thought it was some nutter.'

'Yes, I'm sorry. There's a fault on your phone. It wouldn't let me leave a message, just kept cutting me off.'

'It's ten o'clock. You're not still working?'

'Well… there's a bit of news. I've seen Chandler.'

There was a sound like someone blowing a raspberry, and a little further away, low volume chanting from the television. Then another one: it was the squeak of leather cushions as she moved.

'You *are* still working.' She didn't sound impressed.

'No, no, not really. I though I'd call to see how you're doing. It's been a couple of days.'

Helen sighed. 'That's sweet, Larry, but I'm back in the office with you tomorrow afternoon. Straight after seeing Will.'

'Yeah, OK, point taken. Sorry to be a nuisance.' There was a longish pause. 'So,' I added brightly, 'what are you doing?'

'Nothing. Watching the football.'

'Really? Who's playing?'

'It's… erm… Milan v Padua.'

'What's the score?'

'Oh, er, three two to Milan.'

'Plenty of goals. Good game, then?'

'Well, actually, I've no idea. I'm not really watching it. I'd dozed off.'

'Oh. Bollocks. I really am disturbing you, aren't I?'

I waited for her to protest, to say 'no problem, don't worry about it,' or even (in your dreams, Di Palma!) to suggest I could come over and watch the end of the game anyway. But instead she said she would see me tomorrow. She didn't say anything about looking forward to it. She didn't mention wanting to hear about Chandler. And another thought had worked its way past the booze that was clouding my brain. Who else did I know with big screen international football at home, and brand new leather seats?

'OK, bye then.'

'Bye Larry. See you tomorrow.'

I heard the sofa squeak again and there was a muted roar of passion from the TV. So, someone else had scored. Lucky him.

The phone went dead and I licked a bitter taste from my lips.

CHAPTER TWENTY

I was disappointed.

Yet again I pressed the button marked 'messages.' The red light carried on winking while I went through the rigmarole of pass code, hash key, select options, repeat options, listen and save. It was no good. Chandler's message made no sense.

Diane appeared at my desk, holding a white plastic bag.

'Oh, look,' I whined, 'I said I was sorry about the dog food, didn't I?'

'Apology accepted. But I want you to treat this as a learning experience, Larry, so I've brought you something just so you don't immediately forget.'

She opened the bag and placed before me a small plastic tray in a brightly designed cardboard sleeve.

'Grannie Baker's *Meal for One*?'

'I'm not the only singleton in the office, am I, Larry? Hope you don't feel *too* bad when people point it out.'

'But it was an accident, a mistake! I didn't mean it that way.'

'It still made me upset.'

'Fine, fine,' I muttered, going back to shuffling my notes so that she would take a hint and leave. 'You'll be more upset when I buy you a *Meal for Five*,' I mumbled, once she was out of earshot. Then I felt a bit ashamed.

What else could I try? I started with one of those vehicle check websites, the ones that are supposed to stop you from buying a dodgy second hand car. Shah's registration number matched the correct make, model and colour; the car was not recorded as stolen, scrapped or exported; it had one current owner and no previous owners. So far, so legit. But then I didn't really expect Chandler to be with kidnappers who drove around on false plates…

I rang the DVLA. We have a Phase One Information Sharing Protocol with them, which means we can confirm the ownership of a claimant's private vehicle. Sounds useful? I've used it properly only once in five years, just before I had to follow a gangmaster's minibus to the coast. But I *have* phoned the DVLA on numerous other occasions to try and bend the rules a little, to get something they're not really allowed to share. So I asked for Steve and switched on my best pro to pro banter. We talked Italian football for a bit and then I got to the point.

'You haven't given me his first names,' Steve complained.

'Ah, sorry, mate. I'm in a bit of a rush. I've left the file in my car.'

'And I suppose your computer's down as well.'

'I'm not at my desk,' I lied. 'Come on, just tap in the number, will you?'

'You're in breach of Data Protection.'

'What, for not having a first name?'

'You haven't given me his date of birth, either. How do I know the guy has signed the IS permission sheet when you've not got sight of the file?'

'We always get them to sign it.'

'Oh, yeah? What if the New Claims Adviser forgot?'

'This is bureaucracy gone mad, Steve.'

'You say that every time you ring.'

'I say it *everywhere* I ring.'

Steve chuckled and I heard his fingers on the keyboard. Sharon approached with an internal mail envelope. From the bulge it looked like a card and leaving collection. There was a clink as it dropped onto my desk.

'You're out of luck, mate. It's not registered with a Mr Shah.'

'Of course!' I slapped my forehead in mock exasperation. 'It'll be a pool car he's using. Silly of me. You couldn't tell me the business, could you?'

'Don't ask for much, do you? Let me page forward, there's a code I don't recog- Oh. I can't tell you.'

'Come on, it can't be that secret. I know it's a clinic or a hospital.'

'I really can't tell you, Larry. It doesn't match your claimant. You know the rules.'

'Give me a hint.'

'Alright. It's not some tiny little tin pot business that knows nothing about data security. And they wouldn't be satisfied with a small apology if they found out.'

'I get it. Your supervisor's just going by, is she? Want me to call back?'

'Not at all. Nothing personal, Larry. There's nothing I can do on this one.'

I was surprised by Steve's sudden change of attitude, but I couldn't afford to piss him off for next time, so I decided to drop it. My guess was that Shah's employer had already had cause to make complaints to the DVLA, and an over-cautious supervisor had logged them all onto the database. We get the same sort of thing here; in fact in the old days it was all part of a system of coloured stickers to warn about trouble: red dot – potentially violent; blue dot – previous official complaint upheld; yellow dot – VIP, e.g. married to the local MP. It looked like Shah was driving for a blue dot company. But I was guessing, and the guess was no help to me.

'Thanks anyway, Steve,' I said. 'By the way, how's your trainee coming along?'

'What trainee?'

'I could have sworn you told me about a new trainee last time I rang.'

'Not a chance, mate. We're laying off staff here, not taking on anyone new. I might have to get you to ring the Swansea Jobcentres to put in a good word for me.'

I commiserated, signed off and returned to the internet in a rather desultory way. So there was obviously no point in ringing back, assuming a fake accent and trying to bully the information out of someone less experienced. Shah's car was taking me nowhere.

But there was no joy elsewhere either. No Shah in the local phone books. None on the websites of the local NHS trust. A quick call to the Rehab Centre only gave me access to the answerphone. I shrugged. Maybe Helen would have some more ideas. In the meantime perhaps I would sort out this leaving card and pass it back to Sharon. We didn't want a repeat of the time a card went missing with allegedly nearly a hundred pounds inside, thus proving that financial crime doesn't only exist on the public side of the benefits desk. I emptied my pockets of loose change.

★ ★ ★

Helen was wearing a sort of shimmering green top, tight charcoal skirt and heels. You couldn't miss her coming in, even if it was via the stairwell and not the boss's office as expected. She looked a bit flushed. She seemed happier than the night before, too.

'Don't tell me Will took you out to lunch!'

'Jealous?'

'Yes,' I said firmly. I pushed aside the packaging from a Gregson's *Just Ham* roll.

Helen smiled. 'He was having a – quote, unquote – *target-focussed* lunch with the Regional Director. They asked me to join them for coffee.'

'They didn't ply you with liqueurs, then?'

'No. Mean, eh? I noticed *they'd* had a glass of wine.'

'The RD can probably hide it in his expenses. Nobody else would get away with it, though.'

'Still, better not to when I'm supposed to be working. I wouldn't be much use to you this afternoon if I was drunk, would I?'

I pulled my eyes back up to her face. I would have loved to believe she was being flirty, but it had come out as a quite serious and innocent comment.

'It might have been very useful,' I said, 'if we assume that it takes a drunk to understand one.'

'What?'

'I've got a voicemail for you to decipher.'

Helen listened to Chandler's message twice, lips pursed and frown lines deep. She'd overdone the gloss again; I was surprised the RD hadn't asked her to shadow *him* for the rest of the day. And he hadn't even bought her a proper drink, either! Some managers have the oddest priorities...

'This is what you woke me up about last night, is it?' Helen asked wryly.

'No! Well, alright, yes. But there's more to the story than

this. Except I didn't expect his message to be unintelligible. Stupid of me. He was obviously drunk already when he left it.'

I passed Helen the notes I had made, but she shook her head and said it made the job harder, not easier. I gave her my story of chasing Chandler through the car park and I reluctantly admitted defeat over my research an hour or two before. Helen thought the name 'Shah' was familiar, but she couldn't imagine why.

'Maybe you're thinking of Leroy-*Shaw*,' I said gloomily. 'That's another problem on the horizon.'

'Come on, don't give up,' she suggested. 'You're the one who does cryptic crosswords in the pub. A few sentences should be easy...'

I felt a short glow of pleasure that she had noticed the crossword, and then I remembered that I had only managed two or three answers. But that was two or three more than I had from Chandler's puzzle. I turned the notes round for Helen. 'Have one last look,' I said. She frowned over the words on the pad. I frowned at them upside down. I played the message.

'Your plane 'n fire,' Chandler told us. 'Wash it.'

'Don't flow your inch,' he continued. Well, that's what it sounded like. Or was it 'Don't throw your lunch,' or even 'Don't throw orange?'

'Leave the bacon. Fuck tea. Alone. Pliss.'

A graphologist might have seen frustration and anger in my handwriting as we reached the bottom of the page. *Fuck tea alone? Fuck "T" alone? Fuck tee along? Fuck T Alan?* Then came the one part that made perfect sense: 'Money's running out,' slurred Chandler. And my best guess before the dialling tone returned: *BALLS MINT RUBBLE.*

Helen looked up. 'I don't get it, though.'

'I know that. That's the whole point.'

'No, I mean, I don't get why you're still doing this. You said you wanted to drop this Chandler bloke. Fed up with him wasting your time. But now you've seen him, you know he's safe. He's not drowned in the canal or anything. You don't need to carry on, do you?'

'True... But he contacted us to say he had something–'

'And then he failed to turn up at the pub! You said yourself it was probably nothing.'

'You're right. I ought to get a grip on myself. I'll never get to have coffee with the RD if I don't get on with more important work. Chandler's out of the window. There's someone much more important to track down.'

'Who are we going for?'

'Oswald Mosley.'

'Now I *know* you're taking the piss.'

'Alright. Let's do a random check home visit. You haven't done one of those yet, have you?'

'Aren't I a bit overdressed?'

'You can seduce them into a confession.'

'Don't get fresh, Mister. I've got some jeans in the car. I'll go and get changed.'

'I suggest we try that actor of yours. If he's that good at inhabiting his characters, then maybe he was fooling you all along.'

'Anyone. Just so long as it's not that Jon Smith and his abusive legal representative. After coffee with the RD under Will's scrutiny, I need a restful afternoon.'

'Yes, so do I. In fact, I could do with a relaxing rest of the whole damn week.'

I picked up some files at random and began shovelling them into my briefcase. 'I guess I might need these if I'm...

er, *working from home* after we've done our visit,' I said loudly, just in case any other staff were bothering to listen. I paused briefly and then I also pushed in the Meal for One. 'Just give me a minute to get rid of this card and sack of coins, and then we'll go.'

Helen went into the ladies' toilet to change into her trousers. I added 'home and employer visits' to my diary for the following twenty four hours and logged out of my terminal. Then I concentrated on looking nonchalant as I waited for her to come out.

Meal for One. Though to be really wounding it would have had to be past its sell-by date as well…

CHAPTER TWENTY ONE

There was something very old-fashioned about the Grannie Baker factory that was nothing to do with its products (pastries, pasties, pies), nor even its brand image, with its cartoon logo of a little, grey-haired old lady and its over use of the word 'traditional'. What was old-fashioned was the entire look of the place, from the employees' entrance all the way to the factory floor.

Outside was a neglected job vacancy board, still advertising a possible opening for a packer; though the final letter 'r' had broken off long ago. Inside were abandoned racks for cardboard clocking-on cards, while the office block was still divided by frosted glass partitions displaying lettering from the past: 'Head Foreman,' 'Shop Steward' and the like. They hadn't had a proper refit in thirty years. They'd have to be careful, I thought, or the place would get a preservation order slapped on it.

The security guard hadn't seemed surprised when I said I was from the Jobcentre, but I still had to freeze outside his cabin while he phoned a dozen extensions for help. I suppose it didn't help that Sheena Hardy was apparently still off sick. I could feel a re-run of my previous phone calls coming on, but I decided to stick with it. At least if nothing came of this visit I could honestly say I had tried to do everything I could.

Eventually an elderly man came out to fetch me. He was wearing one of those brown coats you see on shopkeepers in Sunday night TV dramas set in the 1960s, and what with his white moustache and watery eyes I was half hoping he'd introduce himself as Grandpa Baker. His name badge, however, said Walther Gibbs. I'd assumed the 'Wally' in 'Mr Wally' was a surname, but perhaps after all this was the man I'd been looking for. Still, 'Are you Wally?' isn't a question you can easily ask.

'So,' he said, once we were inside. 'You've come from the Jobcentre.'

'Yes. I hope you don't mind me just turning up like this. I've tried to ring several times but couldn't get through to the right person. We could make an appointment if it's not convenient…'

'No, no need for that.' He looked me up and down in an appraising sort of way. 'I could probably start you today if you want. A couple of day's trial to see how you get on.'

'Ah,' I said, 'I'm not sure if you've underst–'

'I have to say that I normally use an employment agency. And we fill such a lot of jobs now by… *recommendation*… People from the Jobcentre often prove unreliable. Even when they are persistent enough to call in person, wearing a collar and tie. The last chap I took on, smartly dressed, polite… and he only lasted a day. Mind you, you do look a bit more on the ball than he did… Look, I'm prepared to give you a chance. It's only operative work, mind, nothing special. What do you think?'

What did I think? I thought this wasn't the right person for me to speak to and that I was never going to find the right person to help me pursue my investigation. I thought that you couldn't tell who did what job here, and nor could security, reception or any of the employees themselves. I thought that communication across this organisation was hopeless and that the old fashioned décor was indicative of an inefficient, moribund business, takeover or no recent takeover.

And I thought that I had just been handed a covert operation on a plate.

I hesitated, worried about what Will would say if he found out I was undercover without proper permission. Seeing me pause, Mr Gibbs said, 'I could do with an extra person on the Danish line, and I really need them right away. But it is a trial period. If it didn't work out, I believe you can continue signing on...'

My ears pricked up. Surely he wasn't familiar with the ancient 'Employment on Trial' rule? So was he hinting at something else? Was that some sort of clue? 'Don't you want the job?' he asked.

'No, no, it's not that,' I said, 'I, er, I just haven't brought any sandwiches, that's all.'

'Don't worry. We have an excellent staff canteen. You'll need to fill in one of these, please.'

It's surprisingly hard to instantly come up with a false surname, address and other details needed for an employee record card, so I was sweating a bit by the time I'd finished, and Mr Gibbs was probably assuming I was semiliterate. Feeling rushed, I had put down Highfield Mansions, Mission Street, since Laura's was the only place where I knew the postcode (apart from my mother's house – and who wants to go undercover pretending they still live with their parents?).

Gibbs left me at a coffee machine in the corridor and returned a few minutes later with a very tall, thin youth, Middle Eastern or North African, with an acne-marked face and a downy moustache. He was wearing an off-white boiler suit a size or two too small. He smiled sadly when introduced and avoided my eye.

'This is–'

'Ali,' I said. 'We've met before.'

'Really? OK, well, he'll show you the ropes. I've had a word with the shift supervisor, too. Finish your coffee and you can pick up some overalls. Best of luck.'

'How long have you worked here?' I asked Ali as we hung around outside the stores.

'About a year and a half.'

'Like it?'

He shrugged and looked unhappy again. I nodded. 'Do they know about the kebab van, or should I keep schtum?'

'What is schtum?'

'Quiet. Secret. You know. You might not want them to know you have two jobs.'

'OK. Schtum is probably best.'

The storeman reappeared, now smelling even more strongly of cigarette smoke than before. I began climbing into the overalls he had brought me, hampered slightly by the awkwardness of having a miniature tape recorder hidden under my armpit. I turned back to face the two of them only when all my fasteners were done up.

'Do you have anything in my size yet?' Ali asked him.

'Sorry, son.' The man caught my eye. 'Not much call for a thirty six chest, extra tall. They're all fat bastards round here.'

'Not being worked hard enough, obviously,' I said, holding his gaze.

'Or eating all the pies themselves.'

'Or going off for a fag instead of doing their job. Don't tell me this lad's been wearing a kiddie's suit for a year and a half?'

'First day, is it?' His face showed a penny had finally dropped. 'I'd watch your back if I were you. Not everyone likes the new regime, you know.' He moved away from the counter and I glanced at Ali who looked even unhappier than before. I supposed that I should try and blend in a bit more; it's the first rule of undercover work. 'Come on,' I said, 'let's get to work.'

The old fashioned impression of Grannie Baker's extended into the production areas, where several huge, dark and tarnished machines dominated the interior, and where the dirty walls held only Health and Safety posters from the 1970s. Squeezed into gaps between the old machinery were occasional shiny, little hi-tech pieces: either they couldn't afford to renew the whole line at once, or the old stuff was still best for the job; I don't know how these things work. The small ones, despite the vast power of their computer chips, looked wimpy and undependable beside the behemoths of mixing and kneading. I remembered reading about a worker who fell into one of these vats: it sounds funny, but he was lucky to escape with his life.

Where I was going turned out to be even more low tech than the oldest of the mechanical mixers, however. Ali and I joined four others around a length of frayed conveyor which carried an endless row of Danish pastry squares. Between the men were battered metal trolleys holding catering sized tins of fruit in syrup: apricot halves and raspberries. Our job was to fill, by hand, the central dip of each pastry, with minimal dripping and with an approved amount of fruit. The others had been going already for a couple of hours. I didn't envy them.

Ali gestured at me, shyly. 'This is Larry,' he said, adding unnecessarily, 'He's new.'

Ali pointed round the group and I tried hard to remember each name. 'Sharif,' he said, 'and Maaz.' Both were older than Ali, in their thirties at a guess, but with similar skin tones. Maaz had a well-trimmed beard under a hygienic net. Both said hello without smiling.

'Terry…'

'I won't shake hands,' Terry joked, waving a red-stained palm at me. 'Welcome to the club.'

'And Kyle.'

'Alright, mate?' Kyle gave a frown and said, 'You don't drink at the Beagle, by any chance, do yer?'

'No.'

'Oh. Thought I recognised you from there.'

I shook my head and smiled amiably as if his face meant nothing to me, which is what you do when you meet a former Jobcentre client. I'd definitely seen Kyle signing on in the past, although whether he still was I didn't know. Still, if I could only get his surname today we could run a check on whether his claim was still live. That wouldn't be a bad start to the day, after all.

'Start on apricots,' said Terry. 'Just one half. Right in the middle of the pastry, light on the juice. OK?'

'OK.'

'It's easier than raspberries. They get squashed easier, and it's harder to judge the amount of fruit. Kyle, you move on to raspberries, will you?'

I wouldn't have guessed that getting raspberries out of a tin was particularly difficult, but I just nodded as if I was carefully taking it all in. It was important not to draw attention to myself after all. I stuck my hand in the tin and winced at the sticky, cold discomfort of it. Everyone laughed.

There was some desultory talk about football and TV as

we worked, and I felt myself gradually being lulled into that semi-hypnotic state that highly repetitive work brings on. Kyle was talking about some early evening programme that he watched, while Terry explained that he never saw it as he was trying to do as much overtime as possible. Maaz, speaking quietly, almost to himself, gave the opinion that overtime was the only way to make a living, especially if providing for a family.

'I didn't know you had children, Maaz,' said Terry. 'I thought you lived in a bedsit in Towbrough Road.'

'I don't live with them at present,' said Maaz, 'but I still have to support them. I send money to them.'

'That fucking Child Support Agency have a lot to answer for,' said Kyle. 'Most of my mates are in the same boat.' Maaz looked as if this was not exactly what he had meant.

'I've got to say,' I said, stretching and letting some pastries go past, 'that on what I've been offered here I'd almost be better off on the dole.'

I glanced around, but nobody looked like they'd been reminded of a guilty secret. 'What d'you reckon, Kyle?' I continued, 'I mean, I don't know if you've ever signed on at all, but what with tax and National Insurance, and maybe losing your Housing Benefit, it's hardly worth it, is it?'

Kyle gave a shrug. 'You're not wrong, mate, really...'

'D'you always do the day shift, Kyle?' I asked. 'Or can you swap around? They'd pay more for night work, wouldn't they?'

'Yeah, I do nights. So does Terry here. Changeover every fortnight, don't we?'

'Really? Fortnightly? Er, doesn't that muck up your sleeping patterns?' I said quickly, trying to disguise my interest.

'Nah. Done it for a year or two now,' said Terry, busily swapping over to a new can of fruit.

'What about you, Kyle?' I asked. 'How long have you been working changing shifts?'

'Longer than you will be if you let any more pastries past. There is quality control on the other side of the hatch, you know.'

'Ah,' I said. 'Sorry.' I had a go at speeding up for a while, but it wasn't easy. My hands already felt frozen, and the syrup kept your fingers stuck together. Terry noticed and sympathised, wondering if there was a way to take our minds off the discomfort. Kyle groaned loudly when he said this.

'Easy one to start,' said Terry looking around the group. 'This one is from the world of sport…'

We were playing a guessing game. Terry had suggested this would make the time pass quicker, and, personally, I was all for anything which might achieve that goal. None of the others had shown any enthusiasm, though, and Kyle had been openly hostile, despite the fact that he had played this with Terry before. It was a form of twenty questions, with only 'yes or no answers' to be given, in order to identify a famous person from history or from the present day.

'From the world of sport…'

Kyle named the England football coach, captain and goalkeeper in quick succession. Terry said, 'You're not supposed to guess at random, you're supposed to work it out. Is it a man? Is it a footballer? Does he still play? Does he advertise organic potato crisps..?'

'Well, you've given it away now…'

'That was just an example, as you well know…'

With ten minutes to lunchtime we had got through two dozen footballers, golfers and media celebrities, with the odd king or queen thrown in. Maaz took us to nineteen questions with Muhammed Ali, while Kyle, insisting we carry on indefinitely, reached forty-one before revealing a troubled pop icon who, it turned out, did not have long left to live.

'Hang on, hang on. Cheat,' Terry complained. 'You said he was white!'

'Michael Jackson *is* white.'

'Is he fuck! He's black. He's an African-American!'

'You didn't ask if he was African-American. You asked if he was white. He is white. He's got white skin. He *used to* be black, I grant you, but you didn't ask that either–'

'Now you're just taking the piss,' Terry argued. He raised his hands. 'I suppose you think I'm not white any more. What am I, a Red Indian?'

'Why don't you give Larry a go?' Kyle said, laughing. 'He's only had one turn so far.'

'Right,' I said. 'It's a politician... and a figure from history. Funnily enough, there was someone who used to work here with the same name.'

'Got to be John Smith,' said Terry. 'There must have been a John Smith in every factory in the country–'

'Don't just guess at random,' said Kyle sarcastically. 'Is it a man?'

'Yes.'

'Is he black?'

'No.'

'Has he ever been black?'

'No.'

'Does he want to be black?'

'Actually, he's dead,' I said. 'But no, he never wanted to be black. That's five questions so far, including John Smith.'

'Was he in the Labour Party?' asked Maaz.

'Yes. But he was more famous for being in a different party.'

'Bloody hell,' groaned Terry, 'This is going to be worse than Michael Jackson.' He frowned. 'Enoch Powell. He was in two parties.'

'Who's Enoch Powell?' asked Kyle.

'Good guess, Terry, and quite close in some ways,' I said. 'Not that Enoch Powell was in Labour.'

'No, there was never an Enoch Powell working here,' Terry was musing. 'Unless the Enoch bit was a nickname, like…'

'Hmm,' I said thoughtfully. 'I'm not sure you're going to believe it when I tell you, then.'

They had still not got it ten minutes later when the bell sounded for lunch break and another small, disconsolate group turned up to take over our places on the line. Kyle was in a hurry to get out for a cigarette and barely listened when I gave away the answer. Maaz and Sharif exchanged comments between themselves in Arabic and I wondered if I had chosen someone too difficult and obscure. Ali looked as unhappy as before, so I asked him if he wanted to go to the canteen. Needless to say it was another drab, downbeat and out of date part of the building.

The food, though, was very cheap, perhaps because a lot of it was produced on the premises; it may even have been the stuff that failed to make it past quality control and I felt guilty that a number of my co-workers might end up with fruitless pastries by teatime. Ali took a steak bake and a Pepsi, but refused the free sausage roll that was part of the deal. I cheekily asked the canteen assistant if I could take it, and I made sure I got a receipt for my own food, since I could make an expenses claim for eating out. If I was careful not to mention what I was really doing here, that is…

'Don't you like these?' I asked Ali, gesturing at the misshaped item on my tray as we sat down. 'Or just not hungry?' I couldn't see Ali staying so slim on this type of food if he filled his plate, so maybe this small lunch wasn't a surprise.

'I don't eat pork,' he replied. 'I am a Muslim.'

'Oh, right. Got you. Does that cause you any difficulties? In work, I mean. You wouldn't want to be on the sausage roll conveyor belt, would you?'

'It's not really a problem. There are lots of us here, and if anyone is concerned about it the management will sort things out.'

'Well, that's pretty positive for an old-fashioned place like this.'

I asked Ali if he had ever met someone called Oswald Mosley in the factory, but he just shook his head without answering. Most of my other small talk elicited only limited replies, and though he seemed like a pleasant young man, I was beginning to think it was a mistake to spend lunchtime with him. I decided to risk one of the blueberry muffins that were piled up beside the till, so I asked Ali if he wanted one. He patted the pockets of his overalls and admitted that he didn't have any more money.

'Don't worry,' I said, 'I'll get it for you. They're pretty good value.'

'Yes.' he agreed sadly. 'They need to be.'

I nodded. 'Probably the only benefit here that makes up for being on the minimum wage.'

'Yes,' he echoed. 'Exactly right. Minimal wages.'

I laughed. '"Minimal" fits the bill even better, doesn't it?'

Ali looked somewhat confused at this. 'That's what you said, isn't it?' he asked. I explained. Ali asked me what a minimum wage was.

'Well, the legal minimum,' I said. 'You're over eighteen, aren't you?' I named the current rate, or possibly the last rate but one; it's hard to keep up to date with these things sometimes, even if you work in that field. Ali looked a bit dazed. 'Don't tell me they're paying you less than the legal minimum?' I asked. 'You could take them to court!'

Ali had decided he had some urgent business to attend to, and I guessed he wasn't the type to stand up for his rights: you only had to look at his work clothes to see that. And no-one else was going to do it for him. There probably hadn't been a real shop steward behind the frosted glass in twenty five years. I wondered about looking on the jobs database for him when I got back to the office: at least then he would receive a genuine minimum wage. How I could find him a new job without blowing my cover was another matter, of course...

I was left thoughtfully chewing my fatty, tasteless muffin alone until the hooter went. I wasn't looking forward to freezing my fingers back on the production line all afternoon. But I hadn't really got anything out of my visit yet, only the suspicion that something was wrong here. Illegally low wages? But *I* had been quoted a reasonable rate by Mr Gibbs. Shift patterns which would fit in with fortnightly visits to a Jobcentre? Could be a simple coincidence. A worker who might still have a live benefit claim? No proof until I checked. If I wanted any more I was going to have to take a bit more discomfort, wasn't I?

Or a *very great deal* more discomfort...

CHAPTER TWENTY TWO

Retrace your steps from the canteen to the dough-mixers and you will pass the employee lockers, which are organised in approximately alphabetical order. Two had been vandalised beyond repair in section M. A large number throughout had name labels in Arabic script.

Turn right from the lockers and you pass another tiny island of modernity in the out-of-date factory: the disabled toilet. Of course, all workplaces must have one, though few even now are progressive enough to employ the sort of staff who really need it. Certainly here the production lines had no jobs accessible to a wheelchair user, and most of the office space was at the top of a flight of rickety stairs, with no sign of any lift. So here, as elsewhere, no doubt, the disabled loo had become a place where girls could make up and change on Friday nights, or where a harassed junior manager could hide out for a while with *Marketing Jobs Monthly*.

Alternatively, it could become a good place to hold a secret meeting. Or to do a little interrogating in peace.

It happened so quickly that it must have been planned, although I didn't think about that at the time. I was on my way back from the canteen when I came across Maaz, Sharif and a third Muslim-looking guy walking the other way. I smiled and stepped aside to let them pass, and was professionally bundled into the disabled toilet before I could open my mouth. Sharif slammed the lock shut and it came off in his hand. I started to laugh at his astonished face, then stifled it as he leaned back against the door, scowling. Lock or no lock, it was still three against one.

I decided to play it innocent but assertive. 'What's going on?' I asked.

Maaz said something in Arabic and Sharif drew a heavy screwdriver from his overall: they weren't exactly subtle, these boys, were they? I took a step forward and was pushed back and down to a sitting position over the toilet bowl. There was no lid, though a hinged handrail helped me to balance.

'What has been your relationship with Oswald Mosley?' Maaz asked in his careful English, staring at me intently. If you think a softly spoken man in a beard net can't be intimidating, you need to think again. I fought back in the British way, with sarcasm.

'Which Mosley?' I asked, 'The dead one?'

There was a flurry of angry Arabic from the third man and then Sharif, which Maaz did his best to quell.

'You know who I mean. You were asking questions this morning–'

'I was asking questions about a historical figure.'

'No, you were asking about someone who worked here.'

'*Did* he work here, then? If you remember, I said I wasn't sure.'

'Tell us how you know of him, please.'

'What's it to you, anyway?' I asked. 'What's *your* interest in Mosley?'

Maaz exhaled angrily and made a frustrated gesture. The third man stepped over and threw on the hot tap to full flow. Steam began to rise. I noticed that my back was pressing hard against the lavatory cistern.

'Look,' I said, conciliatingly. 'There's nothing to it. He drinks in the same pub as me. Then he stopped coming in. When I got offered a job here I thought I'd ask after him. Well, we were playing that word game of Terry's and… It was that that reminded me. Famous people… And he's got the same unusual name…'

'Which pub?'

'Which pub?'

'Which pub do you drink in?'

'Oh. I see… The King's Arms,' I named a pub at random. 'Dene Street.'

'Dene Street.' Maaz thought for a moment, perhaps trying to place this road, or committing my story to memory. 'So,' he said, 'you've… socialised with Mosley in the King's Arms…'

'Not really *with* him. He's with his mates, I'm with mine. I don't know him all that much. You know, you chat at the bar while you're waiting to be served.'

'But you knew him well enough to ask about him here. To be interested when he… When he stopped going to the pub.' Maaz reached out and switched off the tap. 'You knew him by name.'

'Yes, but–'

'If you wanted to know where he was, why not just ask around in the pub? Ask his friends?'

'I don't know them very well.'

'You don't know us very well, either.'

'Look.' I took a deep breath while I tried to replay through my mind anything I had said earlier about Oswald Mosley, to make sure I kept my story straight. 'Look. I didn't make a plan to come asking about a guy I hardly know. We were playing the game and I thought I'd mention it. I was trying to think of a difficult person to catch you all out–'

'Oh, no. That is not going to happen. You're not going to "catch us out." You're going to tell us the truth.'

'I have been.'

'No, you're lying.'

I knew that losing my temper wouldn't help, but I did it anyway. There's only so many weak excuses that you can reasonably offer, so it was either that or get on my knees and beg.

'Well, what are you going to do about it?' I asked nastily. 'Scald my hands under the taps? Shove a screwdriver up my arse? You'll never get away with it.'

'The word of three against one,' said Maaz after a pause. 'Or perhaps we have other friends who would give an alibi.'

Without turning my head I looked around for a weapon. There was nothing but a plastic toilet brush. Could give a nasty poke in the eye, though, especially if it still had some bleach on it. I shifted a little towards it, as if trying to keep my balance. Then I saw the light under the door flicker slightly: was there someone outside?

'I think that's enough now, lads,' I said loudly. 'A joke's a joke. Back to work now for me, though.' Using the handrail I propelled myself towards the door, head down.

There was no way of getting past the three of them, of course, but, as I had hoped, they all moved forward to intercept my sudden dash. With the lock broken, this meant any passer by – or better, someone wanting the toilet – could come straight in. I began screaming for help. Maaz hit the button on the electric hand dryer, but that wasn't going to be loud enough to smother me: there's no place for embarrassment in an unfair fight, so I was bellowing like a yak in an abattoir until Sharif got his hand over my mouth. I bit as hard as I could: he tasted of soap rather than tinned apricots. I was remembering school rugby rucks and mauls as I forced myself further forward towards the door, though the memory didn't last for long.

This sort of fight may feel like a long event but in reality it is over in moments. It would have been even shorter, though, had they not wanted to question me further, which meant the screwdriver stayed out of the way while they made do with fists and boots. I split Sharif's lip with a lucky punch before I was winded and brought to the floor. My ear caught the edge of the wash basin; an inch to the left and I'd have been out cold. Sharif, who was all anger and no technique, tried to stick the boot in and I was able to pull him down onto the tiles with a very satisfying slap. But the other two knew how to keep their distance safely, and by the third kick by the third man I knew my ribcage wouldn't stand any more.

'Jesus Christ,' I wheezed desperately, tears flooding down my face, 'd'you think I'm a neo-Nazi like Mosley is? I'm not, I'm not, I promise!'

I would have given them the truth if I could have, but a complicated story is hard to get out when you've been battered to breathlessness, and a final kick by Sharif jarred my knee painfully enough to shut me up. But this was the last blow that landed. Lying gasping, I became aware that they had stopped kicking amid a fast and intense argument in their own language. And not a three way argument after all, but four voices, one of which came quickly to dominate.

Through my tears I saw a short man in a pinstripe suit standing in the doorway. Thank God someone had come. The three men addressed him as 'Ya Ustaz' which I later found out can mean 'Teacher' but is also a general term of respect, like Professor, Sir or Boss. They also called him 'Ya Walid,' which was his name, and which, when mangled by a young

English temp receptionist sounds just like 'Wally.' The man I had been seeking for weeks had turned up at the disabled facilities just in time.

He didn't look as if he needed the toilet, though, which was lucky because I had suddenly decided that I needed it badly myself.

★ ★ ★

Walid had a blonde, teenage trophy secretary with faultless taste in stockings, but it turned out she wasn't the qualified first-aider, so I spent ten minutes on the couch with a fifty year old homosexual staring deeply into my eyes and trying to run his hands through my hair. He got short shrift: partly because I was in agony, but also as I wanted Girl Friday to come over all solicitous with my cup of tea. After all, I needed some sort of comfort before Walid came back upstairs to question me.

After breaking up the fight, Walid's peremptory 'You there!' down the corridor had turned up Ali, who had been instructed to help me to the Managing Director's office. Since, amazingly, I could still walk, all Ali had to do was hover beside me looking anxious, which was a job he carried out impeccably. I assumed Walid was now grilling the three men who had assaulted me, although as a busy MD he might just as easily have rushed back to checking his sales figures or preparing the next round of redundancies at the works. One thing was certain: I would be a problem he didn't need today, and that thought made me uncomfortable, though not half as uncomfortable as my ribs, knee and the left hand side of my head.

'Your eyes are a bit dilated,' said the First-Aider sweetly. 'That can be a bad sign. Do you feel dizzy, sleepy at all? Confused?'

'I'm always confused,' I said. 'Confusion is my middle name.' He gave a little titter like I was being coy. 'Or do I mean Confucius?' I said to the secretary, who had just walked in. 'It's really hard to be sure…'

'Three sugars,' she said, as if I must have been kidding about that too.

I reached out. 'I hope you'll join me now that you've been to the trouble of making it.' But she was already legging it to the door.

'Actually, sweet tea isn't right for shock,' said the First-Aider seriously. 'It's a myth. You do better not to eat or drink at all at first.'

'Don't worry,' I replied, 'If she comes back in for a chat I won't need the tea at all.'

When Mr Walid appeared I was polite enough to try to stand, but he waved me back down with genial brusqueness and planted himself into his calfskin swivel chair, hands clasped on top of the hardwood desk. This, then, was the one modern and expensive part of the whole factory: superb furniture, discreet lighting; new carpet and wallpaper; tiny, but genuine LS Lowry above the second sofa. I raised my eyes from his gold rings and charm bracelet, up to his impassive face.

'Now Mr… *Fellman*,' he began slowly, and I realised that a file containing my application form, false surname and all, had magically opened out in front of him, somehow without my noticing it before. 'How are you feeling now? Nasty bump you had there. Maurice has had a look at you, has he?'

'Yeah.' I nodded carefully. 'I think I'll survive, though.'

'You don't need the hospital?'

'I hope not.'

'Mmm,' said Walid thoughtfully. I wondered how he was going to play this. I had just been assaulted by three of his employees. Would he take this seriously or try to hush it up? What if he decided to call the police? I couldn't give a statement under a false name, could I? But the alternative would have Will reaching for the Disciplinary Policy faster than you could say 'unauthorised, illegal activity.' Every one of his Seven Signposts to Decisive Management would point to sacking me as fast as procedure allowed.

'You've had a cup of tea? Would you like something stronger? Help to overcome the shock?'

I smiled, painfully. 'I don't think Maurice would approve. And it's a bit early for me, thanks.'

'When we've finished I'll arrange for someone to drive you home.' He looked down at the file again. 'Mission Street, isn't it? We can't possibly have you walking that far.'

'Oh. No.' I didn't want a lift in the wrong direction, much less someone thinking they would see me into a building for which I did not possess a key. 'I'll be fine to drive, honestly.'

'Oh, you have a car? But *are* you fit to drive? Maybe someone could accompany you to make sure you are OK.' I nearly said yes in the hope he would send his secretary, but you can be sure that men like Walid don't inconvenience themselves too much just to smooth over a case of ABH at their premises. Anyway, even allowing for the fantasy that she might prefer what she would call 'older' men (including those with a damaged rib cage), the fact was that the flat wasn't ready for visitors: there were socks and pants all over the place for a start.

'Mr Fellman, you can be assured that I will be treating this matter with the seriousness it deserves.'

'Ah,' I said. 'Look, there's no need for a public enquiry—'

'Oh, I've already started making enquiries,' Walid replied, glancing down again at the file on his desk. 'I understand the trouble started when you asked after a friend, a Mr Oswald Mosley.'

'He's not a friend. Just someone I know—'

'Professionally?'

'Just someone I know slightly.'

'And how is it that you know him?'

I sighed. 'From the pub. The King's Arms.' If Walid had been talking to the others I had better stick to my story, I supposed. 'I thought he worked here. I was just seeing if anyone knew him. I haven't... seen him around recently. That's all.'

'Mr Fellman, the name Oswald Mosley does not figure on our payroll system.' Walid was staring at the ceiling as he spoke. I wondered if he was bored already. 'But it seems the name is familiar to some of my employees.

'You will have seen,' he went on, 'That we have many workers from minority ethnic groups here. Mainly Muslims, though not all. Your... *acquaintance,* Mosley, was... Is...' he shrugged diffidently, 'A member of a certain political party with a certain... *distasteful* agenda. Indeed, I assume he chose his name to match his own political views. A pseudonym, or maybe changed by deed poll...'

There was a pause while Walid shifted his gaze to look directly into my eyes. He was bang on, of course, deed poll it was, shown clearly with all his previous names on his benefit claim forms. I tried to keep a non-committal expression, though, in keeping with someone who wasn't supposed to know Mosley very well. Walid said, 'You can see why this fact might cause people to act rashly. Stress can cause panic... Are you a member of the English Patriot's Party yourself, Mr Fellman?'

'No,' I said. 'No way. I'm much more liberal-minded than that.'

'Unfortunately, your co-workers believe that you are. Not that that excuses anything. I will be dealing with them most severely.'

'Sack them, you mean?'

'I will put them through the disciplinary process, yes.'

'I see.'

Walid bit his lip thoughtfully. Eventually he said, 'You know, it would be quite understandable if you asked me to call the police.'

Another trail of sweat worked its way down the inside of my arm. 'No need for that. As long as they are being dealt with. I couldn't work with them again, obviously.'

'Ye-e-es.' Walid fingered the pages of my file. 'I believe that Mr Gibbs offered you a trial period of two to three days. Unfortunately he has been in error about our staffing levels and we don't actually have any vacancies. I'm arranging a pay packet for you for three days, to cover the trial period you would have had. Plus a small productivity bonus. Cash, just so you won't be inconvenienced too much. If you see what I mean…'

Walid gave me another long, unblinking stare. 'Mr Gibbs informs me that under the usual rules you are entitled to carry on claiming benefits as before.'

'So I'm the one being sacked,' I said, injecting some disappointment into my voice. 'But I haven't done anything wrong.'

'I'm sure you will want to put all this behind you,' said Walid sympathetically. He lifted his phone and dialled briefly. 'Jade, would you pop in for a minute? And is Ali Ibrahim still there? Good. Ask him to come in too, would you? Thanks.'

Jade's paper work bore the new logo Riyadh Foods. *Riyadh!* Not Reed at all. No wonder the management were so helpful to the Muslim employees. There was a nasty moment when I almost signed Di Palma on the receipt for the pay packet, and another very nasty one when Walid asked me if I knew a man called Chandler Wray. Otherwise it seemed I had finally got away with my deception. Walid summarised a few points in front of his two witnesses, including the fact that I didn't want to involve the police. Evidently he hoped this would be enough to deter me from further action or complaint should I change my mind after I had left. He insisted that Ali go with me to my car, and offered a taxi if I did not feel well enough to drive. It was all I could do to stop him ordering Ali to get in with me and see me all the way home, but at least that meant I was on the ball enough to drive off in the direction of Mission Street, before deciding to detour to the drop-in NHS centre along the way. Ali gave me a sad little wave as he disappeared from view.

'You stupid bastard, Di Palma,' I croaked to myself as I drove. 'You stupid bastard. That'll teach you to go into a workplace without a proper, manager-endorsed risk assessment, won't it?' I grimaced with each gear shift and every twist of the wheel, although by the time I had got to the drop-in the pain was subsiding a little, and back at home a shot of whisky improved things further.

Well, it had been a lucky escape, and at least I had a couple of hundred in my pocket for my pains. And a clear vision to ignore Riyadh Foods for the rest of my career. Which also meant a final goodbye to Chandler's half-arsed hints and the question of where Mosley had really been working. OK, I could take a day or two off sick, maybe even a few days annual leave, and then get back to normal. Find some nice and easy investigations to impress Helen with. Deal with Smith and Leroy-Shaw, or better still call in a favour from Herman or somebody else to deal with them. Avoid leaving the office alone after dark. Chill out a little.

Good. I had some extra cash and the feeling that I could maybe take back control of my own work. The metaphorical half empty glass was starting to look like it could be half full after all.

Within four hours Fate would have knocked over my half full glass, smashed it and started slashing at my jugular with the shards.

And people wonder why I occasionally sound like a bit of a pessimist…

CHAPTER TWENTY THREE

When the front door buzzed I nearly ignored it, but having steeled myself to be assertive with the Mormons or a homeless duster salesman I was glad I had made the effort to check.

'Hi, Larry,' said Helen. 'How are you?'

'There was an embarrassing moment when the nurse found a tape recorder strapped to my chest,' I said, 'but otherwise I'm fine, apparently.'

Helen gave me a sideways look. 'Ravi said you'd phoned in sick this afternoon, so I thought I'd call round. You don't mind, do you? I brought you some grapes.' She gave me a plastic bag which clanked heavily; the unexpected weight made me wince.

'You are in a bad way, aren't you?'

'Severe bruising on my ribs, but nothing broken. Probably. The nurse said I should have an x-ray, but I couldn't face a three hour wait.' I pulled out a bottle of Australian Durif. 'This looks nice.'

'I thought you'd prefer your grapes in liquid form.'

'Yes. It's so much easier to get them down.'

We went into my bedsit and I tried hard to block out the shame of it all: the wreckage of old sheets on the unmade sofa bed; the random scatter of coffee mugs wet and dry; the carpet crumbs, the lost socks. Luckily for me, the panorama of the park was compensating well this afternoon, with the tall trees bathed in an orange sunset.

'Lovely flat,' said Helen at the window.

'Isn't it?'

'So, Larry. Are you going to explain what's been going on?'

I turned away. 'I'll get the corkscrew,' I said.

The wine was dark and powerful though it needed to breathe for longer to achieve its potential; I guessed we'd taste its full complexity somewhere below the bottom of the label. On top of the whisky it wakened my appetite, so I started cheese on toast as I summarised my adventure in the factory. Helen multitasked by listening while exploring my bookshelves and shoe boxes of cassette tapes; the roaring of my Calor gas grill intruded on some Bix Beiderbecke I had inherited from my Grandfather and never fully played. I thought of Chandler, the man who thought he knew jazz, and I wondered if he would recognise it.

'So basically they were trying to put the frighteners on you.'

'They succeeded. I won't be going down any dark alleys for a while, I can tell you, or hanging out at the Halal corner shop. And as for going anywhere near Grannie Baker's…'

'You wouldn't have been going back there anyway.'

'Oh, I dunno. I've always fancied a career based on dipping my hands into a freezing vat of fruit and syrup. And now I've gone and thrown it all away! You know, I'm glad they won't be getting off scot free. I hope he sacks the bastards.'

'How serious was this Walid guy about that?'

'Hard to say.'

'Now you're out the way he doesn't have to do anything.'

'Oh, thanks. I thought you'd come to cheer me up.'

'By rights he should have called the police.'

'Well, it's lucky for me that he didn't. And for God's sake keep all this to yourself, won't you? I can't risk Will finding out I was undercover without permission, let alone making clandestine tape recordings. It's a far worse crime than trespassing in a claimant's house... Employers have things like solicitors and PR firms to call on; they can make a lot of the sort of trouble that scares the pants off him. When I do the report I'll just cite a conversation with Mr Walid, and assume it'll never get audited. The rest has to remain- Oops-a-daisy!'

The first thin plume of smoke was rising, which was a signal to deftly pull out the grill pan from the heat, just before the browning Cheddar went too close to black. 'Ouch, ouch,' I said, transferring the slices to a wire rack with my bare fingers. 'Ketchup?'

'Yes, please. But you ought to be careful,' she continued, 'they might still bear a grudge, especially if they're in trouble with the boss.'

'But if they don't think I'm a neo-Nazi they've no more motivation to get me, wouldn't you say?'

Helen chuckled. 'Are you sure you convinced them? I know I shouldn't laugh, but... I can just see it: you're on the toilet floor, and it's "Don't hit me, I'm a Liberal Democrat!" D'you think they believed you?'

'It didn't quite happen like that,' I protested, disgruntled.

I ground the black pepper, picked out the least yellow of the parsley stalks, shook the red plastic bottle and wiped its nozzle with a sheet of kitchen roll. I took a deep breath and carefully squeezed star, moon and heart shapes onto the cheese, then added the final slices of vine tomato at the side. I carried the pre-warmed plates over.

'That looks fantastic.'

'Ah, well,' I replied with fake modesty, 'I am something of an expert in this field. If Will ever succeeds in firing me I could always open a restaurant… serving only cheese on toast.'

She laughed. 'Bit of a limited menu.'

'Not at all. Think Welsh Rarebit, Croque Monsieur, Bruschetta… Think of the hundreds of different types of cheese. And bread for that matter. Plenty of variety. It would appeal to everyone, except perhaps vegans. Or anyone allergic to dairy products. Or people who don't like cheese…'

'How long do you think you'll be off work?' Helen asked, changing the subject with some concern in her voice. 'Only I need some help with my Lifelong Learning folder before my review meeting.'

'I see. Well, I'm glad you value my guidance.'

Helen patted her lips with a napkin. 'Of course I do.'

'Here's some guidance, then. We can wrap up the Mosley investigation. All done. Failed to sign and no longer on the unemployed register. Possibly working, according to a tip off by a political colleague, but unable to trace which employer. No hard evidence of actual benefit fraud. Honour satisfied for both parties, you might say. Will can tell himself his input forced a result, and when he next tries to interfere with my work I'll tell him I can't waste time on any more cases which won't actually lead to a prosecution. Walid told me he'd never worked there. Quote: "Not on our payroll system." Unquote. After today I'll be glad to consign Oswald Mosley to a dormant file, I can tell you. And I'm putting that fucking baking factory into one, too.'

We sat in silence for a few moments, drinking. The wine was already better, and was mixing well with the last three aspirins in the cabinet. I was starting to relax a little.

'Actually,' said Helen quietly, 'That's not quite the same thing.'

'What isn't?'

'"Not on the payroll" doesn't mean he never worked there.'

I frowned and shook my head. Helen continued. 'He paid *you* cash, didn't he? Three days for half a day's work, too. You're not telling me that's gone through the books. Why wouldn't he do the same for Mosley? And others?'

'Oh, come on–'

'How did he seem when he was talking to you? Genuine?'

'Open, empathic?' I said, quoting the *Basic Body Language* video. 'Did he look at me when he was speaking, do you mean? Any visible signs of nerves, any head-scratching, rubbing his chin?'

'There's no need to be sarcastic.'

'I'm closing the file,' I said decisively. 'There's no chance of further co-operation from Mr Walid. He was nearly impossible to track down in the first place. I only met him by accident. And I can't meet him again, he knows me as Larry Fellman, unemployed ex-factory operative.'

'What about Chandler? He went there, and he had some information for you.'

'Yes, Walid mentioned his name, and Walther Gibbs mentioned his description. But so what? He told his homeless friend that he was going to at least two places, and there might have been more... And now he's stuck in some loony bin; no more leads from Chandler. Look, I don't want to talk about this...'

'And what about your tape?'

'*Jazz Greats volume six*?'

'No! The tape you had under your shirt while you were

undercover at the factory. Couldn't that have some useful information on it?'

'Doubtful. Most of it is a rubbish guessing game. The rest's in Arabic.'

'Pour me another glass, Larry,' Helen said, taking out her mobile phone. 'I may be able to help you on this one. We might as well check out our final information source, wouldn't you say? If honour has to be satisfied all round…'

★ ★ ★

The first number Helen had tried proved incorrect, as did the second and third. It seemed the man she was calling changed offices, jobs and addresses with some frequency, but then that's what you get for working in academic research. Helen's investigative skills tracked him from London to the University of Inverness, via Bristol, Blackpool and Bognor. Finally, she got through, mouthing 'ex-boyfriend' at me when he sounded discomfited to hear her name. I grinned wryly. Helen explained her new job and said she would turn on speaker phone as 'My boss is here.' I choked into my wine.

'Nick, I need your help translating something.'

'Oh, right. Fascinating. Which language?'

'I'm pretty sure it's Arabic.'

'OK. I'm more a Modern Farsi man these days, but fax it through if it's short enough. Have you got my fax number?'

'Have I hell. It took twenty minutes to find you on the phone. But listen, it's not written down. It's on tape.'

'Tape, right. You want to send me a tape?'

'Well… Can't I play it for you now? Over the phone? We're in a hurry.'

'I'll try. But I don't think I know the Arabic for girocheque,' said Nick uncertainly.

It wasn't easy for the poor guy, mainly because the men's words were masked by slaps, thumps and the sound of an Englishman begging. We played it several times before he finally stopped us and said, rather uncertainly, 'Right, then.'

'What have you got?' I asked.

'Yes, it's Arabic.'

'OK...'

'There's a lot of swearing.'

'Not a surprise.'

'I can't really tell where they're from by the accents, but I would guess somewhere in North Sudan.'

'But what are they saying? Can you understand it?'

'Not much. The recording's not really clear enough.'

'Anything at all?' asked Helen, who obviously didn't like to see her idea come to nothing. 'You must get some of it.'

'There's a bit that means... I'm translating loosely, "Not here, you tosser." Or *idiot, cretin, wanker*: fill in the insult of your choice.'

'"Not here?" What or who isn't there?'

'No, it's more the sense of "Don't do it here." And there's a bit that comes earlier, where you were talking about Oswald Mosley, and they start saying "How does he know?" Quite agitatedly, I'd say.'

'Yeah, they wanted to know how I'd heard of the man,' I explained. 'What else?'

'Then there's something like, "He's not a something, he's a something else." But I don't know what the somethings are. I don't recognise the words.'

'Great,' I said. 'Sorry. One of the words is probably fascist or neo-Nazi, if you ever get the urge to look it up.'

'Are you sure you're working for *benefit* fraud?' asked Nick, suspiciously.

'Yeah, definitely. It's just a complicated claim, that's all.'

'I'm really sorry, but that's about all I can make out.'

'Thanks, Nick,' said Helen ruefully. 'We must get together for a drink sometime.'

'Yes, thanks for your trouble,' I added. 'I owe you a drink for that.' It felt a pretty safe offer given the distance he would have to travel. We signed off the call and I said to Helen, 'Well, that was worth a try, but I don't think it changes anything, do you?'

'I suppose not.'

I walked over to my shelves and picked up a handful of the papers I had brought home the day before. 'These are going back to the office, asap,' I said. 'End of story.

'Don't be disappointed,' I added, 'There's plenty more investigations to do. Why don't we relax and enjoy another glass of wine?'

Helen had drawn up her legs on the armchair and was emptying the bottle into her glass. 'Mmm,' she said. How is your bruising, by the way? Still painful to the touch?'

'Oh, I'm feeling much better already,' I lied.

★ ★ ★

But when I got back from the chemist I found Helen spreading out my paperwork across the coffee table, with the Dictaphone perched on the arm of her chair. I felt a kick of disappointment, right under my damaged ribs.

'Did you get your painkillers all right?'

'Why have you got that stuff out again?' I complained. 'I thought we were going to relax.'

'Your phone went. I didn't like to answer it. There's a message.'

I gave her a hurt look and went to the machine. It rewound slowly, then I heard the sound of Laura crying. 'Larry, if you're there, can you pick up...' I sighed deeply and waited. 'I think someone's tried to get into my flat. I got back from work and there are marks on my door, like it's been kicked, hard, really hard... The landlord only changed the lock yesterday, and maybe Stephen... He was still refusing to send back the spare key, you see... I'm feeling a bit scared, and I wondered if you could call by... Ring me.'

I faced the wall and screamed, silently. Trust Laura to ring, just when I thought I might be able to foist a bit of charm on Helen. Instead of worrying about tidying up my socks I should have paid attention to turning down the sound of the answer machine, because now she had been sent from a bit of half-drunk flirting right back to a fully professional relationship, shuffling through meaningless paper to cover her embarrassment, or more probably, mine.

'Problems?'

'Sorry about that. Laura's... Well, you know that song by Billy Joel? No? Well, it's about a very needy person who exploits her friends by attention seeking the whole time. Laura thinks her ex-boyfriend's out to get her. She'll be fine, she's a bit of a nutcase, but she'll be fine...' I stopped, thinking this character assassination wasn't exactly making me look good. 'Why don't we just clear away all that paperwork?' I said. I may have sounded a little desperate.

'Listen to this.' Helen lifted up my Dictaphone and pressed 'play.' We heard again the indistinct voices echoing around the disabled toilet.

'What has been your relationship with Oswald Mosley?'

'Which one? The dead one?'

There was a flurry of anxious Arabic. Helen pressed 'pause.'

'Well, what?' I said.

'You say, "The dead one?" don't you?'

'Yes.'

'Nick said they were shouting "How does he know?"'

'Yes, that was the whole point of them interrogating me, wasn't it? How did I know Mosley? What was my connection with him?'

'No,' said Helen excitedly, 'they're asking *how you know he's dead.*'

We shared a moment's silence.

'Mosley's *dead*, Larry. That's why he failed to sign. That's why his so-called mates in the Party haven't seen him. Why d'you think those men reacted so strongly to you and your questions? Not because they were worried about another source of racist jokes on the shop floor. He's dead and they know something about it. Shit, they may even have done it!'

'No, no way!'

'And look at this.' She waved my notes headed 'Chandler' under my nose. 'This is the last message we played the other day, isn't it? You've written "Leave the bacon. Fuck tea. Alan." Which actually sounds, if you read it aloud, a lot like "Leave the baking factory alone." It's a warning.'

'Are you telling me they've killed off Chandler, too?'

'He was taken off by a Mr Shah, right? You said he was Asian. And he refused to say where they were going.'

'I see. You think we've stumbled on a double murder, do you? Or a murder and a kidnapping. Well, what's the motive? *Why* did they do it?'

'I… I don't know.'

I sat back and folded my arms self-importantly. It hurt.

'What about Mr Walid?' Helen continued. 'He didn't want to go to the police about you being assaulted. Guilty conscience…'

'He was the one who broke up the fight! But I guess he didn't want to upset his workers on account of a supposed neo-Nazi temporary operative. He's… What did your friend Nick say? He's Sudanese himself. He wouldn't want to do a fascist any favours. Besides, I didn't exactly encourage him, did I?'

'Or maybe he was as scared as you were of getting the police involved.'

'And the motive?'

'Let's review this. Chandler was seeking information for you. He's disappeared. Mosley could have been working and signing on. He's disappeared. Walid practically told you to keep on signing on. Terry could swap shifts. Kyle, you recognised as a claimant–'

'Employers do not have people killed to protect a benefits scam! And, as senior bloody investigator I can tell you that we still don't have any *solid* evidence that fraud has been committed anyway.' I stared at her. 'God,' I said, 'I mean, I love it that you're so keen, but there's no need to make a conspiracy theory over everything. I'm going to open this other bottle of wine…'

Helen bit her lip while I worked the corkscrew. Then she said in a small voice, 'You know the night we were there? At Mosley's house? Who was that figure in a mask, really?'

Wine slopped wastefully on the table. I thought back to the night of the stakeout: the open back door, *groaning* from upstairs… But the still-hot boiled kettle and the horrible cooking smell… You don't make a cup of tea and a hot sandwich for someone who is going to murder you, do you?

I left the bottle and turned my back on Helen. I tried to tidy the bed sheets without her noticing what I was doing. It's not easy, especially with a damaged rib cage. My latest book on wartime escapes thudded to the floor and I couldn't bend down to pick it up.

'Bedtime reading?' Helen picked up the book for me and opened it at random. 'You said you liked history, didn't you?'

'Don't lose the page… The plane has just been shot up by a German night fighter. It's on fire… A bomber crew's worst nightmare.'

'"Chapter Seven, Jump, Don't Fry." Ugh. That's horrible.'

'Wait a minute!'

The still hot, boiled kettle… The steam from the hot tap in the factory disabled toilet. The still hot iron. The smell of what we thought was burned bacon… Does bacon smell even a tiny bit like a roast pork dinner? Which in turn, smells like...

And there was something else.

'Helen,' I said. 'When Nick translated, he told us Walid said "*Not here.*" Maybe he wasn't breaking up the fight because he didn't want it to happen, maybe he just didn't want it to happen *there*, in his own factory… He could have been *colluding* with them. All that bollocks about disciplinary action. Maybe he's in it with them! Maybe he wants them to finish the job!'

'Thank God you gave a false name and address and so on,' said Helen. 'And that you're not really in the EPP. Shit, you really won't be hanging around any Halal butchers shops now, will you?'

'No, I won't.' I stood up and ran to the answerphone on legs of jelly. 'The Halal butchers know where to come.'

CHAPTER TWENTY FOUR

Fuck knows what good I can do – probably none – but I can't leave Laura deep in shit, so we run down to the car as fast as my dodgy knee will let me. I tell Helen to stay behind as it's dangerous but she slaps me and I can't face having to fight with her as well, so she gets her way and comes. I need a weapon, so I go back for my baseball bat, souvenir of Camp America ten years ago, and being drunk I root out the replica Lüger pistol from my very first Great Escape convention. Nothing else in the bedsit is remotely threatening: even the carving knife is a crappy, wobbly job from the Pound Shop that couldn't stab its way out of a bag. Helen's checking a text or something as I come back out, but she's also got the engine running and turned the car round: don't you just love this girl?

In the Citroën I say, 'Well, I was kidding before about the high speed car chases, and look at us now!' But I'm pale and tired, and my mouth is dry, and it spoils the effect of the joke. I hope I don't get breathalysed and I hope I don't embarrass myself with my driving, but in the event I take it only marginally faster than normal. I slow down for every white van we notice, and when I do cut a red light I nearly kill us both, so I decide to stick to my limits.

Within fifteen minutes we're on Mission Street and I'm looking out for the Africans. There's plenty of traffic but no-one loitering or walking as far as I can see. The only parking space is two hundred yards from Laura's; I pull in and bash the kerb. I tell Helen to stay put just while I have a quick look around, and I reassure myself by telling her we'll call for help as soon as we need it. I even say she can call the cops if I'm not back at the car in fifteen minutes from now, and I mean it this time, it's not a joke deadline like at the stakeout of Mosley's place. I'm scared though, because Laura's number is coming up engaged all the time now and I can't check what's going on. Have they pulled the plug to stop her calling for help? I hobble up the street, thinking, 'How did we get into this mess? How can this sort of thing be happening to me?'

And why haven't we just called the police immediately? I'm insecure; I'm embarrassed. I can't be absolutely sure there's anything to worry about, and I don't want to look stupid or let out the secret of any of my unauthorised activities, at some risk to my job. Under Helen's insistent questioning the weight of evidence has shifted my thoughts and fears, but the evidence is nevertheless still only circumstantial.

There's still hope, then, isn't there?

* * *

Approaching the flats my head began to clear as the fresh air and physical exertion took effect. I scanned the area ahead: pavement, doorways, parked cars. Nothing suspicious or scary. I slipped through the gate and stepped quickly behind the monkey puzzle tree. The front of the building looked clear: no lookout posted outside, then. Should I buzz her, or at least try to get into the block before

I gave away my presence? I moved forward and, from nowhere, a tall figure in dark clothes intercepted me. I gave a short, sharp scream.

'Wait a minute,' said an accented voice. I recognised Ali Ibrahim. I lifted the baseball bat slightly.

'Don't tell me you're part of this, too.' My legs shook, my heart was sinking along with all the hope that I had been dealing with a hypothetical conspiracy. Unless… 'You don't live here, do you?' I asked in some desperation.

'Larry,' he said seriously. 'You are not going home.'

'Oh, Christ!'

'I mean,' he shook his head, 'You are not *to go* home.'

I stared. What was he saying? Was this going to be some sort of order to leave town before midnight and never return? But he was just a kid, unarmed and, for the moment alone. I took one slow, careful step sideways…

'What's going on?' I hissed.

He gestured at the baseball bat. 'I think you know. I'm here to warn you.'

I stopped. If they'd sent their most junior member to warn me off, then didn't that give me a breathing space? Some time to rescue Laura and notify the police? And then end up on some witness protection scheme… No, no, I was thinking like Chandler now, I must keep a clear head…

'They are refugees from a war zone,' Ali was saying. 'They have seen horrible deaths and mutilation. Do you understand? They will do all they can to defend themselves against you.'

'Against *me*? What have *I* done?'

Ali looked at me in disbelief. 'You want to send us all back!'

'Ali, I'm not a neo-Nazi like Oswald Mosley. Really, I'm not.'

'No,' said Ali gravely. 'You are worse. You are a policeman.'

'I swear to you I'm not.'

'An immigration man, then. Or some sort of government man. You have the… the machinery of the state behind you. That makes it so much more dangerous. That's why I took the risk to warn you. And also,' he gave me a shy look, 'you seemed like a nice man.'

Ali began to move away. 'Wait!' I said. I'd read the situation wrongly, but it didn't help me; in fact it made things worse. 'Are they up there already? It's… it's my *friend's* flat, not mine. Is she safe?'

'I'm sorry.'

'Oh, *no!*'

'I mean, I'm sorry, I don't know. They don't share their plans with me. I only know what I overheard this afternoon.'

'But Ali…'

He looked at me one last time before he started to walk. 'If I get caught, remember that I tried to help.'

I looked at my watch. Eight minutes had gone by since I left the car. Laura was still in trouble. I would have to go in.

I made the front door quickly and I buzzed one of the second floor flats with the story that I had some leaflets to deliver and could they let me into the lobby? The guy who answered sounded suspicious, so I told him I was from Pizza Nirvana and there were free samples on offer. We'd just heard the sound of a little two stroke motorbike turning the corner, and I asked him if he could be quick; I'd left my moped running.

Safely inside, I passed a fat guy in a tracksuit on the stairs. I ran on up to Laura's on the third and final floor. While I was hesitating outside the door I could hear some sort of altercation below: I guessed he'd bumped into someone else who hadn't delivered the goods. Serves you right, I thought. If you're obese, don't eat pizza. And anyone who makes you go up and down the stairs a few times is actually doing you a favour…

I was feeling faint now, and it wasn't from the sprint up three flights. I knocked. 'It's me, Larry. Are you all right? Laura? Are you OK?'

Laura opened the door. She was in tears, but that meant nothing, it was pretty much her normal state at the present time, wasn't it? I looked past her, looked over her shoulder and saw there was nobody there. I took her into my arms and even in these circumstances I noticed how soft her skin was, and how good she smelled.

'Has anyone called?' I asked. 'Anyone tried to get in the flat?'

'No. No, I'm sorry,' said Laura. 'I just got a bit frightened again, and–'

'What about the phone? I couldn't get through.'

'I kept trying to ring *you*. And then my mother called. She does go on… I'm fine, really, I was just being silly.' She dabbed a handkerchief at her eyes.

'Talking of sounding *silly*,' I said, ushering her into the flat and shutting the door firmly behind us, 'Listen, what I'm about to say is going to sound very silly indeed, but it's serious. Deadly serious.'

Laura gave me a scared and suspicious look, as well she might on noticing that I was hot and breathless, smelling of booze and holding a baseball bat. 'We don't have much time,' I continued. 'I've become involved with a gang of dangerous… criminals.'

'*Larry–*'

'Shut up and listen. They know they can find me here, so

you and I are in danger. We're in danger right now. We need to leave quickly until all this can be sorted out.'

'How can you joke like this when I'm having such a difficult time?' Laura whined. 'It's not fair.'

'It's *not* a joke. You know that neo-Nazi claimant I told you about? It's to do with him.'

'You're drunk. You're being paranoid.' This was rich coming from *her*. I nearly screamed with frustration.

'No! Laura, for months you've been a drama queen about things of very little importance, but please believe me, this is more important than anything that has ever happened to you in your life. You need to pack an overnight bag so we can get the hell out of here.'

'And stay at yours… This is just a ploy to see me in my pyjamas again, isn't it?'

Laura cowered as I aggressively threw off my jacket and pulled my sweatshirt up over my face. 'See these bruises?' I shouted through the man-made fabric, 'That's what they've done already!' I pulled down the shirt and registered her shocked expression. 'Now get some stuff together quickly or I'll leave you to see what they want to do to *you*. And it won't fucking involve pyjamas!'

★ ★ ★

Laura's only five minutes filling a sports bag with clothing. She doesn't protest when I barge into the bedroom to hurry her and she even asks me to get some pants off the drying rack in the bathroom. But whether it's five, fifteen or fifty minutes makes no difference in the end, because when we open the door, Sharif is waiting patiently outside.

I slam the door in his face and almost shut it, but he gets

a foot in the gap. The door's still closed enough for Laura to slip on the chain, which should hold him off for about two extra seconds, I'd guess, and I keep shoving in the hope he'll withdraw his bruised toes. But he's yelling out for someone called Mohammed, and I know I won't be able to keep out two of them.

'Get out of the fire escape!' I tell her through clenched jaws.

'What about you?'

'Get out! Get help!' I say, thinking the help won't be quick enough, but the idea of it might persuade her to go.

'I can't–' she says from in front of the open sash window. My feet are losing their grip.

'Don't worry about me. Just go!'

'No, I mean it. I can't! There's someone out there!'

I give up on the door and bound back into the living room, picking up the baseball bat and dragging Laura by the wrist into the bathroom, where I turn the key, and sit on the floor with both feet on the door and my back braced against the toilet bowl. Within moments Sharif and Mohammed are putting their shoulders to the wood, but it's a good, strong, solid, original door from the days when this was a Victorian villa, and the lock is pretty sturdy, too. I'm praying Helen has called someone by now or that maybe the fat guy from downstairs will investigate the disturbance, and I'm just thinking I might be able to hold on long enough when one of the panels splits a little, and four blows later the top of a jemmy comes through. Laura screams.

'Sharif!' I call. 'There's money in the flat! Enough to help you get away! Leave us alone and you can have it.'

The banging stops long enough for me to get my hopes

up. I whisper, 'Where's your handbag?' to Laura, and she shakes her head. 'I haven't got any money.' I tell her we'll give them her cashpoint number; she tells me her card has been withdrawn.

'What about yours?' she asks.

'I left it in the car…'

Then the jemmy smashes into the door again. I push with my feet, but it's obvious it's only a matter of time.

'Sharif! The police are already on their way! You haven't got time for this. Quit before they get here!'

This has the wrong effect because they just attack all the harder and the wood around the door knob starts to collapse. With a hole in the upper panel they have a purchase and can use their crowbar to best effect. We've had it, but I'm not giving in.

I stand up and put all my strength into supporting the full height of the door. We strain and strain, then I jump back suddenly and they come tumbling in, unbalanced enough for me to push them down and struggle past. I can't believe they fell for it! Second time around! But it's no help because Laura is still trapped with them. Also, Maaz is in the living room with the still open window behind him; he's wearing thick rubber gloves and has an old fashioned, cut-throat razor held ready at neck height. My neck height. I stop quickly.

Sharif and his friend pull Laura into the room. They look incandescent with shame.

'You're Muslims, aren't you?' I shout, looking Sharif in the eye. 'Are you devout? If you are, remember you mustn't touch a woman.'

Sharif swears and takes a step towards me, but he's waved back into line by Maaz. Beside me on the top of the glasses cabinet I see my pathetic little replica pistol, left there while I helped Laura to pack. 'Let her go,' I say hurriedly. 'She's nobody. She doesn't know anything. This is just the false address I gave your boss and she's totally innocent. You can see I don't live here: it's obviously a woman's flat.'

Maaz is speaking harshly and angrily in Arabic. Mohammed holds Laura's neck and forces her down until she's crouching on all fours; he raises his jemmy. He's not devout: he's fucking well got an erection! Laura whimpers. Maaz gestures impatiently to Sharif, who is moving slowly and carefully around, ready to come and hold me from behind.

I beg. 'Please don't do this. You're giving the fascists what they want! All Mosley's friends will get the public's sympathy!'

But somewhere Maaz has learned to be more professional in his killing than his compatriots will ever be, and he isn't going to waste time arguing, much less indulging in the need to explain himself. And it's no consolation to us that he genuinely doesn't want to gloat.

He takes a step…

I pick up the toy gun and level it at him. 'Stop or I'll blow your fucking head off!' I shriek, as loud as I can manage. He stops; I'm amazed.

'Laura!' I shout. 'Run!' She twists from Mohammed's grasp and is out of the door like an athlete. I'm praying as I follow. But they've seen through it now: they're right behind us.

I'm in the tiny hallway as someone kicks my legs out from under me from behind. Laura's at the front door and I think if I can drag out my own death a bit then she will manage to get away. Then the door bursts inwards with a force that tears it half off its hinges and Laura is thrown backwards on top of me.

'Fuck, fuck!' I shout meaninglessly. I'm ready to give up now.

Except that the big, brutal figures trampling all over us are wearing black uniforms, and, when I strain my neck to look upwards, they have helmets and visor covered faces and clearly they have not just come off shift from the Danish line at Grannie Bakers...

Are we safe? Is it the Cavalry? Someone is shouting in Arabic, deafeningly, using some sort of microphone attached to his riot squad combat suit. I've seen him before... Yes, with Carl in the Jobcentre, and, yes, in the Gasworks car park, too... He's got his name sewn on his uniform, in that American movie style. It's Shah. Or, if I remember my childhood lists of military insignia correctly, *Colonel* Shah...

And this time there's no mistaking the sound of gunshots. Funnily enough they sound nothing like fireworks at all.

* * *

A hard-faced woman in a smart suit was helping Laura out of the front door. I crawled forward myself, mumbling incoherently. On the landing, DS Paul Wodehouse told me that the ambulance was ready and waiting. 'Get a move on, you lazy sod,' he urged, failing to sound as light hearted as he wanted.

Suddenly I realised that I was wet all around the tops of my inner thighs.

'Christ, did the bastards get me after all?' I cried.

'Don't be soft,' said Paul.

Then I saw Helen. She ran up the final steps, knelt down and kissed me on the cheek. 'Thank God you're all right,' she said.

'All right? But I'm bleeding!'

'No, you're not. You're fine.'

The paramedic had probably had rigorous training in reassuring people in an extreme crisis. 'The trouble with this sort of traumatic event,' he said gently, 'is the pressure it puts on your bladder.'

Alright, I thought, get a grip on yourself. Life's too short to be embarrassed about this. In fact, Life was almost too short for anything at all just now…

I saw Laura climb shakily into the ambulance, and saw a uniformed police officer talking to the fat neighbour. Did I imagine hearing the words 'free samples' and 'pizzas'?

Hard to say, because then I passed out.

CHAPTER TWENTY FIVE

Despite a costly revamp and a strong local advertising campaign, Hampton's art gallery remains almost deserted most of the time. That's the way I like it when I want some peace and quiet alone, and that's also the way I like it when I have a pretty girl with me.

The special exhibition was titled 'Radical Feminist Artists Today,' which meant that Stephen had had to enter under a false name. I personally thought that a male artist's work on display could be nicely radical and even some sort of victory for inclusive feminism, but the promoters wouldn't have agreed. They had tried to insist on female-only staffing for the duration, since a surfeit of testosterone would apparently damage the integrity of certain pieces. God knows what they would have done had they known that a male exhibitor was in the show.

Reading about this in the *Chronicle*, I couldn't help thinking of Chandler's first little fraud-related anecdote, so I told him the story when I visited. He didn't really take it in. Depression can do that to you: it makes it impossible to find any interest in anything that's not immediately related to yourself. All he kept saying was that he didn't want to go back on the streets and I could see why when I saw how comfortable the safe house was. I tried to console him with the reminder that he had been classified by the ATU as 'Informer, grade D.' His career was making progress.

I had been feeling OK in the gallery until my eye was caught by an installation on the theme of domestic violence. The baseball bat looked just like mine. I shivered and looked around for Helen. She smiled.

'Listen,' I said, 'I want to thank you. Thank you for coming to meet me today, and also–'

'That's OK. It's... interesting. Not an obvious choice. I was surprised you wanted to come, actually.'

'Are you saying I'm some sort of uncultured chauvinist?' I tried to joke.

'No, but–'

'I suppose,' I said, 'I'm looking for clues.'

'Very enigmatic. Suppose you give *me* a clue about what you mean?'

'OK. One of the sculptures is by someone I know.'

'Really? Which one?'

'I don't know.'

Helen gave me that look again like I was cracking up. 'Cheeky,' she commented. 'Not telling you which one to look out for.'

'Oh, I haven't spoken to h- The artist. I was ringing h- *them* about something else. It was their flatmate who told me about the exhibition.'

'This isn't someone you know well, then?' she said, not looking at me.

'No,' I agreed, although I was coming round to the idea that, emotionally, we had a few things in common. The questions that had struck me on hearing Stephen's tape had eventually led me to phone him, my excuse being that if I could elicit a get well card for Laura it might help her toward recovery. But he was out when I rang, and after a short chat with his fellow student I had lost confidence and let the matter drop. Maybe there are some investigations it's better not to pursue… I couldn't help wanting to see if he had any artistic talent after all, though.

'But talking of investigative powers… Skills, qualities, whatever…' I took a breath. 'Helen, it's obvious that if you hadn't phoned for help while I went back for my bat and gun… Then, well, I wouldn't be here today, would I? Never mind ten-minute exit deadlines and all that crap. You made a good professional decision. That's what I really want to thank you for. You saved my life.'

'Oh, God,' said Helen, 'it sounds scary when you put it like that.'

'I'm just so sorry to have put you through the experience.'

'Don't be daft. *I* wasn't in any danger. You don't need to apologise to *me*.'

'Yes,' I said, thinking of a number of difficult conversations with Laura recently. 'But I feel I want to. Maybe it's because I've had so much practice just recently. I'm on a bit of a roll now. I'm getting quite good at it. And you're the one person I *want* to apologise to, because everyone else is *expecting* it. Maybe I'll have to write a little list of who needs one next…'

My voice was becoming louder as I continued, not that I noticed. The handful of other visitors were giving us looks. I glared back. 'Yes,' I said, 'I'll have to apologise to Will for being wrong about Mosley working, won't I? And Ravi… I'll apologise to Chandler for doubting that he could ever come up with any useful information. I'll apologise to my mother for worrying her, and for being rude to her last time I visited, and for not having a career like my brother's, and for believing it matters. I'll apologise to everyone here for disturbing their exhibition, what d'you expect when you let in a surfeit of testosterone?'

'Larry!' said Helen sharply. She shook her head slightly at the two suited women who had been approaching us. I recognised them as the exhibition organisers from the picture in the *Chronicle*. Helen touched my arm. 'You're getting hysterical. It's the shock.'

'Yes,' I said. 'Yes. I apologise.'

Helen laughed. 'Let's go and have a glass of wine on the mezzanine.'

Unsurprisingly, the café-bar was busier than the exhibition space below, but I still had no problems finding a quiet table beside the wrought iron balustrade. Helen went to the counter and I stared down at a twisted, crying figure fashioned out of red and black vinyl. At this distance the grooves weren't visible, though what looked like a record label could be seen on the sculpture's bowed neck. I needed more time and a closer look, but the piece seemed surprisingly good. The body was convincing, even though there was no way of telling whether it represented the female or the male. Or indeed a metaphor for both.

'Thanks,' I said as Helen brought over my wine. 'You can see why I shouldn't be let out on my own.'

'Don't be silly.'

'Anyway,' I fished, taking a large mouthful, 'I don't know about me being the one who has to apologise all the time. What about you? Chatting up Paul Wodehouse and getting his phone number while we were supposed to be working together…'

Helen gave me a mock indignant look. 'We weren't really working, because Chandler didn't show up! And it's a good job Paul gave me his number. Without him and his direct link to the Anti Terrorism Unit–'

'I know, I know. We'd have been half decomposed before

any local plod car got there.' I had been praising Helen for her judgement in seeking help early, but the speed of actual response had been vital too. Still, the fact that she had phoned Wodehouse first was a bit of a bitter pill. Wodehouse to the rescue! The man would be even more insufferable from now on.

'You know,' I continued, trying hard to keep any sort of whining tone out of my voice, 'that night at the station after I got beaten up... He seemed so uninterested when I was telling him about Mosley. If I had known the reason he was rushing off was to add my information to his own investigation about illegal immigrant traffic... Well, I'd hardly have risked my neck like I did, would I? Sure his links with the ATU saved me. But you could argue that he put me in danger in the first place! He should have warned me off!'

'But he didn't know what you were going to do. No-one did. You went to Grannie Baker's completely on impulse.'

'Yeah,' I said moodily. 'And I've suddenly decided I'm not going to be acting on impulse any more.'

Helen began discussing some of the exhibits and I was just beginning to relax when a loud voice said, 'Now, then,' behind my ear, and a hand fell heavily on my shoulder. I panicked, spilled my wine and felt my heartbeat accelerate from a standing start. Detective Sergeant Paul Wodehouse leaned across to kiss Helen; I couldn't see if it was on her lips or cheek. I was disappointed. She must have asked him to meet us here.

'Hello, Paul,' she said, while I put down a couple of napkins. 'We were just talking about you.'

'Yeah,' I muttered. 'We were just saying how you needlessly risked my life by not telling me what Oswald Mosley was really up to; not even acknowledging that you knew the name.'

'"Hello, Paul. Nice to see you. Thanks for dropping by,"' said Wodehouse with light sarcasm. '"Thanks for saving my life."'

'It's all in a day's work for you, isn't it?' I said ungraciously.

''Course it is. I just love begging the ATU for help and then bribing them with a case of wine when it turns out that the villains have absolutely no connection with terrorism at all.'

'Well, what d'you call trying to carve up me and Laura with a fucking razor? That's terrorising enough, isn't it?'

'Yeah, I know.' Paul patted my arm with what I really ought to have accepted as genuine sympathy. 'You're doing well to be on your feet, mate, after what's happened.'

'And how do you know there's no connection? None of the different departments will have finished interrogating them yet, will they?'

Wodehouse grinned broadly. 'How right you are. My boss hasn't even finished arguing about who's going first! But seriously, there doesn't seem to be any other evidence on that score. Walid was purely in it for the money. And those guys who knocked you about... They were pretty desperate, it seems.' Paul shrugged and opened his palms. 'The one called... *Mouse*, is it? He's a die hard Communist from way back. You can guess what that means in a war-torn Islamic dictatorship.'

I made some bitter cracks about Paul being an unlikely bleeding-heart liberal and Helen said she would buy him a drink. I half-heartedly offered to go to the counter and then let her insist. I told Paul I wasn't ready to forgive my would-be murderers and he agreed that a few days rest could hardly begin to make up for violent trauma. I said that I hoped the interrogators would go easy on Ali Ibrahim, though, as he had tried to warn me, not kill me.

'To tell you the truth, Larry,' Paul murmured, 'we haven't found him yet.'

Wodehouse had brought a gift which he presented to Helen: a list of employees at the Grannie Baker factory. Of course, it was impossible that any of the illegals had been signing on; how could they, if they didn't officially exist? But Paul, in the course of his enquiries, had demanded the whole payroll, and now had names and National Insurance Numbers to pass on. It was enough for us to run a search across the whole benefits database. It was a highly efficient way of working and a helpful gesture.

I told myself that he wasn't giving it to me because I was still off sick. I told myself Helen was only flirting as a thank you, not because she meant it. And I drank some more Chardonnay and gave a small, left-out cough.

'How's what's his name? Chandler?' Wodehouse asked me politely.

'Depressed. You should know. He's your baby now.'

Paul shook his head. 'Not necessarily. The ATU boys have him now, and we're not in so much of a hurry to get him back. And don't forget he didn't come to me. He dealt directly with my boss from the start.'

This was true. Paul Wodehouse's superior had phoned him about Chandler's evidence on the same night we had bumped into Paul in the pub. It was the call we had seen him take, albeit from a distance. So Chandler had gone straight to the police and had failed to keep his rendezvous with me. I had found his disloyalty painful, but I was also disconcerted that his police connections had turned out to be genuine. I'd always assumed they were no more than a fantasy.

'Last time I tramp round to the homeless hostel worrying about Chandler's safety,' I said, ignoring the fact that, held in an intelligence service safe house, he had still managed to get out and ring my voicemail.

Helen protested, 'But you still haven't explained to *me* about what Chandler had.'

'That's because it's a mite embarrassing for Larry,' Wodehouse laughed. I scowled, but I couldn't very well stop him from telling that part of the story.

'It's like this. Larry wants to phone Oswald Mosley because the guy has failed to sign. He thinks he's got a mobile number on a scrap of paper from when he did a home visit, but, being Larry, he hasn't got round to inputting it onto the guy's benefit record. So the database just has an out of date one on it…

'He finds a number when he's particularly tired and stressed, so he rings it, and someone else answers.'

'*Paul* answers,' I said grudgingly.

'So Larry thinks, "Fuck, I've rung Paul by mistake. Wrong number." And he goes off and has another beer.'

'*Coffee*,' I corrected.

There was a pause. 'I don't follow,' said Helen. It looked to me as if she'd moved her chair slightly away from Paul, so I held onto the idea while I took another sip of wine.

'Mosley had gone to photograph lorries arriving at the factory. He reckoned the illegal immigrants would arrive that way,' I explained. 'He wanted evidence for his dossier.'

'Yes, he was going to go to the media,' said Helen.

'And impress his pals in the neo-Nazi fold,' I agreed. 'He'd borrowed some equipment from the Party Chairman, but he damaged it. So he also had a go at getting something on the camera on his mobile phone.'

Paul Wodehouse laughed. 'But Chandler, who is not as useless as he looks, has turned over the employee lockers at the factory. He's only nicked the bloody phone! He takes it to my boss…'

'It ended up on Paul's desk just at the time I tried calling the number.'

'So that's why Chandler was so confident about having valuable information!' Helen suggested. I shook my head.

'He knew it was a big scam, possibly dangerous to anyone who found out. He was right to try to warn me off. If he hadn't started drinking again I might have got the whole story in time. But he knew nothing definite when I last *saw him*. When I met him in the multi-storey he was bluffing. All his stuff about charging me double was bullshit.'

'You know, Larry,' said Paul, 'The phone thing was the only bit of the whole jigsaw that you never fitted in. All the other stuff… You had it sussed. Smart work, considering.'

'Considering what?'

'That you were working in the dark, of course. And alone. You did pretty well.'

'Thanks.'

'It was a bit last minute, mind, to get the answers fifteen minutes before the bad boys came knocking on Laura's door.'

'Bastard.'

'Just kidding. Your boss should be praising you, you know, not putting you through the disciplinary process.'

'Oh, they're not pursuing that Unauthorised Action stuff,' I said airily, 'at least not while I'm off sick. They may sack me when I get back to work, of course.'

'Rubbish. But if they do, give me a ring. I'll give you a job.'

'Yeah,' I said. 'Thanks very much.'

'No, I mean it,' said Paul, leaning back complacently in his seat. 'If I get my promotion I'll have more say over the budget.'

'I didn't know you were up for promotion,' said Helen, too admiringly, in my opinion.

'Well, I've just smashed a huge illegal immigrant employment scam, haven't I?' said Paul. 'I hope I'm entitled to some reward. And you know the way things work nowadays. There's room in the budget for ad hoc payments to freelance consultants.'

'Or a slush fund for informants,' I said. 'Like Chandler.'

'Well, I can't magically *make* you into a police officer, can I? But your pal Chandler is just a lucky amateur. You'd be the real McCoy.'

'What's the pay like?'

'Don't you dare!' said Helen suddenly. 'I want you back with me.' She blushed lightly. 'You haven't finished my training yet.'

'You could always do something on the side,' said Paul. 'You know, when you're out of the office anyway. Moonlighting... Think about it.' He turned to Helen. 'D'you want a lift back to the office? I'll feel better once you've got that list into a secure place.'

She fingered the papers thoughtfully. 'I suppose I ought to be getting back. Will you be OK, Larry?'

'Sure. I've got something to do this afternoon, anyway.'

Downstairs, the two women we had seen earlier were circling Stephen's piece and frowning admiringly. I smiled to myself. If only you knew, I thought. If only you knew...

And then again, what did it really matter? We interpret art according to what we know. Why shouldn't they have a different interpretation to mine, based on their natural assumption that the sculpture was by a woman. Who was to say that I was right and they were wrong. It wasn't as if I had all the answers myself, was it?'

Paul was halfway to the stairs when Helen turned back towards me. 'I meant it about carrying on working with you,' she said. 'I've enjoyed being with you a lot.'

'I love being with you,' I said, mock-casually. I raised my glass. 'To the next stakeout.'

'I promise to wear tights under my trousers next time,' said Helen, and she winked. Paul was looking back from the staircase with a nonplussed sort of face.

I watched them descend. I finished my wine, and then the mouthful left in Helen's glass. For just a moment, I wondered how soon the doctor would let me go back to work.

CHAPTER TWENTY SIX

Outside the sky was already darkening and the air was raw with cold and damp. It wasn't the best season for rebuilding a sense of optimism, and my eyes were caught by the cards in the travel agent's window. I wondered if the bank would give me a loan based on my claim for compensation from the Criminal Injuries Board. But of course I wasn't allowed to leave the country yet. As Paul had said, the law enforcement agencies were still arguing over how to pursue this case, and no doubt they would all want to interview me again.

At a distance, kids were letting off bangers in the street. I remembered how Maaz and Sharif had used fireworks to frighten Mosley's dog, before they killed it. I thought of the still warm corpse in the bin bag in his yard and I felt a little sick. I thought of Mosley himself and felt sicker.

The local papers were still leading on the story, and, since it so neatly combined violence, benefits and illegal immigration, most of the national tabloids were also in town. Suddenly, it seemed, I had to take heed of every one of Chandler's erstwhile warnings: 'Vary your route,' 'Make an unexpected detour,' 'Avoid using the front entrance.' Thank God we had been able to spend a few days in the ATU safe house. Thank God my own building was so secure and that I'd even been able to move into a room on a different floor…

There was new racist graffiti in the multi-storey, and on the radio Rhys had reported a flurry of interest in membership of the EPP. I didn't expect it to last, but I felt sorry for any ethnic groups who were feeling once again public suspicion that they somehow had no right to be here. But at least some of the media had rubbished Mosley's report of an illegal invasion, and had stuck accurately to the true facts and numbers. Not that the facts weren't bad enough: twenty illegal immigrant workers at Grannie Baker's, and more planned; at least three of them implicated in murder…

Carefully, in view of the wine I had drunk, I drove away in the direction of Towbrough. When I arrived, Laura was doing the washing up with my mum. They were getting on fine. Mum liked her company and Kevin liked having her around too, of course. There was no hurry for her to start looking for a new flat, although Laura did say that the décor in my old room was going to drive her out eventually. I stopped myself from joking that I had finally got her into my bed at last.

I wandered off into the living room and tried to put my anxiety behind me for a while. They were re-running *The Great Escape* on TV. I smiled to myself at the thought of Colin wanting to buy part of a costume from the movie. Of course, the characters leave their uniforms at the camp and tunnel out in secretly made civilian clothes, which got me wondering which particular pair of trousers Colin had been referring to. There had to be some way of finding out the answer…

And then I gave up asking myself questions for once and settled down to simply enjoy the film.

COMING IN 2014

The next Larry Di Palma crime novel:

Live-in Killer

'A refreshing twist on the detective novel'
Anneliese Emmans Dean, www.thebigbuzz.biz

PROLOGUE

You know you're in trouble when you see them stoning the fire engines.

You know it's worse when the firemen get shot.

It had been a mistake to try to cut across Peaseholme, but the ring road resurfacing had been causing huge tailbacks all week, and the radio traffic news reporter was hyping the problem in her usual pant-wettingly over-excitable way. Stupidly, I got fooled into making a last minute turnoff three roundabouts too early, with a view to cutting over the far corner of what is one of the direst housing estates in the country. Which felt a little disconcerting, maybe, at this time of night, but ten to twelve minutes would see me back on the right side of the tracks. Or so I thought...

And why the fuck Radio Hampton wasn't reporting the real story of the evening I'll never know...

It was unusually quiet around the Triple Towers, and further on the bouncers outside the Lord Nelson were looking bored and perplexed. The answer came just beyond Junkie Park: I crossed the mini roundabout and all of a sudden I was stuck behind a Greatways lorry trying a desperate U turn, while up ahead the firefighters tried to save the community centre under a hail of lager cans, hubcaps and stones. A white van pulled up hard behind me. Then my mobile rang.

'Hello?' I lifted it to my ear while still staring at the fire ahead.

'It's Mum. I'm just checking that you got home OK.'

'Ah. Look, I'll call you back...'

The flames had a good hold and there was little to be done, especially as the firefighters had retired, at least two visors shattered by air rifle pellets. A paramedic, we learned later, was treated by his colleagues for concussion, alongside six elderly ladies from the Old Time Dancing Society who had suffered smoke inhalation. The right wing, 'hang 'em and flog 'em' editorials were going to have a field day. And just for once we would all agree with them.

When the van behind had managed to reverse, I had the space to get out. The Citroën was at full lock and I'd just bumped over the kerb when a half brick hit my roof and I panicked. Twisting my neck I could see them, a crowd of silhouettes advancing with the flames behind. Small silhouettes: the tallest was maybe five foot seven, they were young teenagers, *kids*. But when they turned their heads, even if just for an instant, you could see the rage and excitement flickering in their distorted faces. They had found the ultimate bully-boy thrill. I hit the accelerator.

I hit a lamp post.

I didn't let it stop me.

And, amazingly, within minutes I was driving down perfectly normal streets, dodging perfectly normal cyclists, moped-riders and pedestrians who had no idea what was happening only a mile or two away. With dents in my roof, my left wing, and my confidence.

And so the one successful attempt to foster a community in Peaseholme fizzled out beneath the firefighters' foam. The papers were enraged for a day, then lost interest. Councillors wrung their hands for twenty seconds on TV. An old age pensioner remained in hospital for a week, then died.

On the day of her death my work sent me back onto the estate.